THE CONFIDENCE

THE CONFIDENCE

A Novel

Bud Simpson

iUniverse, Inc.
New York Lincoln Shanghai

THE CONFIDENCE
A Novel

Copyright © 2005 by E A Simpson, Jr.

iUniverse books may be ordered through booksellers or by contacting:

iUniverse
2021 Pine Lake Road, Suite 100
Lincoln, NE 68512
www.iuniverse.com
1-800-Authors (1-800-288-4677)

ISBN-13: 978-0-595-37371-0 (pbk)
ISBN-13: 978-0-595-67491-6 (cloth)
ISBN-13: 978-0-595-81768-9 (ebk)
ISBN-10: 0-595-37371-2 (pbk)
ISBN-10: 0-595-67491-7 (cloth)
ISBN-10: 0-595-81768-8 (ebk)

Printed in the United States of America

Epilogue

To every child who has ever been the victim of true abuse: God has reserved a special place for you...and them.

This work is my legacy of love to children everywhere, starting with my own: Cameron, Scott, Tammy, Alera and Foster; but, it would not have been possible without the love, understanding, and encouragement of our wife, mother and friend, Joanie.

Bud Simpson

CHAPTER 1

▼

Clay Delaney was accustomed to waiting for Judge Jack Armbrister. He normally waited in the courtroom for the judge to take the bench. There, he'd argue a motion or ask for some form of relief for a client, always in public, always on the record.

This time it was different. He was alone in the judge's anteroom, waiting anxiously for a private audience in chambers. Now for the first time, he'd be pleading on his own behalf.

Until the judge's secretary had called earlier that morning, Clay wasn't sure that the judge would see him. His relationship with Judge Armbrister had always been strained, and they'd clashed often.

An unexpected letter from Armbrister had kept Clay awake at night for almost a week. It was the letter that had brought him to the judge's chambers. Despite his heated exchanges with Armbrister in the past, he knew that he must stay calm and avoid a confrontation.

He settled into a nearby chair and withdrew the creased, well-read letter from his pocket and read it one more time.

Dear Counselor:

You are hereby appointed to represent Mr. Harco Brewton, recently indicted in this Court for the rape and murder of Carrie Lindsey, a minor.

The District Attorney has announced that he will seek the death penalty.

Mr. Brewton's lack of income and financial worth qualify him for indigent status.

Contact Ms. Crowley in the Public Defender's office for Mr. Brewton's file.

Hon. Jack Armbrister
Judge, Superior Court

Clay's hand trembled as he refolded the letter and carefully returned it to his pocket, hoping somehow that by preserving it and keeping it intact, the next time he pulled it out he'd wake up from a very bad dream.

He'd lost count of the times he'd read it, but each time his reaction was the same. Shock, because his entire legal career had been as a civil trial lawyer. He'd never once tried a criminal case. Revulsion at the thought of being forced to donate his time, energy and considerable talent to defend a child rapist and killer. Anger, because anyone who knew Clay Delaney also knew what'd happened to his only child, especially Jack Armbrister.

Clay was aware that the criminal dockets were so overcrowded that civil trial lawyers were occasionally appointed to handle some of the cases. He'd been appointed once before, but that was for a petty crime that had pled out. A capital felony was in a different professional world from his, and he felt woefully inadequate to handle it. Besides, he knew that his personal tragedy would keep him so emotionally off balance that he couldn't defend someone accused of a similar crime. Armbrister had to know that. So, why was he being assigned the Brewton case?

He reasoned that whatever animosity the judge held for him couldn't be so strong that he'd be forced over his objection to defend the killer of a young girl. Surely, the judge wouldn't do that to him.

Judge Jack Armbrister was the last of a vanishing breed. He'd "read law" while working as a young man in his uncle's law office, took the bar exam four times, and was finally admitted to practice law in Georgia before graduation from law school was a requirement. His admission to the Georgia Bar was marked not so much by his persistence as by his uncle's elevation to chairman of the bar examination committee. While in private practice, Armbrister was known as a three-D lawyer: He handled divorces, DUIs and drug cases.

His subsequent appointment as a judge of the Superior Court of Fulton County had saved him from a mediocre legal career and his few clients from representation of less significance than that. It was no secret that Armbrister had boot licked his way onto the Superior Court bench. Even before he passed the bar, he was serving as a representative in the State legislature. Early on, he became part of the "good-old-boy" network that had dominated Georgia politics for years. The Governor's appointment of Armbrister to the court was clearly pay back for years of faithful partisan politics.

His rise to the bench came as a relief to Armbrister. He was on a fixed salary, had a pension waiting for him at the end of the road, and in the meantime he was king of the hill.

On the bench, he repressed his true feeling of inferiority by exercising the almost unparalleled power a judgeship conferred upon him. Though never in doubt, he was rarely right and seldom polite. Civility came creeping around his courtroom only when an old crony was before him, or when someone was obviously calling in an old marker.

Thirty years after his appointment, he became the Chief Judge of the Superior Court, an event marked solely by time in grade rather than competence, and aided by the well deserved myocardial infarction of his predecessor.

As Chief Judge, Armbrister had the largest chambers and his pick of the courtrooms. He also had first call on the funds the county commission had set aside as a courthouse decorating budget. Miserly in his personal finances, he was lavish in his office spending, and his surroundings at work showed it.

In his chambers, solid walnut wall paneling with trim molding finished in bas-relief surrounded his oversized mahogany desk, and the large windows behind his desk featured a deep purple drape with a matching satin border. He felt the color gave a regal appearance to visitors.

The nostalgic smell of old leather always rose from several rows of carefully selected but seldom read law books stacked flush with the paneled wall in a built-in bookcase to the right of Armbrister's desk.

Abutting his desk directly in front was his settlement table, which was a small conference table that sat at a right angle to the front of his desk with two chairs facing each other on each side. This arrangement allowed him to sit at his desk, looking right up the middle of the table, and preside over a forced settlement conference.

At a slight angle to the left of his desk was a long fabric covered couch and three matching wingback chairs, all of which encircled a mahogany butler's table. When lawyers were summoned to the judge's chambers for less formal conferences, the older ones moved quickly to grab the chairs, leaving the couch for the young and uninitiated—those who hadn't heard the rumors of what Armbrister and his secretary did on it during the noon recess.

Now, though, only the court administrator was present in chambers, standing patiently to the side as Armbrister studied the computer printout spread across his desk.

"All these damned defendants don't need a lawyer, Harold," Armbrister said. "Hell, was a time when we could move twice this many through the criminal docket in a week."

Harold Brockett, the Administrator for the Superior Court, shifted from one foot to the other. "Yes, sir."

"Now it takes three, maybe four months. They're all going to plead out anyway. But them young PDs want to hold out and bargain with the DA like they was buying a car, and—"

"Yes, sir."

"They save their man maybe a year or two, and just as soon as they get out, they're right back in here to start this all over again."

"Yes, sir."

"If it wasn't for that goddamn Supreme Court giving everyone who farts in public a lawyer, I could clean up this calendar, huh, Harold?"

"Yes, sir."

"Like the old days, huh?"

"Yes, sir."

"You bet your ass, yes, sir." Armbrister transferred some notes from the printout to a docket book lying open in front of him, then handed the stack of folded computer paper to Brockett. "That'll be all," he said without looking up.

Brockett hesitated for a moment, then said timidly, "The Director of the Public Defender's office was asking me why the Brewton case hadn't been assigned to his office, and I didn't know what to tell him."

"Of course you didn't, and you still don't. But you can remind him that I'm the one who makes the assignments. I'm the one who keeps him and his office busy, and all he gets is what I send him. Nothing more, nothing less. Think you can remember all that?"

"Yes, sir."

"Good. But just so there's no mistake about it, tell him that I've appointed a lawyer from one of those big fancy law firms to handle the Brewton case. It's high time those boys uptown started pulling their load. Started getting their hands dirty and learning first hand what practicing law's really all about. You tell the Public Defender I don't want his boys down there fucking around with that case. I've already assigned them a gracious plenty. Besides, that silk stocking crowd don't deserve no help."

"Yes, sir."

"Goddamn it, you're really starting to piss me off."

"Yes, sir," Brockett said meekly and exited the chambers, headed for the relative safety of his small office down the hall.

As Brockett disappeared, the intercom function button on Armbrister's phone display lit up. His secretary's voice blared out of the speaker on the front of the phone case, "Your sister's on line one, Judge."

"I'll take it."

Armbrister had never married, but over the years had remained so close to his only sibling that fifteen years earlier his sister and her two-year-old son had moved in with him during a bitter divorce. She never left. Armbrister's influence had kept the boy's father at bay, giving him the opportunity to play father to the son he never had. But just like his judging, his fathering was second rate, and Armbrister's nephew had grown up spoiled and reliant on his uncle to bail him out of one mistake after the other.

"What's he done now?" Armbrister barked.

To Armbrister's relief, the call wasn't a bad report. It was a request that the judge help find work for his nephew for the coming summer. That was easy. He'd just make the boy a "gofer" on his staff for three months. That way, he could keep his eyes on his nephew, and at least keep him out of trouble during the day.

Replacing the phone in its cradle, Armbrister rose from his desk and moved to his bookcase. Running his fingers over the leather spines of several law books, he finally stopped on one well-worn volume. He tapped the back of the book idly several times with one finger, then pulled it from its snug resting place with a deft flick of his wrist.

Holding the volume in one hand, he slowly relaxed his grip on the spine of the book, and it readily spread open at the halfway mark. There in the middle of the book was a rectangular hole neatly cut through all the pages. Resting in the cutout was a half-pint of sour mash bourbon.

He poured two fingers of the amber liquid into a water glass and downed it in one gulp. Pouring another shot, he replaced the bottle in the book and the book back in its slot. He then moved across the room, settled on the couch, and began slowly sipping on his second drink.

After a while, he picked up the phone extension from a highly polished drop-leaf table at one end of the couch and dialed his secretary. "What do we have next, Marsha?"

"Appointment with Attorney Delaney, Judge."

"What time?"

"Eleven-thirty."

"What time is it now?"

"Eleven-forty."

"Is he here yet?"

"Yes, sir."

"Shit."

"Are you ready for him?"

"Not yet. But I will be two fingers from now. Give me ten minutes, then announce him. I wasn't going to give him more than fifteen minutes anyway."

"Yes, sir."

Armbrister leaned back on the couch and propped his feet on the butler's table. He held a small sip of the harsh whiskey on his tongue momentarily, then let it trickle slowly down his throat, shivering from its effect. He smiled at the thought of a big firm lawyer in his office, squirming, needing personal relief and not getting it. Especially this firm. Especially this lawyer.

The firm had rejected him years before when he was first looking for a job. When Armbrister went on the bench, he started a shit list, and put this firm's name at the top of it. The list had grown considerably over the years. The lawyer had made it on his own.

In Armbrister's mind, Clay Delaney had made a fool out of him more than once. The worst time was when the lawyer had requested a recess right in the middle of a trial, just so he could go looking for his missing kid. That was no way to run a courtroom. No self-respecting jurist, he thought, should just stop a trial so some highly paid lawyer could gallivant around the country on personal business, no matter how important it was.

But no, he thought, the lawyer had to have his own way. The son of a bitch had intentionally elicited prejudicial evidence at the trial, and forced his opposing counsel to demand a mistrial. At that point, Armbrister had no choice. He'd had to grant it. Otherwise, he would've been reversed on appeal. Along with the mistrial came the inevitable delay.

Armbrister smiled. Clay Delaney had gotten his recess all right. He'd also earned a place of honor on the judge's list.

Armbrister knew he had to be on his best behavior during the forthcoming visit. Surely, the lawyer wanted out of the assignment the judge had given him in the capital murder case of Harco Brewton.

Armbrister planned to down play the lawyer's personal loss, and lecture him on his sworn duty to the law and to the less fortunate, a duty that transcended personal considerations. It was a canned lecture he'd heard at a Practicing Law Institute seminar years before, and he'd parroted it so many times since then he could deliver it almost verbatim. He especially liked the part that sounded like General Douglas MacArthur's farewell address to the Corps of Cadets at West Point, when MacArthur wistfully pledged his last mortal thought to "…the Corps, the Corps, the Corps."

Armbrister's lecturer, however, had exhorted duty and honor to "…the Law, the Law, the Law."

"Mr. Delaney to see you, Judge," his secretary announced over the intercom. "Send him in."

Desiring the meeting to remain formal, Armbrister had returned to his desk by the time Clay entered the room. Without rising, Armbrister invited him to sit and studied him as he took a chair at the conference table.

Armbrister had never paid much attention to the physical appearance of the lawyers who practiced before him. To him, they all looked alike. All he cared about was whether the manner of their dress showed him proper respect.

The nature of their meeting caused Armbrister to focus more intently on the lawyer sitting in front of him. He was at least six feet tall, tanned, and in remarkably good shape for a man in his mid-forties. He must work out, Armbrister thought. A few wisps of gray had intruded into his faintly blond hair, and his eyes had the look of cold blue steel. A few small creases radiated from the corners of his eyes, and were made more noticeable by the contrast of his tan.

Along with Clay Delaney's success in the courtroom and his obvious status in the Atlanta legal community, Jack Armbrister now began to resent the lawyer's remarkably good looks.

"What can I do for you, Counselor?"

"I need to talk to you about my assignment to the Brewton case, Your Honor. I—"

"Oh, yes. Brewton." Armbrister leaned back in his chair. "I hope you see in the assignment the same distinction I perceive, Counselor. Not every civil lawyer who practices before me gets an assignment so choice as this."

Clay shook his head. "Distinction or not, Your Honor. I can't do it. I'm not trained for it, and with what happened to my daughter, there's no way I can defend that guy. You've got to let me out of his case."

Armbrister rose and walked halfway across the room. He stopped and slowly turned to face Clay. "You have a greater duty to the law than you do to yourself, Mr. Delaney. When you took your oath as a lawyer, you took on an obligation to preserve and protect the very essence of the legal profession: the rule of law. What we have here is not a question of a person's guilt or innocence. It's a question of who's going to defend our system of justice. I've chosen you to do that. Don't let your personal life stand in your way."

"But, Your Honor—"

"I'll hear no more of it, Counselor," Armbrister said as he ushered Clay from his chambers. "One day you'll recognize what I've done and thank me for it."

As Clay Delaney left in obvious disappointment, the Honorable Jack Armbrister quietly gloated at what he had done and at what was yet to come.

"Marsha," Armbrister called out through the now open door to his chambers, "get your soft parts in here. It's time for lunch."

CHAPTER 2

▼

The subtle tones of the wind chime gingerly broke the early morning stillness on Clay Delaney's rear deck. That and the constant murmur of the river that eased past his back door were the first sounds that greeted him as he stepped outside to practice the gentle art of waking up.

The cool mist rising from the river swirled around the steam from his mug of black coffee. The two columns of moisture toyed and flirted with each other then disappeared together into the dawn. Clay wondered which one had lured the other away, but it was just too early to try to figure it out. He was content to simply lean against the railing, sip his coffee and watch the river stretch, yawn and wake up beside him.

He loved the peace and solitude of his unique place on the Chattahoochee, a river born in the ancient hills of North Georgia. Still in adolescence when it bounced its way through the suburbs of Atlanta, it reached the inevitable end of its tiresome journey with a new name just before it sacrificed itself to the Gulf of Mexico at a beautiful spot called Apalachicola—only to start the timeless and endless process of birth, death and renewal all over again. His tastefully designed house of wood and glass sat unpretentiously on the riverbank, settled in comfortably among the hardwoods. It gave Clay the feeling that he'd moved to the country. In many ways he had.

The smells and sounds of the river rejuvenated and sustained him, justifying the man-made part of his life, making his daily trek into downtown a fresh and different experience. By the same token, going home was a short journey to a far-away place.

After he lost his daughter, Chelsea, he could no longer bear to rattle around alone in his midtown home. Even with all her things gone, he still sensed her presence. There were times when he even thought he heard her steps padding along behind him. He had to get out, to put that all away and start over. That's when he'd sold and moved to the river.

Clay shivered slightly at the thought of Chelsea. He always did. At least since that cold, impersonal November day six years before when the call finally came to his law office.

"Mr. Delaney?" the hoarse voice on the line had inquired.

"Yes?"

"This is Sergeant Kauffman, Highland County, Ohio Sheriff's office."

"Yes?"

"We found her. An old vagrant stumbled on her in some woods near a small town above Hillsboro. I don't know how to tell you this, sir, but…well, you'd better get up here. We'll be taking the body down to the hospital morgue in Hillsboro. We're pretty sure it's her from the description, but we'll need you to make the I.D."

Clay's last view of his eight-year-old had been her parting wave as she boarded a plane to visit Anna's mother a half dozen years before.

She'd seemed so grown up, with her small carry-on bag slung over one shoulder and her little matching purse over the other. She always insisted that everything match. She was so much like Anna.

He knew the carry-on was crammed with enough books and games to last well through the Thanksgiving holiday. Lord knew what was in the purse. No doubt a little girl's cornucopia of crayons, mixed with beads, baubles, pretend makeup, and an odd assortment of fast food chain critters.

"I love you," he'd sighed quietly to himself, as Chelsea moved through the aircraft door.

"Who'll be greeting her in Cincinnati, Mr. Delaney?" the young flight attendant who had taken Chelsea in tow inquired.

"Her grandmother," he'd replied. "She's going to spend the holiday with her in Hillsboro. It's her first trip to Ohio. Matter-of-fact this will be her first plane ride."

The attendant's reply that she'd take good care of Chelsea was lost on Clay. It wasn't the plane ride that concerned him—it was the letting go.

The plane was still at the gate, and a feeling of loneliness had already crept over him. That was the first time since Anna died that he and Chelsea had been apart.

When Anna slipped quietly away from them during delivery, the auburn haired little person had been Clay Delaney's only link to sanity. Anna's faint admonition, "Take care of her, Clay," was seared into his being, adding a totally new dimension to his natural instinct to protect. It was a devotion born not only out of his love for the child, but also out of his love for her dying mother.

Since that agonizing day, he and Chelsea had been inseparable. Clay had done the professionally unthinkable. He'd taken a six-month leave of absence from an active law practice to care for his little girl.

Spurning the advice of well-meaning friends, he'd rejected the notion of hiring a nurse, and took upon himself, as he put it, "the bottling, the burping and the bathing."

It was inevitable that an unbreakable bond would join the hearts and souls of Chelsea and Clay. He never stopped to analyze or define it. It simply rose within him and swept warmly through his body as he lay quietly one night after a late feeding, Chelsea asleep on top of him, her perfect little fingers tightly clenched to the hair of his bare chest. It was as if Clay had given birth to her himself.

When he finally hired a nanny and returned to his office, the greatest expectation of both father and daughter was the end of what seemed like an interminable day when they could be together again.

"Get a life, Delaney," one of his friends had cautioned. "You can't play mommy forever."

"You don't get it, do you? I am the mommy."

As Chelsea grew, she'd tottered around behind Clay, desperately trying to keep him in sight as he moved about their spacious home. Wherever he was, little Chelsea wasn't far behind. If she wasn't following him, he was following her. He liked to believe that he was always following her, but sometimes he just happened to be out in front.

In those eight years of innocence, they'd learned so much from each other. He taught her how important it was to color within the lines, and she showed him how much fun it was to not. She'd brought the back yard's brightly colored birds to his attention. He taught her how to house and feed them, so they'd feel welcome and stay. He showed her how to mix brownies. And she taught him that it was okay to eat some of them right out of the bowl. He showed her how to catch fish from a creek bank. She taught him how to throw them back, "so they could go home to their mommies and daddies."

They celebrated birthdays, rode bikes, walked in the woods, skipped stones, collected seashells, read books, watched sunsets, and found four-leaf clovers. Clay was a child again, and he and Chelsea grew up together.

His tie to Chelsea was such that as he stood on the jet ramp watching her disappear into that cavernous aircraft, he'd had the overwhelming urge to cry out, to put an end to the whole trip.

The urge quickly dispelled when the excited girl suddenly reappeared in the doorway, her green eyes glinting like faint emeralds against the cameo of her bright face. Running to his embrace, she exclaimed, "My daddy. I love my daddy. Thank you for letting me visit Gran." Then she disappeared again with a wave of her hand.

She'd made it safely by air to Cincinnati, had even enjoyed a traditional Thanksgiving Day and dinner in Hillsboro. But, while on a short walk with a new little friend just before she was to return to Atlanta, she'd disappeared from her grandmother's quiet, residential street, and from the life of Clay Delaney forever.

His trip to view and identify his daughter's remains was like a distant and blurred memory. He was in a trance. Somewhere along the way, he was informed of the rape and partial mutilation. His mind mercifully protected him from his eyes. He retained no image of what he saw. He simply confirmed the non-existence of his little girl, then left Ohio.

As the years passed, he'd been able to push most thoughts of Anna and Chelsea to the attic of his recollection—a place he rarely visited. He'd consumed himself with his daily work to the point where there was little time to think about the future, much less the past.

His appointment to defend a man accused of harming a child had changed all that. It had revived everything in his life that was ever painful. It had returned to his mind and soul an emptiness that once had overwhelmed him. It had set him on a course where he must again confront and deal with the same emotions that had almost destroyed him.

As he watched the water move slowly by his deck, he winced at the thought of going to work. He was scheduled to be at the Public Defender's office that morning to view the Brewton file. Perhaps that explained why he thought the pull of the river was unusually magnetic. The more his sleepy head cleared, the more he realized he wasn't being attracted by the river. He was being repelled by his intense dislike for a man he'd never met.

Clay had tried to picture him many times, but had failed. He tried venting his anger with imaginary punches, thrown as hard as he could. But, he got no relief hitting a man who had no face. It was time to get on with his dirty chore and learn all the things he didn't want to know about a man called Harco.

For the first time in years, Clay took the granite steps of the county courthouse one at a time. He normally felt a sense of anticipation and excitement when he passed through the imposing columns that formed the facade of the old stone building. That, too, was missing.

The normally slow and cranky elevator seemed unusually swift and efficient, depositing him onto the fifth floor hall well before he was ready.

Looking cautiously through the half-glass door, Delaney watched a harried young woman busily typing on a computer's keyboard at the desk closest to the door. The light from the screen reflecting off her glasses turned her eyes an eerie iridescent blue. He hoped she was Mrs. Crowley. Then he'd simply walk in, get the file he wanted, and leave. To stay longer would naturally result in some conversation, which could reveal an embarrassing gap in his knowledge of criminal procedure, and possibly expose his complete lack of heart in the assignment.

From his safe position out in the hall, he surveyed the room, waiting for it to be clear enough for him to enter casually, make his innocuous request, flip through the file as if he knew what he was reading, and retreat with some semblance of grace.

But the office was alive. Men and women of varying ages and sizes poured over books and papers, blazed away on keyboards, went in and out of doors, engaged in heated exchanges, and stared at the walls transfixed in thought.

From what he saw, he knew it would get no better, but could get worse. What the hell. He moved through the doorway. It was then he saw the name plate on the young woman's desk, "Juanita Crowley." He was safe.

"Mrs. Crowley?"

"Nope," the young woman responded, still engrossed in her computer screen. "She's not here today. Good thing, too. My computer's down and I have a brief due in the morning."

"I'll come back." He turned for the door.

"Don't know how long she'll be out. If you need something, you'd better get it now."

"I'll just come back later." He reached for the door handle.

"Whatever it is, you must not want it very bad," she said, looking up for the first time.

Was he that obvious? He'd spent most of his professional life trying to be inscrutable. Now, at a time when he really wanted to remain obscure, a youngster was seeing right through him. He felt his ears getting warm and worried that they would soon be red. "I needed to get a file from her," he blurted.

"Which one?"

"Harco Brewton. I'm Clay Delaney."

The young woman rose and studied Clay intently for a moment. Then she turned to the busy room and called out, "Anyone know where Juanita put the file on Harco Brewton?"

All conversation ended mid word, keyboards fell silent, and books closed. All heads turned toward the front of the room, and all eyes stopped on Clay standing outlined by the door frame.

"I've got it," a muffled voice finally answered from a glassed-in office off the main room.

"Mr. Solomon has your file," the woman said. "Just go on back."

Clay wound his way back through the crowded maze of office furniture and refocused lawyers and lightly tapped on the inner office door marked, "Director."

"Hi. I'm Clay Delaney," he said, moving into the small room and extending his hand.

"Herb Solomon," the round, balding, cherub faced man at the desk replied. "Find a seat."

The only possible place was a worn out loveseat completely covered with stacks of brown folders, unopened personal mail and framed diplomas. It had obviously been a long time since those old cushions had helped bring out the shine on a blue serge suit.

Very little fabric showed through the cracks separating the randomly stacked folders on half of the loveseat. None were visible under the pile of personal effects on the other half. The presence of unread mail unsettled Delaney. He couldn't determine if the head of the Public Defender's office was irresponsible or simply too busy to get to it. The brown folders might be a clue, though. Their eviction from the comfort of an alphabetical resting place in someone's file cabinet and their placement on the loveseat close to Herb Solomon implied a certain urgency—an urgency, perhaps, that could keep one from his mail.

Rather than disrupt what was probably a very efficient filing system, Clay settled himself onto one of the seat's overstuffed arms. It was then he realized that he hadn't been extended an invitation. He'd been given a challenge. Except for Herb Solomon's chair, there was no other place to sit. It was obvious that whoever conducted business in that office did it on their feet.

Clay quickly surveyed the room. It was windowless with three bare walls. The fourth wall faced the interior and was half glass. Solomon's desk was situated so he could look out over his charges through the glass partition. Bent and scratched navy gray filing cabinets with drawers that wouldn't fully close lined the wall behind the desk. Everything in the room seemed tired and worn, including

Solomon. Clay quickly compared the spartan surroundings to his recollection of the opulence of Judge Armbrister's chambers, and shook his head.

Oblivious to Clay's seat selection, Solomon rummaged through a stack of the same brown folders that layered his desk, cluttered with Styrofoam cups. The cups made Clay nervous because, judging by the stale scent, most of them were partially filled with unsmoked but previously chewed tobacco. He imagined the worst if one of the cups tipped during Solomon's fumbling.

He was greatly relieved when Solomon found the folder he was looking for, and then stuck the stub of an unlit cigar into the side of his mouth.

At least he's not a spitter, Clay thought.

"So, you're Delaney," Solomon finally said. "They were all wondering when you'd show up and what you'd look like. Looks as if they got their good look at you all at once."

"Why am I so popular?"

"You're not. You've just got the case most of these kids would kill to have."

"Figuratively I hope."

"You bet. But I still wouldn't turn my back on any of my little piranhas."

"Why all the interest?"

"It would be a no lose situation for any of them."

"How's that?"

"The guy's obviously guilty. If one of them tries the case and loses it, no one gets upset. That's the way it was supposed to be. But they'll get good press and get quoted a lot by handling such a high profile case. If by some miracle they get the bastard off, they're a hero. Either way, it's a one way ticket to a good job with a private firm. A damn sight better living than down here in the pit. You're the spoiler."

"Listen. Any one of them who wants this case can have it. You can give them the file right now."

"No way. Those kids are in over their heads as it is. They probably have a hundred and fifty cases apiece. They don't need anymore. Least of all this one. Besides, the word has come down from Judge Arm Twister. This is your case, no substitutions. Sorry."

"Well, I'm sure any one of them could do a better job on this case than I can. I don't like this little shit, and I've never met him. As for what he did, I could blow his goddamn brains out myself."

"I've been doing this for thirty years now, and I never met one I liked. Hell, I represented my own son once and I didn't like him either. As for what they do, if you ever get to the point where you don't mind, you'll be needing a lawyer your-self."

"I guess I could hold on long enough to make sure he gets a fair trial."

"Fair trial my ass. If you can't plead him out, it's your job to get him off. It's called 'zealous advocacy.' If you can't get him off, you make damn certain he doesn't get a fair trial. You maneuver the judge or prosecutor into a position where they've got to make an error. You raise every possible defense known to man, and then some. Make them up, pull them out of thin air if you have to, do whatever it takes. You file motions, object to every goddamn piece of evidence the State has, even if you know it's admissible. You request delays and continu-ances. You cry foul both in court and to the media when you don't get your way. Who knows, somewhere along the line somebody's going to fuck up. Then you take that error to the appellate courts and say, 'See, this is what I've been saying all along. My client didn't get a fair trial. His conviction should be set aside.' By that time, the evidence is lost or the witnesses are gone, dead or just too fucking tired of it all. And the State can no longer retry him. That's how it works."

Clay stared at Solomon incredulously.

"I didn't make the rules, Delaney. I just use them to my clients' advantage. It wasn't me who said all these guilty bastards are innocent until twelve people off the street unanimously disagree. The State gives me an 'innocent' client, and that's what I try to give them back."

Clay shook his head. "How can you do this everyday? And for peanuts?"

"Because somewhere down deep in this pile of human crap there truly is an innocent man. And I'd spend a lifetime shoveling through it just to be there for his defense. If Justice were to visit us only once every two hundred years, then it still would've all been worth it."

"You're really serious about this, aren't you?"

"Yeah. My grandfather was hanged from a lamppost in a city in Poland you can't even pronounce. He didn't have a lawyer or a trial. This is my way of mak-ing sure that never happens again."

Clay was fascinated by the intensity he saw in the eyes of this man sitting in front of him. Here was a man he could stand back-to-back with, and fight off anybody. He was touched. He sat in awkward silence as his understanding of Solomon matured into respect.

Clay's eyes moved downward to the disheveled loveseat. There partially hid-den by other unhung diplomas lay a dusty, framed certificate. He could make out only "President, Harvard Law Review," but that was enough. He recognized immediately the distinction for legal excellence Herb Solomon had received long ago as a student. He smiled and hoped that when that innocent son of a bitch finally came along, he'd appreciate the man who'd been waiting for him all these years.

"Listen, I'm real sorry about what happened to your little girl," Solomon said. "And under those circumstances, I'm even more sorry you ended up with this case. When you were appointed, the word went through the courthouse like wildfire. We were all shocked. I want you to know I think it was a shitty thing for Armbrister to do."

Clay nodded.

"What the hell did you ever do to him?"

Clay shook his head. "He was dead wrong once, and I got him reversed. Then, in the middle of a trial my mother-in-law called and said that my daughter and the daughter of one of her neighbors had gone for a walk and were missing. When I asked him for a continuance, he refused."

"What'd you do?" Solomon said.

"Forced a mistrial."

"Good for you. Maybe you should try to see him about letting you off this case."

"I did. Right after I got the assignment."

"What'd he say?"

"That he was glad to see me."

"I'll bet."

"Then he gave me a lecture he'd obviously prepared for the occasion. All about laying aside my personal feelings and meeting my obligations as a lawyer."

"Yeah. That sounds like that two-faced bastard."

"That I shouldn't be concerned with Harco's guilt. But that I should concern myself only with preserving the rule of law."

"Even though he doesn't mean a goddamn word of it, the little prick is right, you know. It galls me no end to admit that he occasionally comes up with something worthwhile. Even the truth can ooze out of a dirty hole."

"I know I'm too close to all this, but how in the hell is he right in this case?"

"Look, it just boils down to this: The State's accused Harco Brewton of a crime. A vicious one, no question about it. But Harco Brewton could be anybody. His identity's unimportant. What matters is that the government has singled out someone, accused him of a crime, and put him in jail. Soon, all the resources available to the State will be marshaled in an attempt to vindicate a wrong by putting someone to death. Your job is simple, really. You must question the charge and the evidence, and submit them to intense scrutiny. If they don't measure up to what the law requires, the accused person should go free."

"Even Harco?"

"Even Harco. You should never concern yourself that a guilty man goes free. Just make damn sure that no innocent man is ever punished. You have to understand the ironic symbiosis that exists in our criminal justice system. Our need to protect someone from being wrongfully convicted gives life to some people we all know are guilty as hell. But if we don't question the charges and the evidence every single time, we'd soon have a system where you're doomed by a mere accusation."

"Your grandfather?"

"My grandfather. And if you think for one second that all the cops and prosecutors who've sworn to uphold the law actually obey it, you're naive as hell. Some of them will plant evidence, hide evidence or even manufacture it. They'll make out false reports and lie under oath. Justifying it all in their minds, because they're convinced they have the right guy, but not enough real evidence to put him away. Guess who's the only one who's going to stand between all that crap and the guy we call the defendant?"

Solomon's lesson on the law wasn't wasted on Clay, nor did it come as any great surprise. Those principles had been pounded into him in law school, and he had no basic disagreement with them. But knowing what he must do and doing it were lifetimes apart for Clay. Lifetimes separated by the now vanished smile of a child.

For the first time in his life, he realized how effortless it had been to be idealistic and driven by altruistic motives when his own life hadn't yet been affected.

For the first time, he began to understand what his parish priest, Father O'Hearn, meant when he'd talked about how difficult it was for a hungry man to care about how hungry someone else was. More than likely he was too preoccupied with the scream of the beast in his own belly to hear the cry of the pack prowling in the bellies of others.

"Well, what do you want to know about Harco Brewton?" Solomon finally asked.

"Everything."

Solomon opened the brown folder in front of him, but Clay noticed he didn't look at it once while spouting Harco's seedy personal history and arrests and convictions.

"Male, Caucasian, thirty-five-years-old. Born and raised in Pascagoula, Mississippi. Dropped out in the tenth grade. Worked at a local shipyard—non-skilled.

Drifted from job to job across the Gulf Coast from Texas to Florida. Part and full-time employment as a truck driver, construction worker and in nighttime building maintenance.

"Arrests and convictions for vagrancy, criminal trespass, breaking and entering, public drunkenness, receiving stolen goods, credit card fraud, bad checks, forgery, assault and battery and burglary. No prior sexual offenses or homicides.

"Never married. No known family. Likes beer. Likes women. Has scars and tattoos. How'm I doing?"

"Fine. Keep it up," Clay replied.

"When arrested for this offense he was driving an old white four door sedan with a rusted roof. A car fitting that description was seen on the victim's street two days before she disappeared. A search of the car turned up the victim's Raggedy Ann doll stuffed under the front passenger's seat. A witness places him at a convenience store between the victim's home and her school on the day she disappeared."

The victim, Clay thought. That's how they handle these cases. The dead are simply given a description that removes their identity, and any sympathy attached to it.

"You look upset," Solomon said.

"I'm fine. What about the little girl?"

"Carrie Lindsey. Thirteen-year-old white female. Eighth grade student. Disappeared on the way home from Hillside Middle School. Same white car seen in the vicinity of the victim's school on the afternoon of the disappearance. Body found five days later by two high school students. Death caused by blunt trauma to the back of the head. Crime scene photos and morgue photos are in the file. There was evidence of forced penetration, but ejaculation couldn't be determined."

Solomon paused to catch his breath. "They've got him cold."

"Has he confessed?"

"Nope. He pled not guilty at the arraignment and asked for a lawyer. He's been through this before, remember."

"Tell me about it."

"We thought this office was going to represent him, so we demanded and got all the pretrial stuff. There wasn't any Brady material."

"Brady material?"

"Yeah, evidence that might exonerate him. All the evidence in this file is going to fry him."

Clay shook his head.

"Anyway, one of our people also did an initial interview of Brewton at the county jail. He claims he was in Montgomery when the Lindsey girl disappeared, but has no one to back him up. Our interviewer was totally turned off by him, and thinks he's a lying sack. He's your baby now. The best thing you can do is try to work a deal with the D.A. Get Brewton to plead guilty in return for a life sentence if you can work it. Otherwise, he's going to burn."

A warm rush suddenly flowed over Clay. Ever since he got this assignment all he could think of was why he, of all people, had to do it. He'd sat around feeling sorry for himself, and when that wore off, he felt anger at Harco Brewton. There he'd remained—immobilized—stuck between rage and self-pity.

He had focused so intensely on Harco's crime that, until now, he'd never once thought about the result of the crime, the other half of Dostoevski's dichotomy: Punishment. And not just any old punishment, but death—the ultimate sanction. They'd cook his twisted brain with 5,000 volts. Maybe he could talk them into connecting one of the electrodes to Harco's balls.

We'll just get rid of the problem, he thought. If there's such a thing as Solomon's notion of Justice, I'm entitled to the negative benefit of it. And I'm destined to lose. When I do, Harco will burn. Then I'll volunteer to go down there and throw the switch. A smile began to form on Clay's face.

"Don't even think of it, Delaney," Solomon said. "We all know where you're coming from."

"Indulge me just a little bit, Herb."

"Nope. Not one iota. You take this as the most serious case of your life."

"It is."

"No, dammit! You're not listening to me. I'm saying don't slack up. Don't screw up. Defend this case as if your own life was on the line. In some ways, it is. If the press or if the Disciplinary Committee of the State Bar ever thinks you're pulling punches because of what happened to your daughter, they'll crucify you. You'll never practice law again—anywhere. And that's not the worst part."

"What could be worse?"

"Any conviction of Harco Brewton would be set aside. He could even walk."

"Damn." Clay's small grin faded completely.

"My sentiments exactly. Why do you think Armbrister assigned you this case? Just to make you feel bad? Hell no. He's obviously waited a long time for the right case to come along. Well, here it is. He's counting on the father in you overpowering the lawyer in you. From what I'm seeing, he may be right. If he is, you're a dead man. And whether he is or not, you're the one who's going to be on trial, not Harco Brewton.

"And no matter how you slice it, you get the smallest piece. Do a great job and Harco walks. Do a poor job and Harco walks. Armbrister had this one pegged right."

Clay sat in subdued silence as the realization of the irony of his assignment dawned on him.

Solomon arose slowly and moved from behind his disheveled desk to stand in front of Clay. Clay's eyes met his, stayed fixed in place for a moment, then moved downward to the brown folder held loosely in Solomon's right hand.

"Walk away with this," Solomon said, extending the folder, "or walk away from the law. You have no other choice. But if you take it, the job is yours to the bitter end. No half-assed performance. No quitting midway through. Do it and do it right, or don't even start."

Clay stood up slowly, looked Solomon in the eyes, and took the file. Turning toward the door, he took a deep breath and wound his way out.

As he crossed the main work-room, it was as if he was emitting some low frequency signal that disrupted the preoccupation of each person he passed. They raised their heads sequentially like dominos in reverse to watch his departure.

Solomon watched from the door of his office.

"He take the file?" one of the young lawyers standing closest to him asked.

"Yeah."

"He going to take the case?"

"I'm not sure."

"Think he'll be able to handle it?"

"I don't know."

"What do you think of him?"

"I think the two of us could stand here asking stupid questions and scratching our asses on the county's time for the rest of our lives and never see another man like that walk through those doors again. Now get back to work and find me some goddamn justice!"

As the young lawyer scampered back to his desk, Solomon stood staring at the vacant front door. "God help you, Clay Delaney. None of the rest of us can."

CHAPTER 3

▼

Clay Delaney's unfamiliarity with the practice of criminal law was highlighted by the most fundamental ignorance. He didn't know how to get to the county jail. He'd looked up the address in the phone book under County Government and then located the street on a city map. Now he found himself cruising slowly through an unfamiliar part of town looking for the ever elusive street address that never seemed to be displayed on buildings he was trying to find.

It looked as if the few visible numbers weren't going as high as the one he needed before the street ended at a railroad spur. He was going to have to double back, find a way around the spur to see if the street picked up on the other side.

He was unwilling to stop and ask for directions. He could see the headlines now, "Defense counsel for Georgia's most infamous killer can't find jail."

As he drove past the bum riddled doorways of several abandoned buildings, he was sure he could read in the otherwise vacant stares of the men slouching there an unvoiced recognition, "There goes Harco Brewton's lawyer. He must be lost."

His frustration had reached the point where he was even imagining what fellow prisoners would say when he finally left the jail he hadn't yet found. "Hey Harco. Some lawyer you got there. Hope he can find the courthouse. It don't look like he can find his own ass with both hands."

Clay wondered if he'd flipped. There he was feeling apologetic to a career criminal and his friends for having difficulty getting to him to provide free legal help—help that was intended to save his life for a crime that warranted a death sentence in the first place. He was sure the shrinks had a name for the syndrome. They had a name and a reason for everything, including why they felt compelled to have a name and a reason for everything.

As the dilapidated buildings slipped past Clay's window, he felt a discomfort that arose from his unfamiliarity with his surroundings. It wasn't a lack of familiarity with the location as such, but rather with the character of it. Careening inside the walls of a middle class existence most of his adult life hadn't sheltered him completely from the blight and decay of the inner city, although it had certainly limited his exposure.

Consequently, he was always surprised to be reminded that the inner city was alive, but still not well. He tended to remain emotionally off balance when he was forced to look squalor right in the face. Now, for some reason, it seemed to be looking back, and he was having a peculiarly difficult time identifying his own feelings. Guilt? Fear? Suspicion? Maybe it was a mixture of all three.

The view unfolding around him was a stark realization that he was truly uncomfortable with both the thought of criminal activity, and his own notion of where it might originate. He wondered how he was going to be objective when he entered the jail itself when he was reacting so negatively to nothing more than its neighborhood.

The sudden ear-piercing shriek of a passing police car brought Clay back to his senses, and at the same time put his heart in his throat. But he recovered sufficiently to speed up and follow the impatient policeman to what he knew should be the county jail.

He didn't see any spots marked "visitor," so he slid into a space in the administrative lot.

"Sorry, you can't park there, Mac," a plainclothes policeman called out as Clay was putting on his coat.

"Where then? I don't see anything for visitors."

"You can put it on the street if you want to risk it. Or, there's a lot three blocks up where you can pay."

"You mean I've got to pay to park?"

"You do if you want to keep your car from getting ripped off."

"From in front of the jail?"

"What better place? Happens everyday. They're not holding Sunday School in there, you know."

"Yeah. Real silly of me." Clay climbed back behind the wheel.

As he pulled away, he said, "Tell me. On the way out, is the minefield on my left or on my right?"

"What?"

"Never mind."

Clay pulled in front of the tarpaper-covered booth at the entrance to the lot up the street and stopped to read the sign.

"That'll be six bucks in advance," the attendant said through the opening.

"But your sign says six dollars for all day."

"You'll get a refund for what you don't use when you come back. Want a receipt?"

"If I'm going to get money back, why would I want a receipt for six dollars?"

The question seemed to spur the lot attendant's interest, and he leaned out the booth window. "For your taxes, of course. It's a legitimate business expense."

"A six dollar deduction isn't legitimate if you don't really pay six dollars."

"But that's the beauty of it," said the attendant. "I give you the receipt. It's a good record and you take the deduction for the full amount. I do this for all my customers. The IRS never knows the difference."

"Oh yes they do."

"How's that?"

"I'm with the IRS. Special Agent Delaney. Listen, I'm going to overlook this if you'll just watch over my car real good while I'm gone. It's government property you know."

"Yes sir, Mr. Delaney. You've got my word. No problem."

Clay struck out for the jail. His briefcase swung in one hand while his suit coat was slung over his shoulder with the other. As he moved up the street, he knew that was the last he'd see of his six dollars or any part of it. He didn't expect to be gone long, but from the look on the attendant's face he expected him to be long gone.

The irony was that he would now have a legitimate six-dollar expense, but no receipt. Well, no one ever told him life was fair. But then, no one ever told him he was going to have to pay to see Harco Brewton, either.

He had a good view of the jail building as he approached. It didn't look anything like he expected. In fact, he was surprised to find himself slightly disappointed. Rather than a stark, imposing multi-story structure of stone and steel, he saw in front of him an innocuous one story brick building which, except for the sign, could've been mistaken for a soft drink bottling plant.

He read, "Fulton County Detention Center."

Detention Center, my ass, he thought. What was wrong with "Jail," all in caps?

He'd heard about catering to criminals, but he didn't know they were doing it with syllables too. There was no doubt that the five syllables that had replaced the one in "Jail" softened the sound of the consequences considerably.

Once inside the door of the jail, he was immediately greeted by a smell that was a mixture of sweat, tobacco smoke and disinfectant, weighted more toward sweat.

Clay understood that one couldn't store people in sealed containers and not expect them to smell rotten. He presumed that the permeating smell of disinfectant resulted from its being used as much to deodorize as to clean. The only problem with that was they were trying to replace one bad odor with another, and it wasn't working. He could smell both. But like all things, he knew he'd soon get used to it. It didn't seem to be bothering anyone else.

"May I help you?" a pleasant voice asked.

"Yes Ma'am," Clay replied to the officer seated behind a glass panel with a metal voice grate. "I'm here to see one of your inmates."

"Name?"

"Delaney. Clay Delaney."

The officer scrolled through a computer screen and looked up. "No Delaney here. You sure he's in County?"

"No, I'm Delaney. I'm here to see Mr. Brewton."

"We don't have no misters in here either, Mister."

"Okay. I'm sorry. Harco Brewton."

The officer turned back to her screen. "All right. We've got him. Fill this out," she said and pushed a five by eight card under the glass.

Clay completed the card and returned it under the panel. The officer picked it up and studied it for a moment.

"Lawyer?"

"Yeah."

"His lawyer?"

"Yeah."

"I need to see your Bar card, please."

Clay fumbled through his wallet past a potpourri of plastic. He hadn't expected that. He received a new Bar card every year, always a different color. He dutifully placed it in his wallet and threw the old one away. In the fourteen years he'd been doing that no one had ever asked to see it before.

"Here it is," he said triumphantly, shoving it under the glass.

The officer viewed it and shoved it back. "Through the door on your left. We'll call him up."

Clay moved toward the metal door. He knew that when he passed through it, he'd really be inside a jail. Up to now it was no different from being in any other government building. This would be his first time. Strange for a lawyer of his age and experience, but true.

A harsh buzzer sounded from the vicinity of the metal door. Clay turned the handle and passed through.

While the door had done little to intercept the smell of the place, it had totally blocked the din on the other side. Once through the door, his ears were assaulted and battered by the heavy clang of steel on steel, unintelligible yells and catcalls, a mournful solo and the sounds of multitudinous conversations, each oblivious to the other. All that was set against a backdrop of competing country music stations.

Despite all the noisy indications of human occupation, he saw no one except another officer seated at a desk beside a metal detector. Behind him was a pair of painted white sliding steel bars separated by a four foot space, with another officer seated on the other side.

"Empty your pockets please," the first officer commanded, "and open your briefcase and place it on the table."

Clay complied. When the inspection was complete, the officer nodded toward the metal detector. "Pass through. I'm going to have to hold the pen knife till you come back."

He'd forgotten all about the little knife. He was upset with himself that he hadn't anticipated the objection, and left it in the car. He was going to have to start thinking more like a criminal.

His passage through the magnetometer was uneventful, and when he cleared he once again heard the harsh electronic release on the first row of sliding steel bars. This time, however, he had to do nothing. The first half of it slammed open on its own.

The first officer yelled over the noise of the retreating bars, "Step in, please."

Clay took two steps forward and was stopped by the unopened second row. Another sound followed and instead of the second row opening, the first row noisily slammed shut behind him, leaving him stuck between the two rows, feeling like a piece of meat in a steel sandwich.

He'd always been claustrophobic. That's why he'd opted for aviation rather than subs when he left the Naval Academy. Even those few seconds in that steel trap caused the hair to rise on the back of his neck.

"Watch your hands and feet," the second officer said.

Then the awful sound came again with the opening and closing of the bars in front of him. He was inside.

"First room on your right," said the second officer.

Clay moved into the small room expecting to find a glass panel with Harco Brewton on the other side, connected safely by a telephone, just like on TV. Instead there was a small table and two straight-back chairs. The only glass panel was the top half of the door. Otherwise, there were simply four bare walls.

Then it dawned on him—he and Harco were going to be in same room. Alone.

An officer suddenly appeared at the door and said, "You've got twenty minutes. I'll be right outside." Then he disappeared, and in his place stood Harco Brewton.

Clay was stunned. Instead of a burly brute of a man whose presence would signal danger to even the most unwary, standing in front of him was a short, skinny, pathetic piece of southern trash.

He stood five feet six inches, and weighed 125 pounds at most. He was bug-eyed, pot-bellied, and had a head too large for the body that was trying to support it. Clay had seen people like that all his life. Every high school had one. Invariably, their front teeth were rotten, and they had a sister in the army. They had big watches, little dicks, and were always trying to cash a two party check. The only thing Harco was missing was a large zit on his chin, but Clay was sure he'd have one by the time of trial.

Harco took the chair on the opposite side of the table—the one facing the door. He looked nervously over his left shoulder, then over his right. There was nothing back there but bare walls, not even one of those fake mirrors they always showed in the movies. Any fool could see that when he walked into the room. Yet, Harco checked and double-checked over his shoulder repeatedly throughout the interview, interspersed by periodic glances up toward the door panel.

When Harco spoke, Clay shook his head. There they were: two rotten front teeth.

"Okay, here's what I know," Harco stated.

"Stop right there," Clay said. "Why are you talking to me?"

"Because you're my lawyer."

"How in the name of God do you know who I am?"

"Because they said my lawyer was here."

"What's your lawyer's name?"

"I don't know."

"What's my name?"

"I don't know."

"I'm going to ask you one more time. Why are you talking to me?"

"I don't know."

"That's what I thought. Well, I am your lawyer. My name's Clay Delaney. Now, have you talked to anyone else?"

"No."

"Anyone?"

"No."

"Good. Don't—"

"Let's get something straight, mister lawyer man. I'm gonna talk to whoever I want to, when I want to."

"You get something straight, mister killer man," Clay said. "Either you do exactly what I say when I say it, or you can get yourself another lawyer."

Clay hoped Harco wouldn't call his bluff. He couldn't quit. But Harco could. If Harco rejected him as counsel, maybe a new one would have to be appointed. That might just be his way out.

But Harco unwittingly called the bluff, at least partially. "I never heard of no appointed lawyer quittin'," he said. "It ain't like I hired you, you know. Seems like you don't have much say-so."

Clay knew Harco was on the right track, and he tried to steer him in a different direction. "If you don't like the way I'm going to handle your case, you can request other counsel."

"How long you been a lawyer?"

"Fourteen years."

"What kind of law do you do?"

"I'm a trial lawyer."

"How many criminal cases you tried?"

There was the one question Clay had prayed would never be asked, by anyone, certainly not by Harco Brewton of all people. He knew that the answer would strip him of all the pride that accompanied fourteen years of accomplishment. How'd this interview get so turned around so quickly?

"How many?" Harco demanded.

"None."

"Well, well, well. They sent me a virgin. I usually like virgins, but not this kind. Looks like you're just another violation of my constitutional rights."

"If that's what you think, ask for a new lawyer."

"Oh no," Harco rejoined with a rotten-toothed grin. "You're my ace in the hole. If you don't win, I'm gonna appeal based on your incompetence."

Before Harco could blink, Clay had reached across the small table and had him firmly by the throat with one hand. The door flew open, and the waiting officer was in the room in a flash, but not before Harco's already bulging eyes bulged a little more and began to glaze over.

"You got a problem in here, colonel?" the advancing guard inquired.

"Oh no," Clay replied. "We were just demonstrating technique. Weren't we?" he said to Harco as he released his grip.

Harco couldn't answer. He only nodded.

"Can't touch the inmates, colonel. If they need touching, we'll do it. Know what I mean?"

"Sorry," Clay said.

Harco sank back into his chair gasping. The guard retreated and closed the door, but remained hovering outside.

Harco and Clay eyed each other. They'd both jockeyed for position, but neither had won.

Finally, Clay broke the silence. "Just so there's no misunderstanding between us. I didn't ask for this job, but I've got it. I don't like it, and I don't like you or your kind. But I'm going to see this through to the end."

Harco cleared his throat and responded briskly. "You highfalutin fuckers don't know me or my kind, or even care to. The only end you want to see this to is mine. So let's cut all the happy horse shit and talk business."

"Let's," Clay said. "From what I've seen you don't have a rat's chance in a barn full of cats. You'd be doing good to get the D.A. to let you plead out."

Harco was silent for a moment, then began to pick at the sparrow brown, bushy mustache that covered his weak upper lip. The rotten grin reappeared. "Not if you prove my alibi."

"What alibi is that?"

"I was in Montgomery when the girl got it." Harco paused and then said with a laugh, "She did get it before she got it, you know."

Clay was taken aback by the callous lack of remorse and Harco's pitiful attempt at grisly humor. He knew he was going to have to get past that to do his job, and the best course was simply to ignore it. He gave it his best shot. "Who can prove that?"

"I can."

"Are you planning to take the stand?"

"I sure am."

"I wouldn't advise that, but we'll talk about it later. Even if you testify that's still not enough. You'll never prove an alibi without the testimony of someone else."

A cocky look appeared on Harco's face. "You must think I'm stupid. You know, I know more about beatin' this shit than you do. I got me a buddy from Montgomery who'll say I was with him all day."

The "who'll say" comment raised a red flag in Delaney's mind. "Just who is this buddy?" he asked cautiously.

"He's my cellmate, but we go way back. And he's from Montgomery. He'll do it for me, and I told him I'd take care of him when I got out."

"No. I don't think you're stupid. You'd have to improve considerably just to be stupid. I think you're crazy. Don't you think it a neat coincidence that two long lost friend cons meet up in jail and one provides an alibi for the other? No way I'm going to let you pull a stunt like that."

"All right. I can get someone on the outside to do it," Harco said.

"That's hardly the point. I can't just stand by and let you solicit perjury. That's a crime. Or haven't you heard?"

"What's one more little old crime when you're already facing a murder rap? After all, I am a criminal. Or haven't you heard?"

"I'm not going to argue with you. I'm just not going to let you do it."

"What are you going to do? Tell on me?" Harco said in a mocking tone. "You can't do that. You're my lawyer. Everything I tell you's a secret."

"Everything you tell me is confidential except your intention to commit a crime in the future. I'm obliged to keep everything in the strictest confidence but that. That's my oath. And make no mistake, I'll live up to it. So why don't you go back to playing inmate, and let me play the part of the lawyer."

Harco sat in brooding silence, staring at Clay. His left hand rested nervously on the table in front of him. For the first time Clay had a clear view of the hand. He immediately noticed that on the back of his hand was a tattooed letter on the uppermost segment of each of his four fingers. Each letter faced inward, back toward the arm. Clay made a quick note of the letters, starting with the left index finger. He wrote L, T, F and C.

Harco fidgeted and glanced about the room and over his shoulders. "What do they have on me?" he finally asked.

"Not much. Just some witnesses who place you on the dead girl's street, and near her school. Then there's the small matter of her personal belongings being in your car. Not much. Just enough to send you to the chair."

"I can't believe some little dead cunt's going to put me away."

"What the hell is the matter with you? Don't you have any feelings at all? Any feelings for that little girl?"

"Like they say, if they're old enough to bleed, they're old enough to butcher."

Clay slammed the table with his hand and glared at Harco, while the sound of his reaction ricocheted violently throughout the tiny cubicle. The noise and the swiftness of his movement startled Harco, and he reflexively straightened up and moved backwards as far as he could go in his chair. The attentive guard who had seen everything through the door panel wasn't so quick to enter this time, but he eventually did and said, "Y'all are going to have to hold it down in here."

"I'm outta here anyway," Clay stated, rising to his feet.

"No," Harco cried, rising with him. Then in a much softer, more pleading tone he said, "Please, don't. Please don't go."

"You've got seven more minutes if you want 'em," the guard said.

"All right," Clay responded. "But I don't want any more of that crap," he said to Harco.

Both men returned to their chairs, and the grinning guard closed the door.

"You think if I pled guilty I could avoid the chair?" Harco asked after a brief pause.

"I don't know if the D.A. will deal, but it's worth a try. Why don't you give me seven minutes of personal information, so I'll have something to present to him."

Clay had no idea what he'd need to know when plea bargaining a murder case. But he felt that if he knew more about Harco, he could at least humanize him to some extent during any negotiations, rather than have the district attorney think of Harco as a number on a docket, or as the cold, brutal killer Clay knew him to be.

"Like what?" Harco inquired.

"Well, for starters, where do you live?"

"A roomin' house downtown. Been there just a few months before all this."

"You have any family?"

"My old man walked out when I was about six. Ain't seen him since. Don't recall too much about him, 'cept he stayed drunk most of the time. Can't say as I blame him, my ma being the way she was and all."

At that point, Harco relaxed somewhat and settled back in his chair, his voice becoming monotone. It was then that his right hand moved into view and rested on the table. Clay noticed more tattoos. Again, there were meaningless letters on the back of the uppermost segment of each of Harco's fingers. Just like the other hand, except these letters faced outward away from the arm. He quickly jotted them down, E, S, U and K. Clay checked his notes. He now had eight letters that meant nothing to him, either in clusters or all together. Left read, "LTFC," while the right read, "ESUK."

Meanwhile, Harco continued. "My ma raised me in a rented three room shotgun shack in Pascagoula, Mississippi. It was one of them long, skinny, frame houses with all the rooms set in a row. When you look in the front door, you see clear through every room and right out the back door. Just like you was looking down the barrel of a shotgun."

"What did your mother do for a living?"

"Mostly waitressed. But she paid for a lot of things with her back. What you'd call layin' down on the job. A whore."

All of a sudden Clay felt a need to take up for this unknown woman and justify to Harco what she did. "Maybe she had to, to get by," he offered weakly.

"Hell, she was a doin' it for free when my old man was still around, 'cept it was behind his back. And until I was thirteen and could leave the house at night when she brought one of 'em home, I could hear 'em in there goin' at it. She was havin' such a good time, I thought for awhile there she was payin' them."

"There are explanations for things like that, you know," Clay offered.

"Yeah? Well you can explain it to your heart's content, but it wasn't your ma I was listenin' to."

"I know, but some women are just different. Just like some men."

"Some? It must run in the family. Her sister's the same way. Once when she was visitin' us and ma was at work, she climbed in bed with me and said she was goin' to give me a early present for my ninth birthday."

"What happened?"

"Nuttin'. At first I didn't know what she was doin'. Then when she started touchin' me and all and rubbin' up on me, I got real scared. I mean she looked more like my ma than my ma. She climbed out when I started to cry. I never told my ma."

"Where's your mother now?"

"I don't rightly know. When I was sixteen she went out to get some cigarettes and never came back. Some years back I heard she might be livin' in Kentucky. Then later, I heard she might be livin' here. I'm really not sure if she's still even livin' at all."

"What did you do after she left?"

"I had to leave the house when I couldn't make the rent. Then I dropped out of school and went to work."

"Where did you live?"

"Here and there."

"You ever try to finish school?"

"Naw. I could never take them bitch teachers anyway."

Harco was interrupted by the guard's tap on the door panel. Clay looked up, raised one open hand, silently requesting five more minutes. The guard nodded and flashed five fingers in return.

Noticing the interplay between the guard and Clay, Harco sat up and started his annoying head and eye movement again.

Trying to glean as much information as he could out of the visit, Clay motioned for Harco to continue.

"What else do you want to know?"

"What kind of work did you do?"

"Drove a forklift and did other odd jobs at Haskins Boat Works in Pascagoula right outta school.

"Weren't you underage?"

"Yeah, but I lied. I was big for my age."

Clay figured he must have been a good liar for his age too, or else he already had that stupid mustache back then, because except for the pot belly, Harco still had the size and build of a sixteen-year-old.

"How long did you work there?"

"Oh, a year or so. Then I did some time in juvie, and they wouldn't take me back."

"What was the time for?"

"Me and some buddies were rollin' winos for spare change."

"What did you do after that?"

"Worked at a car wash, stocked groceries and bused tables."

"All at one time?"

"No. I moved from job to job till I got my Class 'A.'"

"Class 'A?'"

"Yeah. You know, my chauffeur's permit—for trucks."

"Oh. Who'd you drive for?"

"There were a lot of 'em. And I did some hard time in between those jobs. I didn't make the same mistake I made as a kid, though. I didn't tell 'em where I'd been. But long haulin' hasn't been so good in the last few years, so I been outta truckin' for awhile."

"Doing what?"

"You really want to know?"

"Yeah."

"This is one of those things you can't tell on me, right?"

"That's right."

"Okay. I been doin' a little buildin' maintenance with a lot of burglin' on the side."

"Burglin'? Like in robbing?"

"No man. Ain't no robbin' to it. Just good old breakin', enterin' and stealin'. I ain't no robber." It was as if Harco felt he had to draw a moral line somewhere.

With time fast running out, Clay changed the subject. "Tell me," he said, "what do the letters on your hands stand for?"

Harco glanced at the back of his hands then said with a grin, "Let's fuck."

"I beg your pardon?" Clay said in amazement.

"That's what it says if I fold my hands and lock my fingers together in front of me." Which he promptly did.

There staring at Clay from across the table was the clear, unmistakable message emanating from Harco's folded hands.

Clay was floored. The face of the guard outside was split open by a toothy grin. Harco swelled with pride.

Clay regained some of his composure. "Great! That's just great! I suppose you're going to flash that to the jury."

"Depends on if I like any of 'em."

"Well, I'm telling you right now. One of those hands is going to be in a bandage or a cast before we get into a courtroom. Even if I have to break it myself. Now, do you have any more tattoos on you?"

"Just these," Harco responded, as he raised the left sleeve of his inmate's jumpsuit.

There on Harco's left forearm were four names in a column. Starting from the top and going down, Delaney read, "Laura, Maud, Samantha, Amanda."

"Is that it?"

"That's it."

"You must really fancy yourself a lady's man."

"Yeah," Harco said, "you got it."

Clay's first session with Harco came to an abrupt end as the guard moved into the room and began to escort him away. As he was being guided through the door, he looked over his shoulder and called out, "By the way. What'll I call you? Clay? Clayton? Claymore?"

"Let's not be formal. 'Sir' or 'Mr. Delaney' will do just fine."

Clay's return through the steel maze was uneventful. As he suspected, the attendant's tarpaper shack was closed up tight when he returned to the parking lot. And he'd been gone only two dollars worth at most.

After his half hour at the jail he felt a compelling need to go straight home and wash himself—not just his hands. After meeting Harco Brewton, that wouldn't be enough.

CHAPTER 4

▼

There were only two things in the world Herb Solomon couldn't stomach, no matter how hard he tried: beef tripe and Judge Jack Armbrister. He was easily able to avoid the one, but not the other. He had to work in the same profession, the same building, and sometimes in the same room with Armbrister.

It had been that way for thirty years now. The day Armbrister took his oath of office as a Superior Court judge, Herb Solomon had taken his as a member of the Georgia Bar, and immediately thereafter as the first Public Defender of Fulton County, Georgia. From a one-person office, staffed by himself, a part-time secretary, and a broken down Underwood, the office of the Public Defender had grown to a fully-automated, twenty-lawyer operation with Herbert O. Solomon as Director.

Only within the last year, by being elevated to Chief Judge, had Armbrister become Solomon's boss, in the sense that as Chief Judge Armbrister was responsible for appointing lawyers to represent indigent persons under indictment. The power to appoint counsel gave him the power to control Solomon's schedule and workload. The Public Defender was the recipient of ninety percent of the cases assigned. The remainder were parceled out among private practitioners, who were obliged to handle them free of charge as part of their public service duty to the Bar.

The tension between Solomon and Armbrister was as mutual as it was natural. Solomon's love and respect for the law was rejected everyday by Armbrister's abuse of it. Solomon used the law to serve others, while Armbrister used it as a source of power over them.

Consequently, Solomon's knowledge of what made Armbrister tick, coupled with his intuitive suspicion of him, caused Solomon to question the selection of Clay Delaney as appointed counsel in the Brewton case. Delaney's loss of his only child was no secret in Atlanta's tightly knit legal community. One had to be a fool to overlook it, or else sadistic as hell. Whatever else Armbrister was, Solomon knew he was no fool.

Armbrister and Solomon had clashed before, mostly in the courtroom as "his Honor" tried to railroad one of Solomon's clients. Seldom did they have verbal exchanges elsewhere. They astutely avoided any social or occasional contact. Now, though, it seemed appropriate to beard the lion in his den. Solomon would confront the judge in chambers. The subject: Clay Delaney's appointment.

Solomon eyed Armbrister's couch warily as he entered the judge's chambers, hoping he wouldn't be invited to sit there.

"To what do I owe this honor?" Armbrister asked, rising to greet Solomon.

Solomon had once been served "mock chicken" at a high school banquet. It was ground flank steak on a stick, rolled to resemble a drumstick, then fried. It was awful. Since that day, Solomon had known that no matter how much culinary alchemy was involved, one couldn't make fried chicken out of the northern end of a southbound cow. Armbrister's strained greeting was just another tasteless serving.

"Have a seat," Armbrister said as he approached.

Solomon's mind flashed with two alternatives. Should he be openly rude and take a good seat without shaking hands, or should he shake hands first then race the judge for the seat he wanted? He split the difference, selecting a wingback chair as he said, "Thank you," then rose to greet the approaching Armbrister, thinking all the while, I'll let the SOB sit on his own snail tracks.

"I've come to talk about the Brewton case," Solomon stated after the judge had seated himself on the couch.

"Would you like some coffee?" Armbrister asked.

"No, thank you."

"Well, I do. Marsha, bring us two cups of coffee," he said through the open doorway. Then, turning to Solomon, "You may just change your mind. She makes a mean cup of coffee. Now, what did you say you wanted to talk about?"

"Clay Delaney and the Brewton case. The most critical death penalty case in this county in twenty-five years, and you assign it to a lawyer with no criminal experience."

"What are you trying to say?"

"I'm not trying to say anything. I'm saying it flat out. The assignment isn't fair to Delaney, it's not fair to Brewton, and you know it. Brewton should go to a heavyweight, not a novice. With all due respect, you made a piss poor choice, your Honor."

"Just one damn minute, Solomon." Armbrister rose to his feet as if struck across the mouth. "I can have your fucking job for that."

"I answer to the County Commission, not you, your Honor."

"I can still have your job. The Commission Chairman owes me." Turning his head toward the door, he shouted, "Forget about the coffee, Marsha. Mr. Solomon won't be staying."

Armbrister moved toward his desk. "Come in here and criticize me. No— accuse me. You have your damn nerve. Your office is so far behind now, you can't handle the cases you've got. Now you're in here complaining that you should have this one too. Well, you don't. And you're not going to get it."

"That's hardly the point."

"That's exactly the point. You and your little 'can't get a job' do-gooders want all the work just to protect your turf. Afraid someone might find out the county can operate without you and save itself a lot of money. That's exactly the point. You know, I don't have to answer to you. I don't have to answer to anybody. Now get your public service, criminal loving ass out of my office."

Solomon rose and moved toward the door. He stopped and turned back to look at the red faced Armbrister. "Oh, you'll answer up one day. You'll answer the question of who it was you were trying to burn, Clay Delaney or Harco Brewton, or God forbid, both of them."

The distraction caused by Armbrister's appointment of him as counsel for Harco Brewton had kept Clay away from his office for almost two weeks. He'd spent that time confronting his assignment, his client, and his repugnance of both. Fortunately, because summer was fast approaching, business had slowed somewhat, and his presence hadn't been critical. When he returned, however, he was greeted by a mound of correspondence, memos, and court pleadings that had accumulated in the center of his desk during his absence. Also, on the corner of his secretary's desk was a huge pink blob that he recognized as telephone call slips crammed onto a slender metal post. They'd lost all semblance of order by the end of the first week.

He'd come in early one morning, shut his door, and by eleven fifteen had reduced the pile of paper to a manageable stack.

Clay intended to do just enough to stay out of trouble. There was little doubt in his mind that he would have to place his law practice on a back burner so he could ready himself for the impending criminal trial. One thing he'd learned very rapidly was while a civil matter may take years to mature into a trial, a criminal case came to trial almost immediately. It was just as well. He'd always heard that "justice delayed was justice denied." He also knew from experience that justice too soon could work an injustice as well. That could easily happen in this case, as he not only needed time to prepare the case itself, he also needed a lot of personal study time to become minimally ready to deal with the idiosyncrasies of a criminal matter.

The knock on his door came as a welcome relief, and his invitation to come in was accepted by his friend and partner, Bobby. They'd seen little of each other in the past several weeks, and Clay was glad for his company.

"Coffee?" Bobby asked.

"You bet," said Clay.

Together the two wandered off to the break room. Settling in by a window overlooking the city to the west, they chatted quietly as their coffee cooled enough to swallow. It didn't take Clay long to bring Bobby up to date on the facts he'd learned about his case and his meeting with Harco Brewton. Bobby sat in silence as Clay described the man, his manner and demeanor—all with considerable accuracy, a Delaney trademark.

As they talked, Clay looked out over the green expanse of foliage that was Atlanta. It wasn't the green of landscapers' decorative plantings, but the deep, rich green of the proud progeny of an ancient forest. Remnants, yes, but still sufficiently ubiquitous to influence the character of a bustling city and soften its sharp, concrete edges.

Off in the distance, he could see Kennesaw, that small bump on the tail of the Appalachian chain, rising on the near horizon. Hardly a mountain, but high enough to command the surrounding terrain and stalemate Sherman's Army of the Tennessee for two weeks. Only pride kept the general from simply walking past it and leaving its gray rag tag defenders cut off.

"Heard about your case, Clay," a stately voice injected into his thoughts.

"Oh, hi Mr. Morgan," Clay responded, turning from the window and his musing to face his own beloved mentor, now retired as a partner from the firm.

Despite his own height, he had to cock his head upward to look into Lane Morgan's eyes. Morgan was meticulously dressed and wore a fresh flower. His full head of gray hair added just the right touch of distinction to an already imposing figure.

Morgan's retirement was in name only. His presence in the office was metronomically regular. Though his partners no longer required it, Lane Morgan was at his desk and on time every workday, available to give counsel and advice to eager young lawyers fresh out of school as well as to the seasoned veterans of many legal wars.

Clay knew that there were few substitutes for the sage wisdom and tempered logic Mr. Morgan brought to any problem, no matter how intelligent or experienced the inquiring attorney was. There was a resource many law firms, and other businesses as well, either overlooked or disregarded: the advice of their elders. Hell, even aboriginal tribes knew better than that. Clay guessed it was the young bucks and bulls eager to show their individual prowess that precipitated that kind of waste.

As it invariably turned out, they didn't have more talent. They simply had more energy, a bigger mortgage and, without question, considerably less experience.

"Who's your adversary?" Mr. Morgan asked.

"Judge Armbrister."

"I know that much. I mean for the State." Mr. Morgan chuckled, his eyes twinkling against the rosy glow of a face too fresh to be that of a man in his eighties. Clay sometimes referred to it as the affidavit face of Lane Morgan—a true reflection of the character of the man behind it.

"The assistant D.A., Jason Rowland."

"Don't know him. Know about him. Knew his daddy, though. Fine man. He was the solicitor down in Colquitt County for years. One of the finest prosecuting attorneys this state ever saw. He once talked a jury into giving the only death sentence ever handed down in this state for rape. Actually, it was a series of five rapes...by a fella named Grath, Walter Grath. Never will forget it. But that was probably before you were born, Clay."

"You know, Mr. Morgan, you've never told me anything about anything that ever happened while I was alive. Why is it that everything interesting happened before I was born?"

"Well now, you'd better ask your own daddy about that. You'd stand a damn sight better chance of getting a straight answer outta him than outta me. Though I wouldn't put any money on it."

"Come to think of it, I think I read a book about that Grath case."

"Really?" said Morgan. "I never knew they wrote a book about it."

"Yeah. Wasn't it The Rapes of Grath?"

"How long has he been this way, Bobby?" Morgan asked, shaking his head.

"He's always been this way, Mr. Morgan. You just haven't been around him for a while."

"You jest about such things, Clay, but did you know that Catherine and I have been working on a book on gardening?"

"No," Clay exclaimed. "That's terrific. I know how much you two love that garden of yours. It's about time you shared some of that knowledge and inspiration with the rest of us. Have you selected a title?"

"Yeah," Morgan said dryly. "I think we've settled on Weed It and Reap."

"He gotcha, Clay." Bobby laughed.

"I should've known better." Clay rolled his eyes toward the ceiling. "Don't ever turn your back on an old barn rat."

Morgan smiled then turned to Bobby. "Just remember, I taught him everything he knows."

And then as if on a prearranged cue, Bobby and Clay chimed in together, "But not everything that you know."

"Seriously, Clay," Morgan said, "Jason Rowland's weakness may very well be his father's success."

"How's that?"

"Old man Rowland's record for capital convictions and death sentences still stands to this day. As I understand it, the only other person who has ever come close is his son, Jason. The way I see it, young Rowland's out to best that mark."

"There's nothing wrong with wanting to win," Clay said. "You're a prime example of that."

"There's a very big difference between wanting to win and needing to win. Knowing boys and daddies the way I do, I figure Jason Rowland's need to has outrun his want to."

"So?" Clay said.

"So, a man who needs to win is going to take risks he wouldn't ordinarily take. And, sooner or later he'll expose his belly. They cater to people like that in Vegas."

Morgan's remark struck home. Clay could always count on a lesson in humanity from him. That was part of Morgan's uniqueness. A part he had tried to pass on to his protege—the part Clay was ever receptive to and so eager to learn, the part that was never taught in law school. Clay knew that Morgan's observation was pointed directly at Jason Rowland. He also knew that the observation was sufficiently universal to apply to anyone who fell into Morgan's well-defined category, including himself. Clay absorbed the advice. He'd be careful.

Clay then excused himself and headed to the firm library. He wasn't yet ready to make all the telephone calls he needed to make. An uneasiness about his ability to play the hand he'd been dealt by Judge Armbrister still gnawed inside him. He had to go back to the basics.

Finding a quiet, comfortable nook in an out-of-the-way corner of the library, he read with genuine interest through two separate treatises on criminal procedure and one thick three-ring binder of seminar material on current issues affecting a criminal practice. He wasn't looking for anything in particular. Rather, he was seeking exposure, trying to find, understand and adapt to the singular nomenclature of a discipline deceptively familiar, yet almost completely foreign to him.

And when Clay finished the last of the volumes he had selected, he was surprised to find that the firm was closed, the staff had long since departed, and it was almost dark outside. He'd been so absorbed in what he was doing that he'd read through lunch, throughout the afternoon and almost through the dinner hour. Relieved at the thought that it was now too late to return calls, he headed for home and the river.

As Clay maneuvered his car through the expressway traffic, he wasn't racing either the truck on his right or the van on his left. He was racing the sunset, trying to beat the darkness to his front door, trying to salvage something beautiful from an otherwise insipid day. Seeing the sun pushing hard against the horizon on his left, he muttered and tapped the steering wheel impatiently every time the line of cars in front of him slowed to a crawl, or whenever someone changed lanes to fill the gap in front of him.

Arriving home, he hastily shed his suit and donned an old cutoff sweatshirt and a pair of worn, faded jeans. Hesitating only long enough to pour a glass of wine, he moved quickly to his rear deck to catch the last fleeting strands of color that were fast vanishing to the west of him. He stood transfixed, as darkness gently nudged the last recalcitrant light from the horizon.

Night on the river was a strange but reverent world. Even the tone of the river became deeper, and the sound of its rush more subdued, as its passage transitioned dutifully from a carefree allegro to a more respectful andante. An occasional splash signaled the entry of some critter into its coolness or the shattering of its surface tension by a prowling trout.

Clay loved that part of the evening, especially the dark stillness that crept into the woods around him, supplanting the raucous disposition of the departing day. Like a mother's hand, the quiet blackness soothed whatever it touched, stroking it, calming it and slowing it down. Clay could feel his whole body relaxing. This is a unique form of therapy, he thought, both mentally and physically. Too bad there was no one to turn the world's lights off for just a few minutes at the end of each day, while everyone was still awake, so we could relax before all the wheels started to turn again.

Clay slowly sipped on his wine and let all his senses expand and explore the dark void around him. He was aware of the feel of the soft cotton of his sweatshirt and jeans hugging his body.

While not strong enough to move any part of the wind chime, a slight stirring of the night air grazed his face. It wasn't so much the movement that he felt as it was the momentary coolness he detected on his lips still damp with wine.

Of course, there was no mistaking the fresh, clean smell of the river itself, but the trick was in extracting from it the subtle sweet scents of the flowering trees, shrubs and bushes that the river nurtured—and he did, one by one: Magnolia, honeysuckle, wisteria, mimosa, oleander, rhododendron, Cherokee rose and on and on, until he was saturated with the heady aroma of a spring evening near the Georgia woods.

His reverie was broken by the soulful cry of a young owl in the trees across the river. As he tried to focus on its location, he suddenly became aware of a sound not of the night, but magnified and carried by it. A sound not of the wild, but unquestionably at home there—a traditional sound. An instrumental sound. A piano. He was hearing the soft, melodic strain of piano music, deftly playing and perfectly in tune with nature and the night. He didn't recognize the piece, but knew it was concerto quality.

Finding a seat on his deck, he propped his feet on the rail, leaned back and took in the impromptu concert. A perfect end to a perfect evening, but it would be perfect only if he could've shared all this with someone he felt close to.

As much as Clay enjoyed his solitude, he longed for someone to share special moments like this with him. Someone he could sit quietly beside or hold close. Someone he could give love to, and receive it in return. Over the years, he'd had a normal series of relationships, but none ever serious. At least it never got that way for him. Something was always missing. Something that he needed to provide but couldn't. Every time he got too close, something unspoken and undefined made him back away. He seemed to be locked in a paradox—wanting intimacy but repelled by a subliminal aversion to the emotional tie that made it complete.

But stirring deep inside him now for the first time was the haunting memory of what he'd once cherished, what he'd tried so hard to forget: the abiding sense of peace he felt as he lay quietly beside her in the stillness of a summer night.

The piano, rising ever so insistently out of the night heightened the sensuality of his memory, almost to the point of reality. And Clay hung onto every thread of recollection, reliving the beauty of it in his mind, over and over, until the music stopped.

It took a few minutes before he realized that the melody had ended. He was so intent on tasting every drop of sweetness he could from the sudden remembrance, that he didn't realize the music was no longer there. Try as he could, he couldn't rejoin the memory. It was like waking from a beautifully sensual dream and then trying hurriedly to go back to sleep to take up where he'd left off. While many things had come together to make him recall those long forgotten intimate moments, the catalyst had been the music. But now it was gone. And Anna with it.

He rose, his whole body shaking. "Please," he whispered into the blackness, his voice quavering, "don't stop."

Deep down, Clay knew that if he couldn't regain the dream now he never would again. He pleaded in vain for more music, but the keys lay still.

He knew it was over, and he did for the first time what he was unable to do when he lost Anna and hadn't been able to do since; he cried. He cried fourteen years' worth of pain and loneliness. Fourteen years of pretending that no one had ever been truly inside of him, inside his very being. Fourteen years of denial, and of never wanting to be vulnerable again. He cried until he could cry no more. Until both his eyes and his soul were dry, and both swollen. He was drained.

Clay had fought so long to forget, and he'd been successful for years. But, unknown to him, the memory was there all the time, resting quietly just below the surface of his consciousness—resting, waiting to be released, but not until all things were even, all essential factors of Delaney's life in place, and all the right stimuli were acting with the same intensity at the same time. When it really was time for him to forget, he remembered. And if it could've been planned, it would've been Anna's last act of love for him. She allowed him to remember so wonderfully one last time, for only in remembering could he really forget.

The woodland birds came back to life just before sunrise, bringing Clay back with them. Sleeping all night in a deck chair left him sore and damp from the dew. But a hot shower and shave quickly cured that. Then fresh coffee and a toasted English muffin put him on his feet, in his car and on the freeway, headed for town.

Once downtown, he threaded his way through the rush-hour traffic to the Superior Court Annex, the building housing the office of the county District

Attorney. He'd avoided going to his own office first. Chances were high that there he'd get busy or distracted, or both, and never make it to the D.A.'s office.

Two weeks had passed since the assignment, and Clay was feeling confident and composed in his new role. He hadn't called for an appointment, hoping to catch Jason Rowland unprepared to discuss Harco Brewton. That way, he figured that Rowland wouldn't have had time to dwell on the innumerable reasons he shouldn't negotiate a plea with Harco's lawyer.

After locating the proper suite of offices in the Annex, Clay found it much easier to walk right in and state his business than it had been when he first visited the Public Defender. His wait was brief.

"Mr. Rowland will see you now, Mr. Delaney," said the smart looking secretary guarding Rowland's door. "Just go on in."

As Clay entered the room, he saw Jason Rowland staring out the window, idly playing with the cord to the window blinds. He was coatless, suspendered and well pressed. Without turning around and before Clay could speak, Rowland stated flatly, "The answer is no."

Without a word Clay turned completely around and walked out of the room. He was past the bewildered secretary and almost to the door that exited the suite before Rowland caught up with him.

"Hold on there. What's the rush? C'mon back for Christ sake," Rowland said in a slow drawl. "At least state your business."

Clay hesitated briefly, then with a show of reluctance returned to Rowland's office. As he passed the recovering secretary, whose back was to Rowland, she smiled at Clay and silently mouthed the words, "Way to go." Clay winked at her, and as he went past her for the third time whispered, "It's only fifteen Love."

"It's so nice to meet you," Rowland said. "I've been looking forward to it. Won't you have a seat? Can I get you anything? Coffee?"

Clay smiled. Funny what silence and a 180 degree turn would accomplish. Ignore them and they're all over you. He'd seen that tactic work with most cats and some women. He never dreamed it would work with a prosecutor. But this was a far cry from the plea-bargain he wanted to strike. Maybe with time he could massage enough good will out of Jason Rowland to get what he wanted. Perhaps he shouldn't push for too much at one time. Anyway, to ask now would put on the table the question that Rowland had already answered. He'd wait.

"Well, what can I do for you?" Rowland finally asked.

"Nothing, really," Clay replied. "I thought that since we'd be seeing a lot of each other in the near future we should meet. I've heard a lot of nice things about you and your family."

"My family?" Rowland said with a smile.

"Yeah. Aren't you one of the Rowlands from down around Moultrie?" Moultrie was the only city of any size in Colquitt County, and Clay had just used up half of his knowledge about Jason Rowland. He would feign ignorance of the rest and then fudge a little to boot.

"Sure am. You from down that way?"

"Nope," Clay said with a laugh. "There weren't any Delaneys in Georgia before Reconstruction, and those who came here were all afraid to leave Atlanta and venture as far south as Moultrie. They thought the war was still going on down there. Is it?"

"No, but they were probably right, for a good while at least."

Clay made no reference to Rowland's father for fear it might be interpreted as a comparison of sorts, and Rowland might feel upstaged by his father's reputation. The last thing Clay wanted was for Rowland to feel he had to prove his own worth. That would only make Rowland work harder. Clay knew better than to challenge an adversary outright, or back one into a corner he had to fight to get out of. Even a sow would charge to get out of a corner.

During their idle chatter, Clay looked his adversary over. In some ways they were very much alike. In many ways starkly different.

Both were tall. Both were handsome. Clay was fair, Rowland dark. Clay was casually neat with hair disheveled just-so. Rowland was starched and fitted, with every hair manicured and mechanically in place.

Both were bright, well trained and self-confident. Clay expected success. Rowland demanded it. Clay hated failure. Rowland feared it.

They mentally circled each other, carefully observing the other's moves, looking for a weakness, an opening, some place to land a punch when the swinging really started.

Rowland finally broke the silence. "When you came in this morning, I thought you wanted to talk about a plea for your client. I'm sorry I jumped the gun."

"A plea? My client thinks he can win this."

"Your client isn't going to be trying the case. You are. What do you think?"

"I think my opinion doesn't count for very much. I haven't figured it out yet. I don't know about you, but in my civil practice I win the ones I'm supposed to lose, and lose the ones I'm supposed to win. Doesn't make sense, but that's our wonderful jury system. I hope I never see another case that everyone says is a sure winner."

"Yeah. Know what you mean."

"Well, gotta go," said Clay, rising and extending his hand. "It's been a real pleasure. I hope when this is over we can get in some fishing or something."

"I'll pass on the fishing, but I'll give the 'or something' some thought," Rowland said with a smile, returning the handshake.

As they parted, Clay added, "Give my best to your family."

Rowland nodded with a puzzled look. When Clay Delaney came in the door, he was the enemy, but he was leaving like an old friend.

CHAPTER 5

▼

The yellow intercom light on Judge Armbrister's bench flashed, indicating a message from his secretary. Without interrupting the lawyer who was arguing a motion from the lectern in front of him, Armbrister lifted the interoffice telephone from its hook behind the bench, turned to one side and cupped his hand in front of his mouth to shield his voice.

The lawyer slowed his presentation but didn't stop, even though he apparently knew the judge wasn't listening. Lawyers who stopped talking at moments like this angered the judge, because it focused attention on the obvious.

"Commissioner Bishop has dropped by to see you, Judge," his secretary said. "How long do you expect to be on the bench?"

"Tell him I'll be right there. And get him some coffee," Armbrister whispered. Turning back to the array of lawyers seated before him, he announced, "We're going to recess early today, gentlemen. We'll reconvene at nine in the morning."

Armbrister addressed his next remark to the lawyer on his feet. "Just pick up where you left off, Counselor."

The bailiff banged his gavel, and Judge Jack Armbrister left his bench before all the lawyers in the courtroom could get to their feet.

Marshall Bishop, Chairman of the Fulton County Commission, was a stump of a man. His sagging jowls gave him the look of an English bulldog, and he had the reputation of tenacity to match. Not a lawyer, he'd paid his dues on the floor of the Georgia General Assembly when he and Armbrister were both freshman legislators. He remained in state government well after Armbrister became a judge. Eventually, he left the Statehouse to become the first black to win the Fulton County Commission Chairman's seat, a position he'd held for twenty years.

With the exception of judges, magistrates and other elected officials, all county employees ultimately answered to Marshall Bishop.

Bishop, who knew Armbrister well, was already seated in a wing-backed chair when the judge entered his office and shut the door. The pitch of Armbrister's voice rose rapidly when greeting Bishop.

When Bishop was a young state representative facing a divorce with potentially disastrous financial consequences, Armbrister had finagled Bishop's non-jury trial away from the presiding judge, and handled it himself. The decree Armbrister entered set Bishop's child support obligation at the minimum and denied alimony. Later, when Bishop was locked in a close County Commission race, Armbrister leaned on an assistant solicitor to nol-pros an embarrassing marijuana possession charge against Bishop's teenage son.

After Armbrister—still in his robe—had taken a seat in the matching wing-backed chair, Bishop asked, "What is it, Jack? Who do you want me to fuck over today?"

"Now, now, Marshall, have I ever asked you to fuck anyone?"

"Well, no one that I'd enjoy fucking. Let's put it that way."

"That's not it at all. I've been concerned for a long time now about how the County's indigent defense system is running—or not running—depending on how you want to look at it. I thought it was about time I said something to you about it. That's all."

Before Bishop could speak, a light tap on the door announced Armbrister's secretary. On entering the room, she said politely, "I've brought some fresh coffee, Judge."

"Thank you, Marsha. Just leave the tray on the table."

Complying, she moved back through the door and closed it lightly behind her.

Motioning with his head toward the door, Armbrister grinned at Bishop and said, "She'll give you a little of that white stuff, if you want it."

Bishop shook his head. "You know I'm not interested in that sort of thing."

Starting to chuckle, Armbrister poured himself a cup of coffee, then poured Bishop one. "I was just talking about cream for your coffee, Marshall."

As Bishop hefted his cup, he said dryly, "You're so full of shit, Jack, you must squish when you walk."

Armbrister laughed and rose from his chair. He moved to the bookcase beside his desk and pulled the familiar leather volume from its place in the stack. Removing the small whiskey bottle from its hiding place, he splashed some in his coffee, then held the bottle toward Bishop.

"Not interested in that either," Bishop replied.

"It's good sipping whiskey, but suit yourself." Armbrister returned the bottle and regained his seat.

"What is it about our indigent defense system that's bothering you?"

"It's too expensive, for one thing."

"That shouldn't be your concern. Budgeting is my department."

"Normally, I wouldn't be concerned, unless I perceive waste. Then I get concerned, as any taxpayer would. Spending a big chunk of the county's funds coddling criminals when we don't have enough to shelter the homeless or for other services to needy families is a crying shame."

Bishop took a swallow of coffee and smiled. "I don't believe you give a rat's ass about the homeless or the needy, Jack."

"Well, there's an even bigger problem. We have, what, twenty or so young public defenders down there in that office? They can't handle the load they've got right now. I know, for Christ sake. I handle all the assignments. You probably need to hire twenty more lawyers right now just to deal with the caseload in that office today. And God knows, the volume's going up, not down. Then what are we going to do?"

"How are you handling it now? You are handling it, aren't you?"

"Damn straight, we are. But I'm having to go outside the system to do it. Matter-of-fact, I've had to assign the worst murder case this county has seen in twenty-five years to outside counsel. The Public Defender can't handle it. Or won't, I'm not sure which. At any rate, I've had to enlist the aid of one of our prestigious law firms. Looks like they'll do a real good job."

"What are you suggesting?" Bishop asked.

Armbrister got to his feet and began pacing as he spoke, his robe billowing behind him. "I was thinking that when this year's budget for the Public Defender's office is exhausted, that you not fund it for next year."

Bishop thought for a moment. He set his cup on the table, and cocked his head toward Armbrister. "That would mean that the entire program would collapse."

"Not so. Those young pups down there who we've trained on county money to handle criminal cases, would scatter throughout the city. They'll either set up their own practices, or else they'll get jobs with other firms. I can implement a pro bono assignment schedule that would send cases to all the large firms where there's already an abundance of lawyers, and I can assign cases to all the former public defenders. Marshall, I can get you for free what you've been paying through the nose for."

"You know damn well that those young lawyers can't go into private practice and work for us for free. They'll go under."

"I can keep their caseload down. But we don't have to worry about the big firms. They have plenty of talent and the money to support their own lawyers. I'll spread the work around. Besides, isn't it time those big time lawyers came down from those fancy office towers and walked on the same side of the street as we do?"

Armbrister's voice had become loud and agitated. He stopped pacing and headed straight for his hidden bottle for a refill. This time, instead of mixing it with coffee, he poured straight whiskey into his empty cup.

Bishop waited quietly for the judge to put the bottle away before he spoke. "The overhead for that office isn't all that great, Jack."

"What about the lawyers' salaries?"

"They're our major expense, of course, but they're not as high as you'd think. Those folks are pretty dedicated, and are willing to work for well below the going rate for new lawyers."

"It's a damn sight more than I made when I started out," Armbrister exclaimed.

"That was over thirty-five years ago, Jack."

Armbrister returned to his chair and sat on the edge of it. He took a heavy sip and washed the liquor around in his mouth before swallowing it, then looked Bishop in the eyes. "What about that Harvard jewboy you got running the show? I'll bet he's a real cost to the county."

"You talking about Herb Solomon?" Bishop asked.

"Yeah."

"Granted, the Director's salary is our major single expense, but he gets paid next to nothing compared to what comparable defense attorneys make in private practice."

Armbrister kept his eyes riveted on Bishop. His tone became flat and emotionless. "Maybe that would be a good compromise, then. Move him out at the end of the year and replace him with a younger, less expensive lawyer."

"But he has such a depth of experience, and…isn't there some kind of law against that, your Honor?"

A faint smile flickered across the judge's face. "Don't try to shit a shitter, Marshall. Decisions like that are made everyday in corporate America. I'll bet there are plenty of youngsters out there just itching to show their stuff."

Bishop hesitated for a moment, then rose from his seat. "I don't know, Jack," he finally said. "Let me think about it."

Escorting him to the chamber door, Armbrister put his arm on Bishop's shoulder and said, "You do that. And I know you'll do the right thing. I just know you will." When they shook hands at the door, Bishop said nothing more, but Armbrister finished with, "This really means a lot to me. And by the way, please say 'hello' to your son for me."

Still avoiding that pink morass of phone call slips sulking on the edge of his secretary's desk, Clay by-passed his office and headed instead for the Eleventh Street address he recalled from the Public Defender's file as Harco's. It was time to do a little poking around on his own.

Stretched out and resting coolly in the shade of a million new leaves, Eleventh Street was one of midtown Atlanta's many historic residential avenues. Avenues that had slipped slowly from the elegance that comes with affluence to a tired, down-at-the-heel rest stop for people with no permanent mailing address. The once proud and stately homes were now stoop-shouldered, and humbled by time and neglect—much like many of their inhabitants.

Clay eased his car to the granite curb, a remnant of old Atlanta paving technique; a piece of Stone Mountain perhaps. The foot-worn marble step-stone at the curb in front of number 801 testified to the dignified comfort its original owners offered to carriage-borne guests of yesteryear. It was now relegated to a convenient place for smashing pecans or right side passenger doors.

The petite front yard flourished with discarded fast-food wrappers and soft drink cans rather than grass. Even the few weeds that were able to push through the foot-trampled hardpan dirt of the yard seemed embarrassed to share living space with the litter. Clay figured that if plant lovers who talked sweetly to their leafy green charges everyday were correct about their feelings, then a clump of chickweed could feel humiliation at having a ketchup stained Styrofoam container as a neighbor.

Obviously, the tenants of number 801 weren't as sensitive as their yard weeds. They seemed to have no problem living alongside all the refuse. Or maybe there was real meaning to the old axiom that one man's trash is another man's treasure. If so, Clay figured, somebody was going to get rich—quick.

The old, once-white structure was solidly built of wood and stone. It looked to be three stories, but at a glance, Clay saw the third floor was only an attic. The intricately carved fretwork along the eaves and around the upper story windows, though broken or rotted away in places, was still a silent tribute to a builder's lost art.

As he climbed the stone steps to the broad expanse of a traditional porch, Clay was greeted by the suspicious stare of a shirtless, bearded man seated on the side rail, leaning back against one of the carved wooden columns that supported the porch roof. The man's eyes stayed on Clay while his hand rhythmically stropped a blade on the upper part of his exposed cycle boot. Sitting close by and leaning against the wall in a rusting chrome kitchen chair, picking at the already split green vinyl, was a stringy-haired young woman. The man's companion, Clay figured. The matching greasy jeans and dirty boots gave them away. Her sleeveless jersey provided some containment but no support for the sagging breasts beneath, but it did reveal and highlight the ladybug tattooed on the top of her upper right arm.

Even though Clay had observed and assimilated all that information about the couple in one quick scan of the porch, it still seemed that he might be perceived as gawking. Already feeling overdressed—he was wearing a shirt—Clay didn't also want to appear rude. Hastily he inquired, "Is the manager around?"

Without speaking, the bearded occupant simply stopped stropping long enough to point the knife over his right shoulder toward the house. Then he resumed the chilling rhythm.

Clay nodded his acknowledgment and smiled weakly at the young woman who was now smiling approvingly at him. Hurrying through the beveled glass door, he could still feel the bearded man's persistent gaze until he was fully inside.

It was evident that the spacious old house had been chopped up and arranged so that each former room, with the addition of a door, now served as a private single room for the tenants. Other than a bath at the end of the hall, the only common area was an old family kitchen, located in the middle, and on the right side of the house. Because of the way the house was originally designed, the kitchen occupied its own separate wing. Opening off a hallway on the first floor, it had tall windows on three sides, making it light and airy. It was there Clay found the manager, seated at a wooden table in the center of the room.

"You ain't here for no room, honey," the black woman stated as Clay entered.

"You're right. You the manager?"

"Well now, they never gave me no title. They just told me to collect the rent each week, keep my eyes open, my mouth shut, and I could live here free. So if that's managing, that's me. Everybody calls me Gladdie." She extended her hand.

"Well, Gladdie," he said, taking her hand in his, "everybody calls me Clay." He already liked the warm, straightforward woman.

"How do you do, Mr. Clay? Let's see now, you ain't here for no room, and you ain't a cop. Just what are you here for?"

"How do you know I'm not a cop?"

"Because if you was, you'd be dressed like that dude on the porch. Sometimes I wonder if he is. 'Specially when he lights up one of his joints." She laughed.

"I'm a lawyer for one of your tenants, Harco Brewton. I'd like to look in his room, if I may."

"The police done looked in there twice now. Just what are you all looking for?"

"Nothing in particular. Just want to look around."

"I don't know what kind of trouble that Brewton fella's in, but we don't need it here."

"There won't be any trouble, Gladdie. I assure you. Will you let me in?"

"You look like a nice sort, Mr. Clay, but he's already two weeks behind in his rent, and he ain't been around. Ain't no one else goin' in that room till it's paid up and something paid ahead. Otherwise the room's got to go to someone else, and then I can't let you in."

"How much?" Clay asked.

"It's thirty a week. Ninety dollars will do it."

"I only have sixty."

"Sixty'll do."

Handing over all his cash, Clay then followed Gladdie out of the kitchen to a first-floor back room overlooking the narrow rear yard. She unlocked the door then melted into the darkness of the unlit hall.

An unmade iron bed filled one wall. On a painted night stand beside it was a coffee can filled to the brim with cigarette butts and ashes. The night stand was pockmarked with hundreds of cigarette burns, and the room reeked of stale smoke and dust. A worn out, overstuffed chair sat near the rear window, and a gooseneck floor lamp stood beside it, its yellowed shade cocked to one side.

Clay rummaged through the drawer of the night stand then through several drawers of a small dresser against another wall. He found nothing that meant anything to him—same with the single closet.

Since he didn't know what he was looking for, he wasn't disappointed. But he was driven by an insatiable curiosity about Harco Brewton, and he had to keep looking. Sitting down in the easy chair to think for a moment, Clay heard the distinctive crackle of paper under the seat cushion beneath him. Standing and removing the cushion, he found a coverless, well-read "girlie" magazine.

He casually flipped the pages and found the inevitable array of naked women in assorted positions. Clay's was a typically male reaction to the seductive poses that featured voluptuous paragraphs of skin punctuated by an infinite variety of nipples and pubic hair—he'd thumbed well into the magazine before he thought to take note of the faces. To his great surprise there were none. Someone had taken a black marker and neatly obliterated each face. Not a recognizable facial feature remained.

A sense of foreboding came over Clay. Whatever the reason for what he'd found, it didn't bode well, and it heightened the intensity of his feelings against Harco. He returned the magazine to its place on the bottom of the old chair and replaced the cushion.

As he was about to leave, something shiny lying on the floor under the edge of the bed caught his eye. Partially covered by the fold of a dingy bed sheet hanging to the floor was a tube of lipstick. Clay twisted the bottom of the tube, and a well-used stump of garish pink emerged. It was perfectly coordinated to match Harco's taste in women, he thought as he placed the tube on the night stand.

Finding nothing else of interest, Clay pulled the door closed behind him. To get to the front door, he had to pass the kitchen where Gladdie still sat at the beat-up old table. He smiled and waved as he eased past her, observing that from that vantage point not much would escape her.

When Clay came out onto the street, a marked police car was parked at the curb directly behind his car.

"There a problem, officer?" he asked as he moved between the two vehicles.

"Just checking registrations and stolen reports," the officer replied. "This your automobile?"

"Yes it is."

"And what's your name, Sir?"

"Delaney. Clay Delaney."

"Then there's no problem, Mr. Delaney. Can't be too sure in this neighborhood," the policeman said as he pulled away from the curb.

"Yeah," Clay called after him, "like in front of the jail."

"All right," the shirtless tough on the porch said, giving Clay a thumbs-up with the knife still in his fist.

School was just letting out when Clay arrived at the Hillside Middle School. He found himself drawn there because he had a consuming need to exchange his mental images of the places critical to the life and death of Carrie Lindsey for a view of the real thing. He parked across the street from the school and waited. He was ready to give an explanation to anyone who inquired why he was there, but no one did. Like many well-intentioned people, he felt very conspicuous just sitting there, but he soon realized that either no one was suspicious of his suspicious-looking activity or else no one really cared. No wonder people got away with murder, he thought.

He watched the yellow buses roll up, fill up with animated, chattering pre-teens, then lumber off to preset destinations to systematically disgorge their effervescent cargo. He saw singles, doubles, and little knots of school children disappear in different directions down the sidewalk. He observed ever-obedient mothers arrive in their Volvos, Mercedes, and minivans to pick up youngsters too pampered to share a seat with a non-family member.

Another group, obviously in no hurry, simply moved deeper into the school yard, deposited their belongings on the grass, and assaulted the playground equipment with shouts and squeals.

Not knowing whether Carrie Lindsey was a walker or a rider, but knowing from his city map where she'd lived, Clay started driving slowly in that direction. As he moved toward her neighborhood, he found himself behind a school bus that made frequent stops along the way. Because all traffic came to a halt each time, his movement was slow and methodical, and he was able to keep a lot of walking children in sight as well. Quite a number of them were giggling young girls who seemed to have a collective destination.

Why weren't they riding the bus? It stopped time and time again along their route of travel. It suddenly dawned on him that they might not live in that direction, and they probably were walking away from their own neighborhood. But to where? He'd track them, mostly out in front, just as he'd done with Chelsea.

As Clay progressed, he had the interminably slow school bus in front of him and the gaggle of little girls in his rearview. No one seemed to be paying any attention to him whatsoever. The kids were easy pickings. It's a wonder anyone had ever noticed Harco in the vicinity.

Up ahead, he saw a crowd of kids forming in the parking lot of a corner convenience store. Fifty, sixty or more. But there was something quite different about them. They looked considerably older than the girls approaching on the sidewalk. No wonder; these were high school kids.

As Clay pulled through the parking lot, he could see the high school off in the background on a small hill. So, this was an after school hangout for the high school, and as such it was a magnet for the slightly younger wannabes.

Where was little Carrie abducted? Did she get this far? Was she dragged from the school yard or from somewhere in between? Harco's car was seen in the vicinity of the school, and he was seen at the convenience store on the day it happened. Was there someone out there who actually saw him take her, and was going to come forward and say so?

Clay moved through the lot and turned in the direction of the street that would ultimately lead to the Lindsey residence. He was soon in their subdivision, and he quickly realized that he was in a typically well-to-do Northside Atlanta neighborhood of professionals, executives and business owners. A place not unaccustomed to an occasional daytime break-in, but woefully unfamiliar with violent personal crime.

The two story stucco house at 3415 Sterling Close was nicely landscaped and well-maintained. As Clay slowly passed by he could see a neatly dressed woman in her mid thirties pruning some bushes near a decorative rail fence in the side yard. Her short, bobbed blonde hair bounced quickly back and forth each time she leaned forward to shear off a stem. It must be Carrie's mother. How could he face her?

He drove past the house three more times, each time thinking that he'd scoop up enough courage somewhere along the way to stop and talk to her. What was he going to say? "Hi. I'm defending the brute who raped and murdered your little girl. Got a minute?" He really didn't want to talk to her. He just wanted to walk up, put his arms around her and cry with her.

Sensing that a classic case of approach/avoidance conflict was keeping him at bay, Clay finally pulled into the driveway. Mrs. Lindsey turned toward his car, laid her shears on the top fence rail and began walking toward him as she removed her garden gloves. Clay got out of his car and stood by the open door, lest he frighten her.

"Mrs. Lindsey?"

"Yes?" she replied.

"I'm Clay Delaney."

"What can I do for you, Mr. Delaney?"

"I sincerely hate to disturb you like this, but I need to ask you some questions about Carrie."

Mrs. Lindsey stopped in her tracks, visibly shaken. "Who are you with, Mr. Delaney? The newspaper? I've told them I don't wish to be interviewed."

"No ma'am. The court appointed me to represent Harco Brewton. I'm his lawyer."

"Good day, Mr. Delaney. I have nothing to say to you," she said stiffly.

"I know how you must feel, Mrs. Lindsey, and I'm truly sorry about—"

"How could you possibly know?"

"Believe me. I really do."

"Good day, Mr. Delaney."

Clay moved toward the car, then stopped and turned, "If I could just ask you one question."

"No! Please leave."

Just then another woman's voice rang out. "Celeste, is anything wrong?"

Clay looked to his right and saw a woman about Mrs. Lindsey's age approaching from the neighboring yard.

"Everything's fine, Roberta. I'm going inside now. Mr. Delaney was just leaving." Celeste Lindsey disappeared through the garage into her kitchen.

Clay sensed immediately that this Roberta person was beside herself to learn what had been going on in the Lindsey driveway and wouldn't rest until she did. He moved slowly, giving her ample time to catch up to him before he climbed back inside his automobile.

"Hi," she gushed, "I'm Celeste's friend, Roberta. And you are?"

"Clay Delaney. Nice to meet you, Roberta."

"Are you a friend of Ted's?"

"Ted?"

"Ted Lindsey."

"Oh, no. I was just trying to get some information about her daughter, Carrie."

"I'll bet you're with the press. Different ones have been coming around ever since the funeral, but Celeste just refuses to talk about it. Can't say that I really blame her. Looks like you did no better than the rest of them."

Clay just stood there smiling pleasantly, his mouth closed and his antenna up. He learned a lot this way.

"Take me, for instance," Roberta continued. "The police were very interested in what I had to say, but no one from the media ever talked to me to find out what I knew. They only wanted to talk to Celeste."

"And what was it that you knew?"

"Well, for one thing I saw the killer's car stopped right down there on the street just two days before poor Carrie disappeared."

"How did you know it was the killer's car?"

"Because when she was missing and the police were asking around for anyone who'd seen anything out of the ordinary, I told them about the car. And later, when they said they'd caught him, I went down and they showed me the car, and it was the same one."

"What'd the car look like?"

"It was white. Had four doors. Was all rusty on top, and the license plate wasn't from Georgia."

"What state was it from?"

"I don't know, but it was a different color from ours."

"The driver—did you get a look at the driver?"

"Not really. He was parked in front of Celeste's, so his back was to me. I did notice his head, though."

"What about it?"

"It was rather large. Larger than normal. And, oh yes, once when he turned to look up at Celeste's house, I caught a glimpse of a mustache."

"Did you tell all this to the police?"

"Of course."

"Now, I understand you saw all this two days before Carrie disappeared. Is that right?"

"Yes."

"How are you able to remember that it was two days beforehand?"

"Because Carrie failed to come home from school on a Friday. On the Wednesday morning before that, I had a hair appointment at ten thirty, and I was on my way out when I saw the white car. It didn't belong in this neighborhood. That's why I noticed it. Anyway, he pulled away right after I got out of the house. Guess he noticed me, too."

"Where were you when Carrie disappeared?"

"I was right here, waiting for them to come home."

"Them?"

"Carrie and my daughter, Julie. They normally came home together. They used to ride the bus home, but during the last month or so they started staying after school for something, and they walked home. It's not really that far. Anyway, Julie came home by herself that day. She said Carrie had something else to do, and would be along later. I didn't think anything about it at the time. Later that night, we found out that she was missing."

"May I talk to Julie?"

"She's not home from school yet."

"When do you expect her?"

"You're not going to put her name in the paper are you? She took Carrie's death really hard, and that might upset her all over again."

The opening of the Lindsey kitchen door interrupted Clay, and saved him from having to lie or confess the inappropriate conclusion hastily jumped to by this nosey neighbor. "Roberta, may I see you a minute?" Celeste called out.

The two women conferred quietly in the garage as Clay stood patiently by his car door, knowing that the spontaneous interview was over. Sure enough, when the huddle broke, Celeste returned to her kitchen and Roberta, like a scolded child, retreated sullenly across the two adjoining driveways to the comfort and solace of her own house. Clay knew from her glare that he wouldn't be talking to Julie. At least not that day.

After leaving the Lindsey driveway, Clay backtracked to the corner convenience store. Once there, he observed the now dwindling crowd of teenagers still moving around in the parking lot and on the sidewalk, but by and large they'd begun to drift home or to other interests. Pulling to one side of the lot, he opened the brown file folder beside him on the front seat.

Flipping the pages, Clay located the names of the several potential witnesses. "Jaynelle Eubanks," he read to himself, "cashier, Zip 'N Mart. Observed man fitting the description of Harco Brewton at her Northside mart location on Friday, April third, the date decedent was reported missing. Mart location is six blocks from decedent's middle school on direct route to decedent's home. Witness picked Brewton out of police lineup on April twenty-third."

Clay got out of his car and positioned himself in the phone booth nearest the front window of the little market. When he saw the cashier alone at the counter, he dialed the Zip 'N Mart number in the file. For a moment, he thought he had the wrong location, but after the fifth ring the woman behind the counter finally waddled over to the wall phone and, out of breath, announced through her nose, "Zip 'N Mart."

"Jaynelle?"

"She ain't here."

"When will she be working?" he asked.

"She won't. Leastways, not here. She quit last week."

"Oh. Do you know how I can reach her?"

"Same way as always," she said. "Just leave a message with her sister, and she'll call you."

"Do you have that number?"

"You'll have to look it up. It's Doris Fleeman in Mableton."

Using a directory in a phone booth was always an unwelcome challenge for Clay. If he ever got it opened and held in place long enough to find anything, invariably the page he wanted was ripped out. He suspected that someone surreptitiously preceded him, and did that on purpose. But how did this mysterious person know who he was going to call?

He struggled with the gravity-loaded container holding the thick volume. He held it in place with his left knee and left elbow, and turned the pages with his right hand. "Flack, Flagg, Flaherty, Fleck, fuck!" The son of a bitch had done it again. How did he always know the exact page?

Reaching Doris Fleeman through the operator was easy, and the ensuing conversation with Doris was brief but informative.

Clay learned that Jaynelle Eubanks had quit the mart after a run-in with her boss over scheduling. Apparently, they had a disagreement over her being off work in time each day to pick up her first-grader from school in a neighboring county.

Jaynelle had told her sister all about her involvement in the Lindsey investigation: her visit from a detective who had a photo of Harco, her having seen him at the store earlier, and her identifying him in the lineup. Much to Clay's surprise, however, he learned for the first time that Jaynelle claimed to have seen Harco, "with the dead girl," as Doris said. That damning piece of evidence made Jaynelle Eubanks a crucial eyewitness, and he knew he had to talk to her face to face.

Apparently, Jaynelle was now working nights as a cocktail waitress in a local tavern. Doris wouldn't say where. Clay left his number with Doris, but doubted that Jaynelle would call. He'd have to find her.

When Clay got off the phone, no kids were milling about, but a few young couples and a foursome were seated in parked cars on the side of the popular little mart. A lone teenager was slowly cruising past for one last chance to see or be seen. Clay decided to call it a day. His pursuit of information about his case had yielded quite a bit. All of it bad, but then what did he expect?

At least he was a little better prepared for the onslaught he was sure Jason Rowland was going to steer his way. What he was going to do about it was another matter. Maybe he shouldn't have been so cute in avoiding plea-bargain discussions with Rowland. What the hell, he thought, Rowland was going to bargain or he wasn't. He already knew the kind of case he had against Harco. Clay was doing nothing more than learning it piece by piece. He certainly wasn't making it worse. He was just finding out first-hand how bad it really was.

CHAPTER 6

▼

Returning to his house, Clay wound his way up the long driveway that snaked through the woods to his back door. As he rounded the last bend, his progress was slowed by the nonchalant ambling of his yard cat, Fraidy, who was moving tail-high down the center of the driveway. Fraidy paid little heed to the approaching car and continued steadfastly on his plodding course, even more so after Clay honked once.

When Clay finally arrived on his back steps, Fraidy was seated expectantly beside the metal box that received and insulated Clay's weekly milk delivery. It was then he realized that he'd left in such a rush that morning he'd forgotten it was delivery day, and the milk had probably become too warm to keep.

"Looks like you've got yourself a treat, Fraidy." Clay reached down and opened the box. When he did, he was surprised to find that the half gallon of milk had already been opened and was partially gone. Living off the beaten path the way he did, Clay didn't expect to have children roaming about, nor did he envision strangers coming uninvited to his door. But who drank his milk? The clever little raccoon family that lived in the woods nearby was certainly capable of pilfering any available edibles, including milk, and any one of them would have the dexterity to unscrew the top from the bottle. But they wouldn't have the discipline to return it. But what kind of a jerk would take several big swigs of someone else's milk? And right out of the bottle too.

He retrieved a bowl from the kitchen and poured a grateful Fraidy a large portion, discarding the rest. "Don't get used to this, mister," Clay said to the lapping Fraidy. But he knew his words would go unheeded. He was aware of the scientific fact that a cat slurping milk, like a Doberman eating raw meat, was temporarily struck deaf.

As Clay changed clothes and began to prepare dinner, he continued to be puzzled over the missing milk. He was irritated at the thought that someone would go through his things and help himself, but he was more concerned that someone was prowling about in his absence. If that wasn't a joke or an isolated incident, he feared that whoever had taken the milk was so bold he would surely end up in the house one day while he was gone. Clay wasn't quite sure what to make of it, and he was at a loss as to what to do. He needed to run it by someone, but who? Who did he know who knew anything about prowlers? Harco.

"Well I'll be damned." Had his life gone so completely haywire in the last two weeks that he would now be going to Harco for advice? He began to laugh. When he recovered he threw open the back door and shouted out into the dimming light, "Just come on in and take what you want. You'd better not wait too long or old Harco Brewton will get out of jail and beat you to it. What? No takers? Well, don't ever say I didn't tell you so."

Before Clay could close the door, he heard the clatter of something falling to the wooden floor of his porch, and he heard and sensed the rush of something moving swiftly toward him out of the darkness. He felt a sinking sensation in the pit of his stomach, and like an animal he could feel the hair beginning to stand up on the back of his neck. His whole body tensed as he instinctively readied himself to receive a blow. Through clenched teeth he let loose an uncontrolled grunt formed by the air involuntarily expelling from his lungs. Flashing into view with incredible speed and then turning away just before impact was Fraidy, now walking sideways and forward all at the same time, as only a true attack cat could do.

"You little shit. You scared me half to death," Clay yelled, slamming the door in the triumphant feline's face. His heart continued to pound wildly.

That wasn't the first time Fraidy had attacked out of the night. It wasn't the first time he'd scared Clay in the process, either. But it was the first time his timing had been so good. Considering the milk treat, in all it had been a very successful evening for Fraidy.

By the time his dinner was over, Clay was chuckling about being bested by his cat. It was that kind of intelligent playfulness that made him appreciate the delicate creature. It had come a long way from the frightened, starving wild kitten he'd found in the woods one rainy Saturday, its fright so great it almost overcame its hunger. For more than two weeks Clay had been unable to coax it out of the thick undergrowth but had to leave milk for it and walk away.

After regular visits to its makeshift den and with a gentle voice and even gentler touch, Clay was finally able to pick it up and comfort it. In doing so he saw what remained of the body of its mother, who'd obviously died soon after giving birth. Fraidy now occupied a unique place in Clay Delaney's order of things.

The only benefit of eating alone was the small amount of cleanup required. Clay was still chewing while drying his last plate. This gave him plenty of time for more important things, such as piddling around. Sometimes he'd organize his nuts and bolts by size in various containers to be stored systematically in the basement.

Now though, he was piddling around the laundry room, separating blue socks from black ones while half listening to the evening news on the small TV in his kitchen. Even though he could hear it clearly, his pilot trained ears filtered out anything that didn't directly interest or affect him. Consequently, nothing got through to his brain until he heard a newscaster say something about "an exclusive interview with the man accused in the brutal murder of Northsider, Carrie Lindsey."

Exploding through a pile of black and blue socks, Clay raced for the kitchen, only to find the station occupied by a commercial. Reacting quickly, he dashed into his great room, searching frantically for a blank tape to stick into the VCR on the larger TV there. Without knowing what was coming, he instinctively knew to preserve it for study later. God forbid that Harco should talk on TV, but if he was going to, Clay knew that Jason Rowland already knew about it, and would tape it for use against him. He had to be ready to counter that.

Finding the tape was easier than getting the cellophane off it. But he succeeded just in time to slam it into the slot and punch the record button.

The chipped white bars inside the county jail faded into view, framing the bulbous head of Harco Brewton.

His smugness was evidenced by the smirk peering out from under his unkempt mustache and contradicted by the furtive darting of his eyes.

As the camera stayed focused on Harco's face, the reporter gave her off-camera version of the rape and murder, never once saying anything about Harco except that he'd been indicted for the crime. But the combination of the close-up camera work and narrative voice-over caught Harco smiling and acting self-important while the grisly facts were being detailed. At one point, he even clasped both hands over his head and shook them, all the while grinning from ear to ear. The interviewee was a casting director's dream, and the effect was repulsively brilliant.

The subliminal message, "Guilty! Guilty! Guilty!" couldn't have been more indelibly presented if the words had been stenciled across his face.

Harco's protestations of innocence seemed more like taunts than denials. His claims of, "They can't pin that on me," and, "They'll never make it stick," were interspersed with bleeps covering his colorful language. In all, his five-minute interview earned six bleeps. But the harm wasn't the masked words themselves. It was the fact that his obscenities were all directed at women.

Feeling helpless, Clay shook his head. In frustration he finally yelled at the TV, "Ask him about his tattoos. Go ahead. I dare you. Show 'em, Harco! Show 'em, man!"

Relief of sorts came when the camera finally returned to the studio. But much to Clay's chagrin the subject switched from Harco to him. His picture was plastered across the screen, subtitled as the lawyer for Harco Brewton. No mention was made of the fact that Harco was indigent, and that Clay had been assigned by the court to represent him. Rather, the newscaster was intent on emphasizing that even Harco's lawyer was "no stranger to the crisis of crimes against children."

Clay sat in stunned silence as he watched old news footage of himself walking numbly out of church many years before behind a small casket of polished mahogany, a view he neither recalled nor had ever seen before. It was as if he'd suddenly become detached from himself and was standing outside his body, eavesdropping on his own grief. He knew he'd never again watch a scene like that featuring someone else, without feeling some shame at being a voyeur to their pain. Being present out of love and respect is one thing, watching strangers bury their dead while resting comfortably in your living room was quite another.

The program was hardly over when the phone calls began. He was caught by surprise by the first two. After that, he turned on his answering machine. He was told he must be a pervert like his client. He was told that God probably took away his little girl as punishment for defending criminals. He was accused of killing his own daughter. And one rather loud and obnoxious caller told him to stay out of an adjoining county, or he'd kill him.

Morning found Clay back in the small interview room at the county jail, facing Harco across the table.

"I can't believe you gave a TV interview."

"They show that last night?" Harco asked nonchalantly.

"They sure as hell did, and you were at your very best."

"Well then, sorry I missed it." Harco grinned slightly.

"You were the only person in Atlanta who did. What in heaven's name possessed you to do that?"

"It's all part of my plan," Harco replied still grinning.

"Your plan."

"If I can get enough pre-trial publicity, you can file a motion to have my case tried somewhere else. Maybe even in another state. Like they did for that guy who killed the federal judge."

"For starters, we're not in federal court, so you'll never get this case out of Georgia. Second, you can't go around giving press conferences and then complain about the publicity you've created in the process. This case isn't going anywhere but to trial. Your plan just went down the toilet it obviously came out of to start with. What jailhouse lawyer have you been talking to? Let me guess, you recently got a new cellmate. He's real interested in your case. He's been asking you a lot of questions and giving you a lot of advice. Am I close?"

Harco nodded.

"And he's the one who suggested you go on TV and tell your side of it. How am I doing?"

Harco nodded again.

"I told you not to talk to anyone. I didn't say that just to hear my head rattle. You realize, of course, that this guy, whoever he is, has a direct line to the D.A.'s office, don't you?"

By this time, Harco had become quite passive and, once more, could only nod his understanding.

"And you know we'll probably see him again at trial—testifying for the State?"

Nodding one more time but struggling to speak, Harco finally said, "But what'll I do about it now?"

"Find some way to get him out of your cell. Start a fight with him, or better yet kiss him in front of his friends. Maybe he'll ask to be moved."

Harco indicated that he understood, and would do as he was told.

"Now," said Clay, "not that it really matters, but did you tell him anything they can use against you?"

A pained expression came over Harco's face. "You really think I did it, don't you?"

Clay simply stared at Harco, his eyebrows rising slightly.

"You know," Harco said, "you've never asked me if I killed that girl."

"That's right," Clay replied.

"Why not?"

"What difference would that make? My job is to defend you whether you did it or not. How I feel about you should be of no consequence. But knowing the truth might complicate things."

"Well, it might make a difference in the way you look at things," Harco replied. "You might not believe what those bitches are saying about me."

"Whoa," said Clay, forming a time out sign with his hands. "Hold on. The way you feel about women is very clear, and it's not going to help your case at all. This 'bitch' shit has got to stop. You understand me?"

Harco nodded. "Anyway, if you didn't believe their stories you might check them out better to show that what they're saying isn't so, or something. Well, you know what I mean."

"I'm not so sure I do. But if I do, I'm not so sure I agree with you. But let's go over some of it. What color is your car?"

"White."

"Older model?"

"Yeah."

"Is there rust on it?"

"The floorboard is rusted out real bad."

"What about the top?"

"Yeah. There's a lot of rust on top. It's a Pascagoula special," Harco said with a grin.

Looking the grinning Harco in the eyes, Clay bored in. "Did you stalk Carrie Lindsey?"

"What do you mean by 'stalk?'"

"Don't split hairs with me."

"I don't know what 'stalk' means."

"Did you shadow her? Follow her?"

"No!"

Clay rose to his feet, placed both hands on the table, and leaned toward Harco. "What were you doing parked in front of her house two days before she disappeared?"

Harco began to fidget. "I don't even know where she lives," he said weakly.

"On Sterling Close in Northside Atlanta."

Averting his eyes from Clay's, Harco continued. "If that's one of them rich neighborhoods near Dunwoody, I was probably crusin' and casin'. I do a lot of that, you know. I hit three houses up there the week before it happened. I could've been in front of her house and never knowed it."

Clay paused from the rapid-fire tempo that had paced his earlier questions. Lowering his tone and his volume, he asked sternly, "Did you kill Carrie Lindsey?"

"No."

Slamming the table with the palm of his hand, Clay shouted in Harco's face, "I don't believe you!"

"But I didn't."

"I don't believe you! I don't believe a goddamn word you've said."

"But I'm telling you the truth," Harco replied, his voice shaking.

Clay began gathering his papers. "You wouldn't know the truth if it bit you in the ass," he said.

"Hear me out, Mr. Delaney, please."

Clay stopped what he was doing, gazed quietly at Harco, and sat down. "Okay," he said. "Let's finish this little old examination and see where it takes us. I've got plenty of time and you have more than that. Where were you on April third?"

"Is that when the bitch—uh—the kid got it?"

"Yes."

"I was in Montgomery. I'd been there a couple of days."

"If you don't know the date it happened, how can you say you were in Montgomery?"

"Because on the night I came back to Atlanta I saw on the evening news that she'd disappeared the day before."

"What day of the week do you say you came back?"

"On a Saturday."

"Who knows you were in Montgomery?"

Harco paused briefly and looked away. "No one that I know of."

"You sure?"

Harco still didn't look at Clay. He simply shook his head.

"What were you doing there?" Clay continued.

"Same thing I do everywhere. Breakin', enterin' and stealin'. After I hit those houses in Atlanta, I drove over to Montgomery, stashed the stuff, and hit a few places over there." Harco seemed to relax, and he spoke casually about criminal activity that was obviously a way of life for him. He looked directly at Clay without any apparent embarrassment or remorse. "I move back and forth to avoid the heat. It ain't smart to hang around too long."

"You saying you hid the stuff you stole in Atlanta somewhere in Montgomery?" Clay asked.

"Yeah. I swap states with it, so it won't be easy to trace if somebody finds me with it. It's also easier to hock that way. Unless it's a car, nobody in Alabama is on the lookout for something that's been stole in Georgia."

"Where do you put it?"

Harco began to pick at his moustache with one hand. "Got me a room over there."

"You keep a room in Atlanta and in Montgomery?"

"Yeah."

"And you bring the Alabama stuff over here?"

Harco's face lit up, and his eyes seemed to sparkle. "Sure do. Smart, huh?"

Clay raised the palms of his hands. "So, you just bounce back and forth stealing from people?"

A self-satisfied smirk crossed Harco's face. "Yeah," he said.

"Harco," Clay asked, "just out of curiosity, how many people do you think you've stolen from?"

"Well Mr. Delaney, the way I figure it, if you had a bumper sticker that said, 'Honk if you've ever been burglarized by Harco Brewton,' it would sound like the projector just broke down at a drive-in movie."

For the first time since he met Harco, Clay found one of his comments humorous, and he smiled and shook his head at the tragic comic sitting in front of him. Noticing Clay's reaction, Harco smiled back.

That was a mistake. Sensing that the momentary joviality would be mistaken for comradeship, Clay regained the initiative. "Tell me about the doll."

"What doll?"

"Just when I thought we were making some progress."

"What do you mean? What are you talking about?"

"Are you telling me you don't know anything about the doll?"

"What doll?"

"The Raggedy Ann doll. The one the police found under the seat of your car. The doll that may very well convict you. The one that belongs to the little girl you say you never saw. The little girl you claim you didn't kill. That doll!"

"I swear, I don't know nothing about it," Harco protested.

"That's not good enough, Harco. You'd better lie to me or something. I'm not buying 'I don't know' today. Not on the doll, I'm not."

"I swear."

"One more time. Did you kidnap Carrie Lindsey?"

"No!"

"Did you rape her?"

"No!"

"Did you kill her?"

"No!"

"Bullshit!" Clay turned and walked out. Harco was left sitting helplessly alone.

The rest of Clay's week passed quickly. He devoted his remaining time to his private practice, but gnawing away in the back of his mind was the question of Harco Brewton's guilt. Every time he took a mental break from his work, he could see the look on Harco's face when he'd walked away from him. Harco's story was plausible, but to believe it he had to believe Harco—not a smart thing to do. There was a man who placed a lifetime of dishonesty on the table in front of Clay, and asked him to carve out two days' worth and believe it. With all the emotional baggage Clay piled on that same table, he wasn't the most likely candidate to find Harco's story credible.

Regardless of his own personal feelings, ultimately a jury had to believe it or Harco would surely die. Clay knew it would be a rare jury to convict for the rape and murder of a very young girl and not order a death sentence as well. But to get to that point collectively, they each had to resolve some doubts. Would they resolve them in favor of a dead child or a career criminal? He was personally opting for the child, but he was having difficulty resolving them for himself, or dispelling them from his mind.

Earlier, when he was so upset and angry about the assignment, he'd had no difficulty suspecting Harco. Now he wasn't quite so sure. The light that had shined so starkly on the answer earlier was diffusing over time, bringing into focus more things he hadn't seen before—things that had always been there, but not in the spotlight.

The threads of logic that were inextricably woven throughout the fabric of Clay Delaney's judgment were a barrier to hasty conclusions. How volatile he was. Impetuous too. Even hot-headed at times. But premature? Never. Sound logic shielded him from premature action. No matter how deeply involved his feelings were, the logic side of his brain kept on clicking, telling him to slow down, turn left, turn right, stop. He was getting those messages now. His heart had already found Harco guilty, but his mind was beginning to have reasonable doubt.

The pieces of evidence all fit so well together that there should be no puzzle. But what if there were? What if he made it a puzzle with the last piece—Harco's guilt—really missing? Would the other pieces still fit so nicely? What if they did, but other pieces fit as well? What if some of those other pieces fit better? Would the last piece still be missing?

Clay was intrigued by the thought. The only troubling aspect was in giving Harco the benefit of the doubt. But in reality he wasn't really giving it to Harco. He was giving it to Carrie Lindsey. Whoever killed her shouldn't be able to walk away. If it was Harco, so be it. But if it wasn't, doubting his guilt was one step closer to avenging her. It was worth it. He'd give it a try. But first he was going fishing.

CHAPTER 7

▼

Sunlight crashed through Clay's bedroom window, shattering his sleep and showering slivers of light all across his king-sized bed. It had all the markings of a roll over, stick your head under the pillow and snooze some more Saturday morning. But he promised himself he'd go fishing. His dad had always told him to forget about the early bird, it was the early worm that got the fish. He loved to fish, but he also loved to sleep in. He lay for just a bit longer, enjoying the coolness of the sheets on his bare skin, then forced himself out of bed.

The rattling of fishing rods on the rear deck as Clay prepared his tackle brought Fraidy out of the dew-laden woods. Fraidy often followed him to the riverbank and paced impatiently nearby, waiting for a still-wriggling morsel to be deposited at his feet. Normally, the only fish he kept out of the water was the first one—the one he gave Fraidy. The rest of them he returned—a trick he'd learned from a little auburn-haired girl years earlier. Now, he simply enjoyed the challenge of finding them, the thrill of luring them to strike, and the excitement of landing them.

"Not today, Fraidy. I'm taking the kayak. I'll bring one back to you if I can."

He rummaged through a pocket-sized tackle box, sorting small river lures and making sure he had a sufficient assortment on hand for the day. Actually, he had more than any ten people would need, but he felt ill prepared if he didn't take them all along. Someone once accused him of buying lures just to keep other fishermen from having them. He never thought about it that way, but when he did it sounded like a great idea.

Besides the lures, he always took along some natural bait. Earthworms were plentiful, and no digging was necessary. He just pushed aside the moist, dead leaves that had fallen on the edge of his asphalt driveway and there they were, making dirt. Bass loved them. Trout would take a worm, but seemed to prefer insects.

He was ready. The night before, he had spread a little honey in the bottom of his bug box and left it under a bush at the edge of the woods. Bingo! Every fish in the river would have to have lockjaw for him not to score now.

As Clay examined the contents of his little box, something shiny on the ground nearby caught his attention. He reached down and picked it up. It was the foil wrapper from a stick of chewing gum. He neither chewed gum nor threw trash in his own yard. The chances of it blowing there from the road were minimal at best because of how far away it was. It was unlikely it would've come from someone on the river, because access from the river to this point in his yard was limited. No, it must have been dropped right where he found it. But he was at that very spot the evening before and hadn't seen it.

Someone must have been in the yard last night. But why? First the milk incident, now this. Clay was getting a little edgy about it all. He took a quick spin around the yard, looking for any other sign of someone's presence, but found nothing.

His bewilderment was sidetracked by the jangling of his phone. He hated the phone. It rang all day at the office, and at night someone was always trying to sell him something. Now they were calling him at home to tell him that he and Harco were assholes. They were half right. He'd give them that, but he surely didn't want to have to listen to it. He was reluctant to answer, but since he was about to get out on the river for a good while, he decided he'd better.

It was Bobby. "Hey, Clay, buddy. You gotta help me out, man. You know, uh, since the kids are both in preschool now, Claire is enrolled at Georgia State to finish her degree."

"Yeah?"

"Well, she's taking a psychology course from this visiting clinical psychologist."

"Yeah?"

"Anyway, they've been discussing the psychological aspects of the Brewton case in class."

"Yeah?"

"And Claire talked knowledgeably about the case and all."

"Yeah?"

"And the professor wanted to know how she knew so much."

"Yeah?"

"Can't you say anything but 'yeah?'"

"Yeah."

"Well, Claire kind of said that I was working on the case."

"'Kind of said?'"

"Yeah. Now you've got me saying it, damn it."

"What do you want, Bobby?"

"We want you to come to dinner. Tonight."

"Why?"

"Because the professor is coming, and I need you here to talk about the case. I'll say we work together, and you can sort of take over the discussion."

"'Sort of?'"

"Yeah. Oh hell, Clay, will you do it? Please?"

"Yeah."

That was all Clay needed: a dull after dinner conversation with a semi-shrink. A college professor, no less. More than likely he was just an adjunct, but a stuffy "professa" nonetheless. He probably smoked a pipe for effect. Clay loved the aroma, but hated that sucking sound they made. But he was very fond of Bobby, and he loved Claire to death. He'd just have to put up with it for the evening.

After hanging up with Bobby, Clay picked up his old Charleston-born folding kayak from where he stored it under his rear deck, and with just a few steps was at the water's edge. The bow of the stable little kayak eased into the current, and Clay began paddling effortlessly upstream.

Except after a heavy rain, the water of the river was always very clear, but had a beautiful light-green shade to it. That came from the healthy growth of aquatic vegetation on the many rocks that formed its bottom. The combination of all sizes of rocks and vegetation provided habitat for all manner of river critters for the fish to feed on. That made the fish abundant, and the fishing delightful.

A broken layer of puffy white clouds lay overhead, and alternating patches of sun and shade varied the hues of green on the river, as did the varying depths of the water. Exhilarated, Clay felt fresh and free as he and his sturdy old kayak knifed their way against the current. Weaving his way in and out of the numerous rocky obstacles, he'd occasionally misjudge the strength of the flow and graze the side of a protruding rock. The tough, flexible skin of the old boat would give just enough to absorb the blow, then return to its original shape when the force subsided. The unique hull shape of the well-designed vessel kept it steady and upright, even in the roughest conditions. He could leave the roomy cockpit and sit or lie on the long stern, or he could enter and exit from the side without fear of capsizing.

As he moved farther up river, he felt a slight breeze blowing on his back. He looked over his shoulder and noticed a few towering clouds way off in the distance. Having the wind behind him was good—it made moving against the current a lot easier. He intended to go upstream until he found a good place to start, then float back down the river, fishing as he went. Better keep his eyes on the weather, though. A wind out of the southwest could easily bring thunderstorms up from the Gulf Coast.

The rock he was looking for was between a double bend in the river. When he rounded the first bend, he saw that a lone fisherman already occupied it. He didn't see a boat or canoe. The river was shallow in many places, but not so there, and the rock was too far out into the stream for someone to have waded.

Then he saw it sitting on the far end of the rock, a float tube. A piece of green canvas fitted over a truck-size inner tube, forming a sling-type seat that slipped down into the hole of the tube. A fisherman could sit comfortably in the sling while floating down-river, fishing merrily all the way.

Clay had tried this only once. What the sellers of those handy little devices failed to tell him was that this part of the Chattahoochee wasn't the ideal place for that type of fishing. The water there was drawn from the lower regions of Lake Lanier to the north, and the cold temperature caused by the lake's hundred and twenty-foot depth made the river water sufferable for just a few minutes. The only way one could bear it was to wear waders while sitting in the tube. But Clay felt one had to have big brass balls to wear the waders. One was in danger of drowning should anything ever happen to the tube while it was in deep water. He had tried it once without the waders, and he got so cold it took two days for his common, garden-variety everyday balls to re-descend. He wouldn't be doing that again.

Clay veered way out to the left to avoid disturbing the fisherman's area and passed swiftly by. Up ahead, he saw the outer bank of the second bend in the river.

He nudged around several rocks upstream and found a place to wedge his boat. It was such a nice fit, he had stable footing on either side and was able to climb out and stand up. Looking back downstream, he saw the fisherman below him wave his slender fly rod gracefully back and forth several times, then arc the yellow-tinted line gently out over the current. The splash of the business end was imperceptible. That was a feat Clay hadn't yet mastered.

After several casts, instead of sweeping back over the fisherman's head, the line grew taut and the tip of the slender rod curled toward the water. For four or five minutes, Clay watched the battle between the stalwart fish and the solitary figure on the rock. The harsh clicking of the fly reel signaled the line being taken out by the fish and then back in by its would-be captor. Clay could tell the fish was losing. He saw the bend in the rod getting sharper, indicating that the fish was slowly nearing the rock. At last, the fish lay exhausted near the fisherman's feet, just under the surface of the water. Holding the rod in one hand, the victorious fisherman scooped up a gleaming, trophy-sized brown trout with the other. Then, loosening the tiny hook from the fish's mouth, the fisherman quickly lowered the trout to the water and gently nudged it back into the current.

Clay's reaction was instantaneous. He clenched his fist, pumped it up and down a few times and cried out, "All right," over the water. He was hailing not only the skill demonstrated in catching it but also the class shown in setting it free. The surprised fisherman looked up, and acknowledged the compliment with a slight tip of his hat.

Clay stayed at his spot for about an hour, catching and releasing bass. As he fished quietly, he noticed that the temperature had dropped slightly and he hadn't seen the sun for a while. The wind had been steadily increasing, and was now at a worrisome pitch. He decided to pack up and head home. As beautiful as the river was, it wasn't the place to be during a thunderstorm, and Clay suspected that the ominous darkness he now noticed in the sky to the west was just that—a big thunder bumper.

As he stowed his gear into the bow of the kayak, a sudden gust of wind blew spray all over him. When he looked up, he saw that the wind had caught the other fisherman's float tube, and was blowing it crazily upstream as if it were a piece of paper. At times, the tube was actually rolling along on top of the water. Clay knew that it would be sheer folly to try to retrieve the tube with the wind, so he launched his kayak in the lee of the rocks and turned downstream, then across river to where the fisherman was now stranded.

He thought the trip across would be simple, but the wind was roaring right up the river with ever increasing velocity. He had to fight to keep his little craft going in a straight line. Within seconds, the storm was on him, and he was caught in a torrential downpour. He could barely see, and the crack of lightning striking a tree on the far shore sent a chill up his spine.

The noise of the storm was so intense that when Clay reached the spot where the fisherman was huddled, all he could do was motion for him to discard his waders and jump into the kayak behind him. He was using a double paddle, and because the kayak was designed as a single there wouldn't be enough room for anyone to sit in front of him while he paddled. What had earlier been a comfortable cockpit for one was now cramped quarters for two.

Clay reached out, taking long, steady strokes. He wiped the rain from his eyes and pulled again, moving farther downstream. With the wind in his face, he leaned forward to reduce the drag and he felt the man behind move with him. There was some water in the boat, but it was rain and nothing to worry about. The rough water of the river swept across the bow, but was deflected to each side by a little guard protecting the front of the cockpit.

Every time he started to ask how his passenger was doing, either the crack of lightning stopped him, or thunder drowned him out. He figured all was well back there, and they could talk later.

The ferocity of the storm was lessening. The threat of the lightning seemed to be gone, and the wind had died down considerably, but the rain continued fairly strong. Clay's shoulder muscles ached from the rapid and difficult paddling, and he paused to rest and let the current continue to move him downstream.

It was then he first sensed the body of his rider push up against his back, shivering with cold. Arms pulled tight around his stomach. Legs stretched out alongside his. Very soft breasts pressed into his shoulder blades. Breasts? With the wind gone he could now detect the delicate fragrance that was all woman. I'll be a son of a bitch, Clay thought. The guy with the trout was no guy at all.

Only a light rain fell when Clay beached the kayak at his house. He lifted his chilled passenger from the back of his boat and helped her inside. They had yet to speak, and he had no idea what she looked like. She was drenched. Her khaki clothes stuck to her shivering body.

Once inside, Clay realized that the storm had knocked out the power, so he led her to his room overlooking the river, where one wall was almost all glass. There was sufficient natural light for her to see, and he directed her to get out of her wet things and into the shower while he still had hot water. She neither questioned nor hesitated, and soon steam was pouring out of his bath.

"There are plenty of towels in there," he said, "and when you come out grab something of mine that might fit you from my dressing room."

"Okay," she said from the shower.

"I'll shower in the guest room then build a fire to knock the chill off the house."

"All right."

Clay took some dry jeans and a pullover from his room, and quickly showered and dressed. He had plenty of dry, seasoned firewood left over from the winter, and soon a roaring fire lighted the great room and began to warm Clay and his house. He rummaged around and came up with some tea bags and hot chocolate, and began heating water in an old black kettle in the fireplace.

He hadn't heard the shower in his room for a while and wondered how his guest was doing and whether she needed anything. It was so unusual for a woman to be in his house, he hardly knew how to act, especially under the circumstances. But then he heard the faint sound of her singing and figured everything was under control. The water was now hot enough, so he poured a cup of tea and one of hot chocolate, and headed for his room. He'd give her whichever one she wanted.

As he reached the closed door and was getting ready to knock with his foot, he was startled by a piercing scream. Dropping both cups on the hardwood floor, he pushed the door aside and raced into the room. His newfound fishing buddy was standing in the middle of the floor wrapped in a towel screaming at something furry moving in the semi-darkness of one corner. When Clay burst in, she wheeled around and rushed into his arms. He pulled her around behind him just in time to see Fraidy move out into the room. Apparently, he'd been asleep when they first came in and was reluctant to approach this stranger after he woke.

"What are you doing in here?" Clay said to the yawning cat. Then he turned to face his guest. "I'm sorry. I don't know how he got in here. I left him outside. He only comes in by invitation." She was still trembling from the scare, and he put his arms around her and pulled her to him.

She responded genuinely, placing her face against his soft shirt and wrapping her arms tightly around him. It was the same embrace he'd felt in the kayak, only now they were dry and warm, and all the softness was in front. As they stood in the dim light clinging to each other, he could feel her heart beating against his chest, and he sensed a warmth emanating from her body.

Ever since they'd come into the house he'd been trying to see what she looked like but was afraid to stare. Now it seemed all right to do so. Her short hair was coal black. He was exactly a head taller. The top of her head fit neatly right under his chin. He nuzzled his face in her hair and enjoyed the soft aroma he found there. Her features were very delicate, and her skin the color of coffee with a lot of cream. She had small but full breasts, and as the towel slipped aside a little he could see that her skin color remained constant as far as he could see.

As he held her, a warm glow began deep inside him and he sensed an excitement and arousal he'd known long before, but thought was gone forever. He tried to fight the feeling, and told himself it wasn't proper. It wasn't right. He didn't know her. How could he think something like that? But nothing worked. His feelings grew stronger as he stood there, and he felt a hot and tingling sensation course through him. A similar glow was coming to him from the other side of the towel, and he knew he could stand it no longer.

He reached down, removed the towel from her, and picked her up into his arms. "Will you come with me?"

"Yes," she said, kissing him warmly on the neck, "I want to be with you."

While still holding her in his arms, Clay removed the fluffy comforter from his bed and carried it and her to the great room, where he made a soft pallet on the carpet in front of the fireplace.

As they lay naked by the fire, they kissed easily and sweetly, and touched each other all over as if they'd known the other intimately for years. Clay sensed her need for gentleness.

As they lay facing each other, slowly moving in sensual simulation of the love making to come, his arousal was such that without any effort by either of them he gently became a part of her. He felt her warm moistness open up to him. He was suddenly surrounded by the softness of velvet, while little hot spokes of pleasure radiated outward in all directions.

They moved together as one. Clay was lost in a world of pleasant darkness with sharp, bright lights popping and sparkling all about. A world of intense pleasure radiated outward from where they were joined together, undulating and pulsing with each movement. Faster and faster they moved, until they could each sense that the other was so close to the edge that there was no pulling back. So, faster and faster they moved, and closer and closer they got to ecstasy.

So intense had been their pleasure, that they had to now lie perfectly still in each other's arms, for any further movement brought something akin to pain. But they bathed in the afterglow of the tenderness of each other.

As they lay there, Clay was filled to the brim with this astonishing woman he'd discovered on the river. After some soft caressing and nuzzling, the two of them drifted off to a restful sleep on the floor in front of the fire.

When Clay awakened, she stood in front of him, dressed in one of his flannel shirts and a pair of his sweatpants rolled up.

"I really must go," she said. "May I borrow your kayak? I live just downstream from here. I'll bring it back tomorrow."

"Sure," Clay replied. "What time is it?"

"Six-thirty. The power's back on, but your clocks are about three hours behind. See you tomorrow." She kissed him on the cheek and bounced out the door.

Clay lay there for a moment, then leaped to his feet and ran for the door. He suddenly remembered he was naked, so he raced back and picked up the comforter and wrapped it around himself, then went stumbling out onto the deck.

"Wait," he called out to the kayak disappearing around a bend down-river, "I don't even know your name."

Six-thirty. He had to be at Bobby's in an hour, and he still had to dress and pick up a bottle of wine.

Showered, shaved, dressed, and bearing wine, Clay was right on time.

"Come on in and fix yourself a drink, Clay," Claire said, hugging him. "My professor will be here any minute."

"I'll need several drinks if I'm going to make it through the evening. You guys really know how to put me on the hot seat, don't you?" Clay responded, following her to the kitchen.

As he mixed a drink at a kitchen counter, the door bell rang.

"Will you get the door, Bobby? Just introduce yourself then y'all come on back to the kitchen. We're going to be very informal tonight. And Clay's fixing drinks."

Clay was just beginning to turn the corkscrew when he heard the kitchen door swing open.

"Clay," Claire said, "I want you to meet Professor Gallagher. Professor Gallagher, this is our good friend, Clay Delaney."

Clay turned around and found himself extending his hand to the same beautiful woman who had taken his breath away on the floor in front of his fireplace.

"It's a pleasure to meet you, Mr. Delaney," she said, taking his hand. "I'm Callie Gallagher."

"The pleasure's all mine, Professor Gallagher. And please call me Clay. May I fix you a drink?"

"A glass of that wine will do fine. Please call me Callie. Just a little something to warm the spirit. It's been an unusual day."

"Indeed."

Clay and Callie carried on their little banter as if no one else was in the room, so Bobby and Claire slipped out of the kitchen.

When Callie returned the next day with the kayak tied to the top of her car, her meeting with Clay was somewhat strained. Gone was the buffer provided the night before by Bobby and Claire. Gone too was the need to speak in code. Now that the two of them could talk openly, words, at first, were hard to come by. After a little small talk, they simultaneously tried to offer each other an apology for their conduct, but ended up laughing together at their overlapping awkwardness.

They spent that Sunday sitting by the fire, talking and drinking the tea and chocolate that had been so delightfully ignored the day before. Words now flowed freely between them. For the first time, Clay felt comfortable enough with someone to talk openly about his past and his pain. He felt as safe in Callie's mind as he had in her arms. He was beginning to realize that there was something much worse than being vulnerable. It was being truly alone.

By the time the last glowing coal was snuggled under a blanket of ash in the sleeping fire, Callie and Clay were snuggled together under a blanket of mutual trust in a tender affection that was just awakening.

When Monday crept silently across Clay's big bed and gently nudged him into a new week, he could feel the slight impression Callie had left behind, and smell her fragrance rising from the pillow beside him. Opening his eyes, he smiled, reliving the previous night.

CHAPTER 8

▼

When Herb Solomon finished reading Chairman Bishop's letter, his first inclination was to crush it into a wad and fling it against the half-glass wall in front of him. Instead, he yelled through the open door of his office, "Crowley, get in here."

Whenever Herb Solomon felt pressed or under-the-gun, he called for Juanita Crowley. Only three years out of law school, she'd matured rapidly under Solomon's guidance. Despite her own caseload, she always found time to deliver when he called upon her.

"Yeah, Chief," Juanita said when she arrived at his doorway.

"Don't call me Chief. I hate that."

She smiled. "Okay. Chief."

Solomon grimaced, shook his head, and handed her the letter. "Take this and start gathering the information they've asked for. Looks as if the County Commission is off on another efficiency tear."

Juanita looked at the two pages in her hand and said, "This is asking for some detailed stuff: cases handled per lawyer per quarter, cases nol-prossed, cases pled out, cases tried, average hours per lawyer per case per quarter, et cetera."

"It gets worse," Solomon said. "We need to back our fixed expenses out of overhead, and give an adjusted overhead figure per attorney hour for the last four years."

"What's up, Herb?"

"I'm not sure. This has all the markings of a productivity study. I have no idea how the County Commission's going to use this information."

"When do you need it?"

"Yesterday. Get on it, will you."

Solomon had been around county government long enough to know that productivity reports generally preceded funding decisions. He didn't quarrel with that concept, but experience had taught him that the decisions had already been made, and the Commission needed some way to justify them—especially if they were likely to arouse public concern.

What he wanted to know was the scope of the study and how many of the court-related activities paid for by the county were being reviewed.

"Rutledge," Solomon called through his doorway.

A lanky young lawyer, pecking away at a keyboard, raised his head and glanced toward Solomon's office. Solomon motioned with his head and his hand for him to come. The lawyer unfolded his bony frame from a swivel chair in front of a computer and moved slowly over to Solomon's door.

"You keep callin' folks over here, Mr. Solomon. You givin' out awards today?"

"I'm going to pin an award smack dab on your Dewey button, Rutledge, if you can't move any faster than that."

"Dewey button? Is that one of those sayings you learned up at Harvard, or did you make it up all by yourself?"

Solomon studied the young man he affectionately called "The Lean Machine." Billy Rutledge had two special talents: he was the best on-line researcher in the office, and he knew every nobody in county government. Billy didn't know one county official or department head, but he was on a first name basis with the people who delivered their mail, typed their memos, and emptied their trash.

On any given day, Billy was unaware of what was happening in the county office complex, but he could find out during one casual stroll down its busy corridors.

"What are you lookin' at, Mr. Solomon?" he said with a broad grin, which Solomon returned in kind.

"I'd replace you in an instant, Rutledge, if it wasn't for the fact that you're nothing but brains and bones."

"You didn't call me over here to comment on my intelligent good looks. What is it you want?"

"Someone's doing an efficiency or productivity study for the Commission, and I want to know how broad it is. Can you find out what departments are being studied?"

"You want to know right now, or can you wait long enough for me to get back to my desk?"

"Since you put it that way, right now, wise ass."

Billy pushed his way between Solomon and a computer on a small table beside Solomon's desk. Some rapid tapping and he'd prepared and sent an e-mail message to someone he called Peach Fuzz in the Commission secretarial pool.

While they waited for a reply, Solomon asked, "How in the world did you know who to send it to?"

"Those kinds of reports require spread sheets and bar graphs. There are only two ladies on the Commission payroll who can put data in those formats. One of them is on vacation. I contacted the other one. Wait a second, she's answering."

A two-letter answer appeared on the blue screen in front of them. It read, "UR."

Solomon stared at the tiny white letters. "Does that say what I think it says?"

"Let me double check," Billy said, and he typed, "Who else?"

In a moment, the symbols for two half notes and a full note flashed across the screen, followed by the words, "Only you."

A bewildered Billy Rutledge returned to his desk, while Herb Solomon placed a call to Marshall Bishop, looking for an explanation of why his office was the sole subject of a study. He didn't get through, and after several tries, he decided that he was getting the runaround. The Commission Chairman was, no doubt, a busy man, but Herb Solomon had been around long enough to warrant a return call. He didn't get it.

In the weeks that passed, Clay spent his days handling his private practice the best he could and spent his evenings either studying criminal law or buying beer and quizzing his friends who already knew it. His weekends were taken up reviewing the evidence against Harco, then checking it out with personal investigation.

Callie was an occasional weekend visitor, but her time with Clay was limited by his absorption with Harco's case. He'd summarized the evidence for her, and she'd sat with him while he reviewed the videotape of Harco's TV appearance. But when he wasn't talking about the case, he was reading something on criminal law. Consequently, Callie and Fraidy spent a lot of time together and became fast friends.

Once while struggling to get Clay's head out of a brown folder marked "Brewton," Callie finally said in mock exasperation, "Why are you putting yourself through all this? He's obviously guilty."

Clay looked up slowly from the material in front of him. "How can you say that? I've read this file at least a dozen times now and talked to half the people involved, including Harco himself, and I can't say one way or the other. At one time, I was positive he did it, now I'm not so sure."

"The videotape you showed me of his television interview was proof enough for me."

"That was network hype. They set it up that way."

"No," Callie exclaimed. "Don't let this guy get to you, Clay. He's a liar and a killer. He does both without compunction or remorse. I don't have to read your file. Reading people is what I do. It's my life's work. It's as much a part of me as my arms and legs. Watching him and listening to him on that tape made my skin crawl. It's clear to me he has a controlled and calculated hate for women. Sufficient enough from what I see to kill them."

"But how does that balance with what appears to be his open sexuality?" Clay asked. "He gives all the outward signs of wanting to be down and dirty all the time."

"He's a classic case of a sheep in wolf's clothing. He howls and prowls, but when it gets down to it, all he can do is nibble grass."

"What about the rape, then?" Clay asked.

"He focuses on their sexual vulnerability to hurt and degrade them. Actually he abhors sex, so he uses it as a means of punishment—probably the final punishment."

"How's that?"

"While he may sexually violate his victim in some way while she's conscious, more than likely he doesn't enter her until she's already dead."

"That's really sick. Do I have an insanity issue here?" Clay asked.

"What he does is sick. He's not. He knows exactly what he's doing, and he knows it's wrong. He just doesn't care. He's a sociopath, not insane. Anyone with training who saw that tape would come to the same conclusion. I imagine they already have."

"Damn."

"What's the matter?" Callie asked.

"No wonder the district attorney conned Harco into going on television. It was to get a voluntary psychological profile of him and have Harco provide his own evidence of motive."

"Well," said Callie, "it'll become a textbook classic. When this is over, I'd like to use it when I lecture."

"I know it shows he's capable of committing this crime, but being capable is hardly enough. You need much more than that."

"From what I hear, everything else needed was already there, all cut and dried."

"The interview did kind of tie it all up in one neat bundle, didn't it?"

"Yes, it did," she answered.

Clay thought quietly for a moment then said, "Maybe that's what's been bothering me. It's too cut and dried. It's just too simple."

"Well, I'll leave that to you lawyers. But as far as I'm concerned, you have a killer behind bars. Don't help turn him loose."

As much as Clay admired Callie's professional instinct and reasoning, he remained troubled about his assessment of Harco. He'd gotten over the hurdle of Harco's presumed guilt and was finally working on the possibility of his innocence. Callie's feelings were at the same place his had been when he first became involved with the case. Maybe she too would soften with time.

It wasn't long before word came down from Judge Armbrister's office that Harco's trial was scheduled to begin in three weeks. That notice rocketed Clay into action. He had yet to talk to several potential witnesses—including Jaynelle Eubanks and the teenage daughter of the Lindsey's neighbor—nor had he visited Harco's rooming house in Montgomery in search of anybody or anything that could link Harco to that city on April third. Actually, if what Harco was saying about switching cities with his stolen goods was so, then any of the stolen goods with a Montgomery connection would've been stashed in the room in Atlanta. But that room was empty. Either Harco had already hocked them, or Jason Rowland had them.

Now, there was a dilemma. Any stolen articles he might find in Montgomery would further connect Harco to the Lindsey neighborhood in the days just before the murder. If Rowland had taken anything from the room in Atlanta that might tend to prove Harco was in Montgomery, in order to use it as evidence at the trial, Clay would have to prove that Harco was a thief. In deciding Harco's guilt or innocence, the jury would never be allowed to know of his previous criminal record, unless Harco actually testified in his own defense.

If he did testify, then Rowland could introduce evidence of his life of crime to show that Harco was dishonest, was devoid of any moral character, and shouldn't be believed when he denied raping and killing Carrie Lindsey. As long as Harco didn't take the witness stand, the law would keep the jury in the dark about his past while they were trying to decide if he did it.

Putting Harco on the stand was extremely dangerous to begin with, but to put him up there to prove that he was in another city stealing from folks when Carrie

Lindsey died was crazy. Then as soon as that was done, Jason Rowland would lay a dozen or more criminal convictions for God knows what under Harco's nose, and it would all be over. No juror in his right mind would believe Harco after that, and rightly so.

Nevertheless, Clay needed to know if anything helpful to him had been taken from Harco's room on Eleventh Street, and to find that out he had to face Rowland again. Maybe he could use that as an excuse to subtly reopen the plea-bargain discussion he had avoided earlier.

"Good morning, Mr. Delaney," Rowland's secretary said with a broad smile as he approached her desk in the Annex.

"Good morning. He in today?"

"Yes. Let me see if he's available." She rose and eased toward the partially opened office door.

Clay busied himself with a year-old issue of a Fraternal Order of Police magazine while he waited. He had time to learn the price of a kevlar bulletproof vest before Rowland appeared at his door looking somewhat stern and slightly unsettled. Clay could sense something was amiss. But not knowing what was bothering Rowland, he broke the ice with an over-dramatized southern inquiry. "How do? How's your momma and them?"

Rowland responded with a weak smile. "I'm fine, Delaney, but my momma has never heard of you or your momma. So cut the crap. What's on your mind?"

"I don't have to know your momma to be respectful and inquire about her health. She knows that even if you don't. Be a dutiful son and tell her I asked next time you talk to her."

Once again Clay had put Rowland slightly off balance, but he was already a little that way when Clay came in. He continued. "To answer your question, I came to talk to you about taking a look at Harco Brewton's car and anything you found in it, and—"

"That's easy enough," Rowland said, looking somewhat relieved.

"And to inspect anything your boys took from his room."

"We took! We took! You've got a lot of gall, Delaney."

"What the hell are you talking about?"

"Surely you're putting me on."

"You know what?" said Clay. "You've acted strange ever since I arrived, and it's getting worse. You've gone from strange to weird."

"You really don't know, do you?"

"Know what?" Clay asked.

"Never mind. You'll find out soon enough." Rowland turned away from Clay, pushed a button and spoke into his intercom. "Please see to it that Mr. Delaney gets access to the Brewton car in the garage downstairs." Then turning to Clay, he asked, "Today?" Clay nodded. "Today," Rowland said into the speaker-box. "I'll have to accompany you to the evidence room for the other stuff. We can do that first."

Clay followed Rowland to the elevator then down several floors to a room marked, "Property." Rowland told the officer behind the screen what he wanted, and in just a moment he returned and handed Rowland two plastic bags.

One bag contained a porno magazine. In the other lay Carrie Lindsey's red-tressed Raggedy Ann doll. Clay noted the black marker writing on a label on each bag with Harco's name, a date, a description of the article, the place where it was found, and some initials. The bag with the doll indicated it had been found in Harco's car, "under the right front passenger seat," and the magazine, "in the rear seat."

When Clay went to unseal the bag with the magazine, Rowland grabbed it, saying, "Look, but don't touch."

"Won't do me any good if I can't look inside," Clay complained.

"Seen one, you've seen 'em all."

"Open the damn bag."

Rowland did and handed the magazine to Clay. As he flipped through the pages, he wasn't surprised to find all the faces blacked out as before. But this time there was something new. All the crotches and nipples had been slashed with a very sharp knife or razor. A chill slipped up Clay's spine. He knew this was going to be Exhibit "B." Exhibit "A" would be the doll.

Rowland steadfastly refused to allow Clay to open the doll bag, but in examining it closely he noted beads of condensation on the inside of the bag. "Has someone tested or tampered with this doll?"

"You know, I don't have to answer your questions, Delaney. But, just so you'll know I'm an okay guy, no. That's the way we found it. Wet."

"Thanks, okay guy. Now, where's the rest of his stuff?"

"The rest of it? Delaney, you amaze me. You really do. I was hoping to get it all back from you."

"From me?"

"Yeah. The rooming house manager said you had been in Brewton's room just a while back."

"So?"

"So, the stuff we first saw in there is all gone, and you're the only one to go in there except us."

"What kind of stuff?"

"The VCR, TV, calculator, CD player. You know what I'm talking about."

"No, I don't."

"The stuff we now think may have come from some burglaries near the Lindseys' house just before Carrie disappeared. That could be hard evidence to link Brewton to the kid's neighborhood, and you could be facing an obstruction of justice charge."

"You're serious, aren't you?"

"Like a heart attack."

"Go to hell."

"I hear you, Delaney. But don't forget the first rule of criminal law. 'If anybody's going to go to jail, make sure it's your client.' Now, do you want to plea-bargain?"

"I thought you'd already said, 'No.'"

"I was talking about your case. Not Brewton's."

"Go to hell!" Clay wheeled and disappeared down the corridor.

In the dim light of the Annex basement, Clay could barely make out the dingy, white four-door sedan parked behind a small section of chain link fence. But even in the poor light, he could see considerable rust exposing itself through the roof, hood and trunk. It wasn't an easy car to miss or forget, Clay thought.

The guard noisily unlocked the double gate and without speaking, gestured for Clay to enter the enclosure. In passing the rear of the car, he noticed the tag was from Kentucky. Kentucky? Why Kentucky?

"You sure this is Harco Brewton's car?" he asked the guard.

"Yeah. I helped 'em bring it in. The only white one we got."

Clay jotted down the tag number to check out later.

"May I see inside?"

"Help yourself," the guard replied. "It's unlocked, but I have to stay here till you're finished and lock the gate."

Clay climbed in the driver's side and was greeted by a musty odor and the same stale tobacco smell he'd found in Harco's room. The ashtray was overflowing, and the seat and dash were littered with cookie, gum, and candy wrappers, as well as an assortment of stained hot-and-cold-cups. The back seat was much the same, but the emphasis there seemed to be on empty cigarette packs rolled into balls and, based on where they were located, seemingly tossed over the driver's right shoulder.

He leaned over to his right and felt up under the front passenger seat with his left hand. The carpet all under the seat was damp and his fingers easily poked several holes in the rotting fabric and rusting floorboard. That explained why the doll was wet when found. It was a straight shot from the street to the interior of the car, indiscriminately allowing roadway water a way in.

A quick view into the trunk satisfied Clay that the beat-up old car contained nothing but trash, including any memory of the presence of Harco Brewton. He thanked the unobtrusive guard, and started out of the basement to the cadence of the clanging metal gates and rattling fence.

The thought that little Carrie Lindsey might have been dragged screaming into the old sedan and possibly silenced forever in its filthy interior chilled Clay to the bone. But, no, he was supposed to be giving Harco the benefit of the doubt, and working to show his innocence. It was hard being objective—so hard.

Before entering his driveway, Clay pulled up and stopped at his roadside mailbox that marked its entrance. As he stood flipping through the various postal pieces, he was suddenly confronted with a stream of police vehicles exiting his driveway out onto the main road. He was so startled that before he could regain his composure and flag one of them down they were gone. Leaping back into his car, he raced up the winding driveway to his house. He saw one unmarked police car parked near the rear of the house as he roared to a stop near his back door. A plainclothes detective stood just inside.

"What's happened?" Clay asked excitedly, as he rushed in.

"You Clay Delaney?" the detective asked.

"Yeah. What's wrong?"

"Here," the detective said, handing him a folded document. "We just finished executing this."

Clay unfolded the paper and, incredulous, read a search warrant signed by Judge Armbrister, describing articles of personal property "known to be the property of other persons and believed to have recently been in the possession of Harco Brewton."

"District Attorney Rowland wanted me to call as soon as we finished," the detective said. "Mind if I use your phone?"

Clay was still too stunned to speak, and simply nodded and pointed to the wall phone in the kitchen.

"Nothing," the detective said into the phone. "We're on our way in." He then bid Clay a perfunctory "Good day," and left.

Clay stared in disbelief at the disarray of what had earlier been his neat and orderly home. From the kitchen to the basement, not a room or a drawer had been spared. Furnishings and personal belongings were scattered everywhere.

Clay had never before been subjected to a search warrant, a burglary or any vandalism. If he hadn't personally seen the police, he would now be on the phone calling them to report what he believed to have been a crime.

He was too dumbfounded to be angry, so he sat down on the now pillow-less couch in his great room, and waited for the waves of shock and humiliation to stop crashing over him. He felt violated, vulnerable, and too helpless to fight back.

As he sat there, he noticed an eight-by-ten silver picture frame lying face down on the floor beside him. He reached over and picked it up. The glass was badly cracked from a careless footstep, but the last school photo of Chelsea Delaney was still intact. When he moved to the river, he'd relegated the photo to an end table drawer as part of his effort to cleanse his memory.

Now as he gazed at the sweet, innocent face of his auburn-haired child, he wondered how violated, vulnerable, and helpless she must've felt in her final moments. He knew his feelings were nothing in comparison.

Reaching up and straightening the crooked shade on the end table lamp, he placed the silver-bordered photo, broken glass and all, beside it. It was time to clean up.

He knew when he met Jason Rowland that he was in for a tough fight. What he didn't know was that it was going to be as bad as a back-stabbing knife fight in a dirt-floored bar. He wasn't ready for that. He needed someone to cover him from behind. Solomon.

"What do you mean 'cover your back?'" Solomon barked into the phone. "He did what? That's a crock. Look, Delaney, I'm already up to my ears in cases as it is. I simply don't have the time. So? Of course I've heard of Thomas Edison and Albert Einstein. Go to hell, Delaney." He slammed down the phone.

"What was that all about?" the young lawyer standing in Solomon's doorway inquired.

Removing the well-chewed cigar stump from his mouth, Solomon growled, "Clay Delaney wants me to help him with the Brewton case, and I just don't have the time."

"Why was he asking you about Thomas Edison and Albert Einstein?" the youngster said.

"Because he says I have the same amount of time as they did."

"Well, you going to help him or do I have to add Helen Keller to his list?"

"Haven't I run you off before?" Solomon snarled, as his young charge back-pedaled out of his office, smiling as he went.

"Smart aleks and wise asses. Why am I always surrounded by smart aleks and wise asses?" Solomon rummaged through the clutter of brown folders on his desk. "Crowley," he called out, "have you seen my personal copy of the Brewton file?"

CHAPTER 9

▼

In the waning days before trial—in order to keep Jason Rowland at bay and give Clay the time he needed to get ready—Herb Solomon went into high gear. He prepared five separate motions for Clay to sign and file in the case. Each had an accompanying brief, and each had to be responded to in writing by Rowland before trial. They ranged from a motion to grant bail through motions to suppress evidence, to a motion to dismiss all charges for prosecutorial misconduct.

When all the motions and briefs were prepared and ready to go, Solomon had them filed one day apart. A new motion was delivered to Rowland's office each day for five days in a row. Everyone on Rowland's floor of the Annex knew when the mail arrived that week. Each morning his curses flooded the hallways like clockwork. They grew louder and more profane as the week progressed, because only a few early morning hours separated his finishing touches on one brief from the arrival of a another motion.

"He probably has a horde of young talent up there responding to all our stuff," Clay said, over the line of empty beer bottles separating him and Solomon.

"No way," Solomon replied with a broad grin. "My mole tells me he has only two assistants. One has a new baby and is working part-time, and the other is still recuperating from a skiing accident. Looks like Mr. Fancy Pants is having to do most of the work himself. Don't you just love it?"

"Another round?" the approaching cocktail waitress asked.

"I thought you said Jaynelle was working tonight," Solomon said.

"She is. Must be running late. That kid of hers always screws up her schedule. She'll be along shortly."

"Give us one more," he said. Then he turned to Clay. "If she doesn't come soon, we're going to be too shit-faced to talk to her."

Their table along the side wall gave them a good view of the door and the darkened interior of the small, suburban tavern. They were as far from the juke-box as they could get, but still had to strain to hear each other over the blare of country music.

Clay glanced at his watch. It was almost nine p.m. They'd been there since seven, hoping to catch Jaynelle Eubanks when she came to work.

"How'd you find out she worked here?" Clay asked.

"I told her sister I had an insurance check for Jaynelle that I could either drop in the mail or deliver to her at work. She told me about this place."

"What if she said to drop it in the mail?"

"She'd still be waiting on it," Solomon replied. "But then I'd have her home address. And you and I would be waiting over there without any beer—"

"That must be her," Clay said, nodding toward the door, where their waitress and another woman were talking and looking their way.

The woman started toward them, and Clay rose to greet her.

In the dim light of the tavern, Jaynelle Eubanks was a looker. Tall, lithe and looking extremely well-built in a too tight blouse. But even in the poor light Clay could see the crow's feet at the corners of her eyes and the hard lines around her mouth; harsh evidence of a tough life.

"You the guy that called about the insurance check?" she asked.

"No," Clay replied. "Are you Jaynelle Eubanks?"

"Yeah?" she said with some hesitancy. "What do you fellas want?"

Solomon rose, extended his hand. "I'm with Fulton County, and we need to talk to you about the Carrie Lindsey murder."

Clay looked at Solomon inquisitively.

"I've told y'all all I know already," she said, "and I'm plumb talked out about it. And I haven't talked to that murderer's lawyer like you folks said. What else do you want?"

Solomon glanced at Clay and continued. "We just want to go over it one more time. There's some confusion about what you said."

"One more time? I've got to go to work. I don't make nothing just standing here."

"Well, we can do it here or we can do it in my office at the courthouse," Solomon said. "It's up to you."

"Can I sit down, then?"

"By all means," Solomon and Clay said simultaneously, both scrambling to get her a chair.

"Darlene," Jaynelle cried out to the other waitress. "Would you cover for me till I finish with these guys?"

Her friend nodded.

Once the trio was seated, Solomon took the lead. Despite his frumpy looks, grumpy manner, and outward gruffness, he had a big heart, a tender soul, and he was smooth as silk with Jaynelle Eubanks. He got her life's story in the first fifteen minutes, had her laughing for the next ten, then drained every ounce of useful information out of her in the remaining twenty, all the while ordering and downing his share of several rounds of drinks for the three of them.

Clay sat in silent awe. The two were laughing and calling each other "Herbie" and "Jaynelle, honey." Clay wasn't sure if Solomon was conducting an interview or a seduction. But, whatever it was, it was working. Jaynelle Eubanks had come alive in the stale dimness of the little tavern, and was chirping merrily away like a mockingbird just before sunrise.

It was clear from her description that she had definitely seen Harco Brewton at her corner mart. It was also readily apparent that Jaynelle was very impressionable. While she stood firm on events she was sure of, she was easily swayed on matters not so certain in her memory. What she wasn't sure of was when she'd seen Harco. It was obvious that when the investigating detectives suggested that it must have been the day Carrie disappeared, she went along with it. Clay surmised that if any doubt could be injected into that thought, Jaynelle might waver. Maybe just enough to start a crack in Rowland's tightly structured theory.

If it was true that Harco Brewton had been in the Lindsey neighborhood two days before Carrie disappeared, then it wouldn't have been unusual for him to have been at the market that same day. Before Clay could concede that the Lindseys' neighbor was right about seeing Harco, however, he had to prove that Jaynelle was wrong, but only by two days.

As Clay had earlier observed, Jaynelle described the little mart as an afternoon gathering and mixing place for the local teenagers. A place where chance meetings were arranged, dates made, and liaisons begun or ended. It was a place to show off new clothes, varsity jackets, and new wheels.

"I'll bet Friday afternoons were hectic," Solomon said.

"Every afternoon when school let out was hectic. Fridays weren't any worse than other days. When that bell rang, we'd make over a hundred sales in the first forty-five minutes, and then some."

"I guess that made your boss happy."

"I guess. He never said. Mostly, he complained about the stealing that went on when the store was so full of kids. There wasn't nothing I could do about it. I never saw it. I had all I could do just ringing up the sales."

Jaynelle slowed down in her story, and Solomon said, "Of all the people who came in and out of your store, how did you know to pick out the killer and describe him to the police?"

"Oh, I didn't pick him out. The police came in one day, said they were looking for the killer of the Lindsey girl, showed me a photo of him and asked me if I'd ever seen him. Of course I had, and I told them so."

Solomon pressed on. "Mr. Rowland says that when you saw the killer in your store, he was with the little girl. Is that right?"

"Oh yeah. They came in, looked around and picked up a few things. He paid for them, and they left."

"They came in together?"

"Yeah."

"Shopped together?"

"Yeah."

"And then left together?" Solomon continued. "Yeah. Sure."

"Had you ever seen them together before?"

"Nope. That day was the first and only time I ever saw them. Either together or by themselves," Jaynelle said.

"How did you know the little girl was Carrie Lindsey?"

"Well, the police said that's who it must've been."

"Did they show you a picture of her?"

"Yeah, but it was made at the..."

"At the morgue?" Solomon added.

"Yeah," she continued. "It was hard for me to look at, and all, but she looked familiar. Really, I didn't remember her as much as I remembered him. He was weird looking."

"Mr. Rowland also says you saw the two of them together on the afternoon the little girl disappeared. Is that right?"

"Yeah."

"How do you remember that?"

"Well, he definitely was in the store very close to the time the girl disappeared, and since they were in there together, we all figured it had to be the day it happened."

"We?"

"The police and me."

"What days did you work at the market?"

"Monday to Friday."

"What hours?"

"Seven in the morning to four in the afternoon."

"Well, Jaynelle," Solomon said, rising to his feet, "I guess that's all for now."

Jaynelle and Clay also stood up, Jaynelle looking at her watch. After appropriate pleasantries and as he was turning to leave, Solomon thrust his hand into his pocket and retrieved two twenty dollar bills. Pressing them into her hand, he said, "I hope this makes up for what you lost talking to us tonight."

The look of relief and gratitude in her eyes spoke louder than the quietly polite "Thank you," she directed at the departing Solomon. As Clay started to follow, Jaynelle reached out and touched his arm. "I'm sorry," she said. "I didn't catch your name."

"Delaney," he said. "Clay Delaney."

Jaynelle stood there with a puzzled look on her face as the two went out the door. Then, shrugging her shoulders, she stuffed the two twenties into the center of her bra and went to work.

Outside in the parking lot, as the two were approaching Clay's car, Solomon said, "I don't know about you, but after that, I need a drink."

"A drink?" Clay laughed.

"Hell, yeah. We need to celebrate your first break."

"My break?"

"It's your case, isn't it?"

"Not anymore, Herb darling. Not anymore. It's ours."

"Well, let's not argue about that. Let's just celebrate a crack in Rowland's case, then."

"You're on," Clay said. "But you'll have to drive. I've had too much to drink already."

They proceeded back toward the city to find a suitable watering hole.

"You hungry too?" Clay asked, as they cruised into the lighted streets of downtown Atlanta.

"Yeah. What'd you have in mind?"

"How 'bout some pasta?"

"Where you going to find good pasta at this time of night?"

"At My Aunt Emma's Place."

"We're not going to somebody's house, are we?" Solomon moaned.

"No. That's the name of a small Italian place across town."

"They still serving this time of night?"

"Probably not, but they'll serve us."

"Why do you say that?"

"Because the owner's my aunt," Clay replied.

"Don't tell me. Your Aunt Emma."

"That's right, and I was the one who suggested the name to her, too."

"Let me get this straight. Your Irish aunt owns an Italian restaurant?"

"Who said my aunt was Irish? She's as Italian as they come."

"But I thought 'Delaney' was—"

"Irish? It is. My father was a 'Delaney.' My mother was a 'Gambini.' This is my mother's sister."

Clay guided Solomon to a small, white frame house on Highland Avenue, in a mixed residential and small business neighborhood. A petite red and green neon sign in a window near the door announced the establishment's name. The pervading smell of garlic reached as far as the street.

The ring of the bell on the door provoked, "Kitchen's closed," from the rotund little woman standing behind the register.

Peering out from behind Solomon, Clay said, "To your favorite nephew?"

"My God, it's Clay," Aunt Emma said. Then, turning to the two waiters who were cleaning up, she said, "Anthony. Jerry. Fix a table and get some wine for your cousin." Turning back to Clay, she held out her chubby arms to him, then enveloped and kissed him affectionately when he got within range. Clay introduced Solomon to her, and she greeted him with a hug.

In the hours that followed, Emma and family joined Clay and Solomon, and laughter, animated conversation, good food, wine and multicolored liqueurs abounded at the little table in the closed restaurant.

It was two a.m. when Clay and Solomon left the little restaurant to return to the county courthouse where Solomon's car was parked. Solomon was feeling no pain. He'd gotten into a drinking contest with Cousin Anthony, and lost. Clay was in slightly better shape.

As their car moved down Ponce de Leon Avenue, a straight shot to downtown, it suddenly picked up speed. Soon the vacant street was passing faster and faster under its headlights.

"Slow down, Clay," Solomon shouted, "or you'll kill us both!"

"Herb," Clay said, "you're the one who's driving."

"Oh," Solomon said sheepishly, and eased back on the accelerator.

When Solomon stopped the car in front of the courthouse, Clay questioned him about whether he should be driving himself home.

"Don't worry, I'm not going home. I've got some work to do."

"Work?"

"Right. You see that?" Solomon said, pointing unsteadily up to a lone light burning in a corner of the third floor of the Superior Court Annex. "That's Jason Rowland's office. He's still working on one of my motions. I'm gonna have another one on the bastard's desk in the morning.

"For what?" Clay asked.

"To suppress Jaynelle's I.D. of Brewton." Solomon heaved a half-empty wine bottle against the stone side of the Annex. "Hey Jason," he shouted upwards over the shattering glass. "Search warrant, huh? I'll show you search warrant. I'm gonna keep your suspendered ass so busy, you'll need a search warrant to find your own pecker."

"Goddamn winos," Jason Rowland growled at the tinkling of glass and faint shouts on the street below his window. "Can't they see we're still working up here?"

CHAPTER 10

▼

In spite of the distasteful search warrant experience, Clay felt drawn back to Harco's rooming house on Eleventh Street, if for no other reason than to take one more look and to quiz Gladdie, the manager. He knew he'd find her at the kitchen table, facing the door.

"How you doin', Mr. Clay?" Gladdie said as he entered unannounced into the old kitchen.

"Just fine, Gladdie."

Clay seated himself at the bare table across from her and began to chat quietly. Before long, she brought out an old perc pot of fresh, black coffee.

"Have you rented the room?" Clay asked.

"No. The police raised such a ruckus after you was here that I decided to leave it be."

"Have you ever seen anyone else go in or out of that room?"

"No, sir. Only Mr. Brewton, the police, and you."

"Think I could take another look?"

"If that's all you take." She laughed heartily.

"Did the police ask you if I had taken anything the last time I was here?"

"Oh, yes."

"Didn't you tell them 'no?'"

"Oh, yes."

"Well, you weren't very convincing, then," Clay said with a grin. "How about it? Can I go in?"

"Only if I stay with you."

"No problem."

Gladdie led Clay back down the hall to the end room. Something about the room seemed different from the last time he saw it, but he couldn't quite put his finger on it. He stood in the center of the room and looked around intently. He suddenly realized that the bedside table was different. The coffee can that he recalled overflowing with cigarette butts and ashes was now empty. Gone too was the lipstick tube he remembered placing on the table.

He questioned Gladdie about whether she was letting anyone use the room, but she denied it. He believed her. Maybe the police took those items when they returned the second time. As before, he still saw nothing of value in the room. If there had been any stolen goods in the room when the police first came by, they had to have been taken out before his first visit. And, except for the small differences he noticed, the room was the same as before. Even the porno magazine was still safely stashed under the armchair cushion. Whoever had searched there wasn't as thorough as the ones who'd searched his house.

There was still a loose end—Harco's room in Montgomery. That was bugging Clay, so he decided to head directly there from Eleventh Street. It was about a two and a half hour drive. He could be there and back before the rush hour traffic started.

A call to Callie to let her know he was leaving town for the day, and he was on his way. He liked the idea of someone as special as she knowing where he was and looking forward to his return.

The trip was quick. He took the interstate all the way from downtown Atlanta to downtown Montgomery and made it in the allotted time without breaking the speed limit. He grimaced at the thought that if he could make the trip so easily, so could Harco. If the killing of Carrie Lindsey was premeditated, one could easily establish an alibi in Montgomery, drive over to Atlanta, and return without being seriously missed. But Harco had no alibi, and catching Carrie Lindsey on the way home from school couldn't have been planned or timed. To just drive over, kill, and drive back made no sense. If pure killing was the motive, there were too many people in Alabama who needed killing. If killing young girls was the key, Montgomery had its own supply. If Harco was a killer and had really been in Montgomery, then its short distance from Atlanta was irrelevant.

While Harco's Atlanta domicile had enjoyed a former stateliness, the one in Montgomery had always been trashy. Built years ago as a low-rent boarding house near a now abandoned textile mill, the spartan edifice had steadily deteriorated. Unpainted clapboard covered the sides of the rambling structure, and cardboard squares substituted for missing windowpanes. The grass-less red clay yard between the building and the street had eroded so severely that it was entirely below the level of the curb.

Other tired old buildings bordered the cracked concrete street, and the occupants' similarly rundown or jacked up automobiles formed a gauntlet that made passage arduous. Clay maneuvered his way through the narrow lane, looking for a place to stop. Finding the old house had been easy. Finding a place to park wasn't.

No drug dealers or pimps around here, he thought. The condition of the cars proved that.

After squeezing into a space between a mud-splattered pickup and a Harley, Clay walked self-consciously back up the street. He sensed the probing curiosity of hidden eyes, and would feel relieved when he was finally off the street and inside. One thing was for sure—dealing with Harco Brewton had taken Clay out of the comforting security of his own world, and caused him to walk paths he never would've thought of, much less selected.

The front door of the old building was open. A badly torn screen door sagged on its hinges, allowing free access to cool air, insects, and the pollen of late spring. The rusty hinges of the old screen door rebelled loudly as Clay slowly pulled it open. A mixture of red clay dust and yellow pollen formed a thin film on the wooden floor of the downstairs hallway, clearly recording the footprints and dog paws of the inhabitants.

The first door on his right was marked "Mgr," in pencil on a piece of torn cardboard. Clay knocked. Then again, but louder. The door opened cautiously, and he was greeted in silence by a wide-eyed little boy, barefoot and dirty-faced. The static-laced beat of AM radio rock began to escape the small apartment, closely followed by the smell of beans cooking.

Clay's inquiries received only head-shaking replies from the child. It was clear from the nods, however, that the mother wasn't at home, but the father was somewhere close by. Just as Clay was about to give up and go in search of Harco's room on his own, the boy's father suddenly arose from where he'd been asleep in a beat-up old recliner, partially hidden from Clay's view.

The man was frail, sunken chested and clothed only in gray work trousers and a dingy, sleeveless undershirt. He announced that he was the husband of the resident manager. It was obvious that he stayed at home while the wife worked elsewhere, then came home to handle her manager's duties after dinner. It was also quite obvious that he prided himself in his wife's managerial accomplishment, and was set to milk it for all the perceived glory he could.

Clay introduced himself as Harco Brewton's lawyer, and asked to be let into his room.

"That Brewton fellow quit showing up around here and stopped paying his rent. My wife figured he'd abandoned it, so she rented it out to someone else."

"What happened to all of his things?"

"What little there was, we sold off to pay the back rent."

"How much did he owe you?"

"I don't know exactly, but it was right near a hundred dollars."

"Hell, he had a television, a VCR, and probably a CD player or two. Any one of those would've covered the rent. Where's the rest of it?"

"Now, there weren't nothing like that in the room when we went up there. But then, there'd been a break-in the week before, and a few of our tenants lost a bunch of stuff. They must've hit his room too."

Clay believed him, but was amused at the irony of Harco Brewton being the victim of a burglary.

Clay learned that "a shoebox full of stuff" with no real value remained, and they'd given it to the little boy, who was now peeking shyly from behind his father's legs. Clay asked to see the contents, and the man barked at the youngster to get the box.

The little fellow scampered from the room, and Clay was asked to step inside to keep the flies out.

With the door closed behind him, he took in the clutter of the cramped apartment. Sitting in the living room window was a gallon jar of water with a half dozen or more tea bags suspended from the rim. The sun's rays filtered through the slowly brewing tea, bathing the furniture near the window with a reddish-brown glow. Strung throughout the small kitchen was an assortment of household clothing hung up to dry. A half-empty fifty-pound sack of rice leaned against the leg of what appeared to be an old free-standing cupboard. It was apparent what would be for dinner that night. The same as it had probably been for many nights—rice and beans, with iced tea.

The logos on a handful of individual sugar packets piled in the center of the small family table indicated that one or more of Montgomery's fast-food restaurants would be supplying the sugar for the tea.

A tug on Clay's trouser leg broke his concentration, and he looked down on the wide-eyed little boy with his shoebox. Gently taking the box from him, Clay flipped quickly through its contents. He could feel those big brown eyes on him, watching every move, fearing the very worst—the loss of his precious possessions. Realizing the boy's fearful insecurity, Clay kneeled beside him so he could watch while he foraged through his treasures. Clay faced the child on his own level and assured him that his things were safe. He just needed to look at them for a moment. That seemed to bring some relief to those apprehensive eyes.

The box was a potpourri of personal items that a man would throw into a top dresser drawer: buttons, safety pins, a Kenworth key ring, stir sticks, a plastic spoon, a pen knife, one triple-A battery, and so forth.

Flattened out on the bottom of the box were some papers. When Clay pulled them out, a small photo fell to the floor. It was a picture of what appeared to be a young woman kneeling beside a small boy dressed in a cowboy outfit, complete with double-holstered six guns. But the face of the woman had been completely blacked out. Clay turned the picture over. "Lovie and Harco," was written on the back. For whatever it was worth, he now knew Harco's mother's name.

Sifting through the papers, Clay found little of interest except some old settlement pay receipts from a trucking company in Lexington, Kentucky. What was it about Kentucky? he thought. He made a note of the company's address.

Clay never believed that those watchful wide eyes could get any wider. But they did when the promise was kept, and the tired old shoebox was closed and placed safely back in eagerly awaiting hands. A smile flashed across the little dirty face, and was mirrored by Clay. He fully understood. He'd had a box like that many years ago that even had a big toenail in it. The box and the boy quickly disappeared.

The boy's father confirmed that, except for some "real bad nudie books" which he'd trashed, what Clay had seen was all that remained of Harco's possessions.

Clay questioned the father at length about Harco's comings and goings, but got nowhere. The man knew where he was both before and after April third. He was at home, but he had no idea where Harco was.

Harco's former room was on the second floor. Clay found the occupants of the rooms on each side and across the hall at home, but got no useful information from them. They all agreed Harco was very private and came and went at odd hours. Two had seen him only once. The other had never seen him but heard him arguing with a woman once in his room. Clay wondered if she was one of the ones whose names were tattooed on his arm.

Frustrated, Clay started back to Atlanta. Just before getting on the interstate, he spotted a convenience store near the entrance ramp and decided to grab some crackers and a soft drink. It wasn't until he pulled into the parking lot that he recognized the store as another Zip 'N Mart.

He was surprised to find the store in Alabama. That chain was a well-known Atlanta family success story which began in the mid sixties, and had always remained local. Clay had traveled Georgia extensively, but had never seen a Zip 'N Mart outside the five-county Atlanta metropolitan area. That was consistent with the founder's oft-quoted statement that he attributed the chain's success to short lines of supply and constant home office supervision.

"What are you folks doing outside Atlanta?" Clay asked the neatly dressed young man standing behind the counter talking to the cashier. "I thought old man Pilcher always kept one foot on home base to be safe."

"That was daddy's concept." The young man laughed. "But he retired at the end of the year, and my older brother thought it was time to venture a little farther out. You from Atlanta?"

"Yeah," Clay responded, placing his purchases on the counter in front of the register. "So, you're a Pilcher too. Sorry about the 'old man' bit."

"That's all right. Nobody ever calls him that to his face, but he loves it. I'm Jeff Pilcher."

"Nice to meet you, Jeff. Clay Delaney."

As the two men shook hands and chatted, the cashier rang up the purchase, took Clay's money, then bagged his snacks.

"How many stores have you opened outside Atlanta?"

"This is the only one. It's a pilot we opened three months ago to test the change in the way we've always done business."

"You live in Montgomery?"

"No, but I might as well. My brother sends me over here all the time. He wants to branch out, but he still wants constant supervision. Only thing is, he wants me to do it. He wants to prove daddy wrong, but I think deep down inside he's afraid daddy might've been right all these years. He doesn't intend to let anyone in Atlanta know we've opened this store until it's running in the black, and he can claim it's a success."

"Doesn't sound as if a lot's really changed."

"Not as long as I live on I-eighty-five between Atlanta and Montgomery." Jeff laughed.

"Nice to have met you, Jeff," Clay said as he walked out.

"Same here."

Clay munched peanut butter crackers and sipped a diet drink as he drove back toward Atlanta. The monotony of interstate travel took over, and he was almost lulled to sleep by the never-changing scenery of evenly spaced pine trees, the same culvert seen again and again, and a continuous fence interrupted only by an occasional exit ramp. He rolled his window halfway down. The fresh air would keep his head clear.

With the window open, Clay was tempted to keep his car clean by tossing out the wadded-up brown paper bag that contained his cracker wrappers and empty drink can. Superimposed over this temptation was the sudden recollection of a stubby little finger being shaken in his direction and the stern admonition, "Don't be a litterbug, Daddy." He smiled. He knew better of course, but like everyone else he occasionally needed to be reminded not to make exceptions to his own little rules. He laughed and, a' la Harco Brewton, grandly tossed the paper bag over his shoulder into the back seat.

Then he wondered if Harco was really environmentally sensitive, or just plain trashy. He surmised the latter was more accurate. He'd have to remember to dispose of the bag later, or someone would be asking themselves that same question about him.

The long drive gave Clay more time to think about Harco than he wanted. He'd already burned too much emotional energy worrying about his case, but try as he may, he couldn't get him off of his mind.

What made the man tick? What set him off? He was a cheap crook who obviously hated women. Yet his rap sheet showed no priors for any type of violent behavior. Had his anger and hatred finally boiled over onto Carrie Lindsey? Or was he getting a bum rap? But damn it, he had the kid's doll. How could he ever justify that?

As before, Clay chased the illusive logic about Harco's guilt around in a circle, ending up right where he'd started.

He didn't quite avoid the rush hour traffic that afternoon, but it wasn't bad for a Friday. And, with daylight savings time in effect, he still had some light left to putter about outside after he got home. He hated getting home after dark, which it seemed he did most of the time.

As he walked about his yard, he checked the condition of the few bushes and shrubs the builder had placed around his home. Being in the woods as it was, not too much landscaping was necessary. There was just enough around the border of the house to break up any harsh lines of the structure and blend it into its natural setting. The shrubbery appeared somewhat distressed, probably from a lack of water. The only rain he could recall that spring was the drenching the day he met Callie.

Clay smiled at the thought of Callie. He'd call her when he finished watering so she'd know he was back.

He unreeled a hose and moved slowly around to the front of his house, watering as he went. Out of the corner of his eye he spotted Fraidy crouched on the deck railing, intently watching a squirrel on the other side of the deck. The tip of his tail twitched back and forth, totally oblivious to Clay's presence. Fraidy hated water. Having been raised by an Italian mother, Clay always contended that he fully understood only three things: sex, spaghetti, and revenge. Well, Fraidy, he thought. It's payback time.

Releasing the trigger on the hose nozzle, Clay moved silently under the deck. When he was in position, he placed the nozzle between two deck boards and took careful aim at the unsuspecting stalker. The hose hissed as he unleashed the water. Fraidy screeched, and his body arced into the air as he desperately tried to avoid further contact with the water. Twisting as he went, he was now in no position to land back on the deck. Instead, he landed feet first on the ground beside Clay.

Seeing his attacker up close, Fraidy raised his back and started his sideways walk in Clay's direction. Clay figured the cat needed one more good squirt for good measure and squeezed the nozzle once more. Nothing. He squeezed again. Nothing. He looked for a kink in the hose—none.

He dropped the nozzle and retraced the hose around the house to the spigot. It was off. He looked about and saw nothing out of place, no one else around. He had no idea what was happening, but felt an eerie sensation as he opened the valve again and returned to the front of the house, checking uneasily over his shoulder.

As he rounded the corner, he was hit full in the face by a stream of cold water. Now in control of the business end of the hose was a wildly laughing Callie. "That'll teach you to mess with my cat, Clay Delaney. How do you like it, mister? There, take that, you monster." She soaked the approaching Clay.

She screamed with delight as Clay wrestled the hose from her, took her to the ground, and drenched her. They fought for the hose as they rolled around in the soft grass. It traded hands several times. Callie was strong, and it was clear that she wasn't going to be bested without a fight. She got it.

As they lay together out of breath and soaked, Clay could feel her warmth emanating through the wet clothing that was now clinging to her. He felt the exquisite softness of her body against him, and his head spun with the thought of making love right there.

Not realizing that Callie could possibly feel the same way at that moment, Clay was totally unprepared when she rolled him over, sat on top of him, and began to unbutton his shirt.

"What are you doing?" he asked.

"I'm unbuttoning your shirt, dummy." She continued to strip Clay, stopping only long enough to pull off her own blouse and bra.

Clay was dumbfounded, but too aroused to put up much argument. "Right here in the yard?"

"There's got to be some advantage of living in the woods," Callie said. "Now, please shut up. Can't you see I'm busy?"

That was the last thing Clay remembered hearing before finding himself engulfed once more in the delirious sensations of Callie's touch.

Saturday morning, Clay sat in a deck chair, studying Harco's file and making notes. Callie stumbled out onto the deck half-awake, carrying two cups of coffee. She looked as if she were being swallowed alive by Clay's terrycloth robe.

"I made some fresh," she said. "How long you been up?"

"An hour. The judge is going to hear our motions Monday morning, and we could start the trial the next week. I'm trying to get everything ready."

"Maybe I should go home and let you have some peace and quiet."

"No. I'd like to have you stay around for awhile. There are a few things I'd like your advice about. And besides, I may need to water the shrubs again."

"God's going to get you, Clay Delaney."

"Seriously, would you stay? I really want to bounce a few things off of you, and I think you can help me."

"Okay," Callie replied with a satisfied grin, as she curled up with her coffee mug in a chair beside Clay.

As Saturday morning wore on, Clay worked quietly on the deck while Callie puttered about. Finally, he looked up from his work and asked her if she'd study his file and give him a professional analysis of Harco.

Callie smiled. "I thought you'd never ask." She quickly took a seat beside Clay. "Do I get to charge you?" she asked mischievously.

"You know," he said, "that's not a bad idea." Reaching into his pocket, he pulled out a dollar. "This makes you my consultant—officially. And what you learn from me remains confidential and protected. This will keep Jason Rowland from calling you as a witness."

"Would he do something like that?"

"In a heartbeat, if he could. He doesn't miss a trick."

"You don't seem to miss many yourself."

"Well, I need all the help I can get."

"You'll have to give me the focus of the analysis you want," she said.

"I fully expect Rowland to put up an expert to present psychological evidence against Harco. To help prove he's guilty. I need to have a profile on Harco myself, so I'll know if the expert is shooting straight or just blowing smoke."

Callie took the hefty file from Clay, handing him her empty coffee cup in return. As Clay disappeared into the house to get her a refill, Callie placed the file on the deck, pulled her feet into the deck chair to get comfortable and selected a folder from the file.

After delivering her coffee, Clay wandered down to the yard to roll up the hose that had been left lying on the ground. As he reached for the nozzle, he spied another foil gum wrapper on the ground. It was right where he and Callie had been rolling around. He picked it up. It was fresh, and the smell of gum was still there. He knew from its condition that it couldn't have been there when the water fight started.

"Callie," he called up to the deck. "Do you chew gum?"

"Never touch the stuff," she called back, not looking up from her reading.

"Me either."

It was becoming painfully clear to Clay that his house and yard didn't have the privacy he'd always thought existed, and certainly not as much as Callie assumed when the laughing stopped and the loving started the day before. But why was someone watching him?

That was the fourth time in the month he'd detected something out of the ordinary. Surely, it wasn't simply his imagination. Whoever it was must've gotten an eyeful if they were watching the hose fight. He decided not to say anything to Callie just yet, but to keep his eyes open until he could learn more.

Callie kept her head buried in the file for the rest of the day. She blithely ignored occasional overtures by Clay and Fraidy, who were both vying for her attention.

"Come on, you guys. Can't you see I'm busy here?"

Clay sheepishly retreated, but realized what it was like just to hang around while someone was engrossed in their work.

"Come on, Fraidy," he said, "let's go make dinner."

Clay busied himself in the kitchen, preparing the evening meal. He pretended to have invited the cat inside to keep him from bothering Callie. Actually, it was for company.

Darkness and a few insects succeeded in driving Callie inside. There she was confronted by an apron-clad Clay and a candle-lit table for two. With her finally inside, he unceremoniously discharged Fraidy to the yard, and pulled the cork from a wine bottle.

"You have time to change while this wine is breathing," he said as he pulled Harco's file from her hands. "I've washed, dried and folded your things. They're on my bed."

"You do good work, counselor. You treat all your consultants this way?"

"No. And I don't sleep with them either."

"Is that extra?"

"No. That's special."

Dinner was quiet and relaxed, the mood gentle and warm. Soft conversation moved between them. As the evening matured, Callie became pensive and began idly rubbing the rim of her wine glass.

"You all right?" Clay finally asked.

"Oh, yes," she replied quickly. "I just can't seem to get my mind out of that file. Your notes on Harco are fascinating. He really is a piece of work."

"I know. How about a quick preview?"

"Okay," she said. She paused in thought for a moment, then started. "There's no question that he was bent at a very early age. Whether he was broken is another question entirely. His life at home lacked any real care or nurturing. This would've left him feeling unloved and insecure, with very low self-esteem. The situation with his aunt probably made him feel vulnerable and unprotected— even in his own home. What few feelings of self-worth he might have had, would have been severely damaged by the humiliation brought on by his mother banging sailors for bucks at home. When he tried to avoid the shame of that by leaving the house when it was going on, she eventually rejected him completely by walking out on him. He was so emotionally traumatized by this that he can't separate the resentment he has for her from other women. He sees them as all alike."

"Do you see him as being capable of raping and killing?"

"Yes, I do. It would either be his way of fighting back and saying, 'I really am somebody and worth something, and you're nothing.' Or, it would simply be his way of getting even. Of repaying the emotional debt, as it were."

"You seem troubled. What's wrong?" Clay was genuinely concerned.

"The analysis you wanted was easy. But something's not quite right."

"Like what?"

"I'm not sure, but my view of Harco doesn't fit with what appears to have happened."

"How so?"

"I can show you better than I can tell you," Callie said as she rose from the table and moved into the great room. Clay dutifully followed and watched silently as Callie pulled a folder of eight-by-ten photographs from the file. Finding an open space, she began dropping them on the floor in an ordered sequence. All of the photographs were of the body of Carrie Lindsey, first as she was found in the woods, and later as she was seen by the medical examiner.

With the pictures forming two rows on the floor, Callie guided Clay between them, talking and pointing as she went.

"Look at her, Clay—look at how she was found. It's as if she was asleep. She's fully clothed, and her clothes aren't even messed up. There's still a bow in her hair, and her dress hem is down over her knees where it should be.

Now look at the first morgue photo. It shows her wearing panties, but the panties are on inside out. See how the seam stands out? It's like someone put them back on her after she was dead, then laid her out. It's as if they were trying to conceal the rape."

"What are you saying?"

"What I'm saying is, the kind of rape Harco Brewton is capable of didn't happen to this little girl."

"Why do you say that?"

"Because there's no sign of the reasons that would've moved him to do it in the first place. In other words, if my profile of him is correct and his anger had progressed far enough for him to do it, he wouldn't have attempted to cover up the rape. He would've reveled in it. The body would've screamed out, 'I've been raped.' He would make sure he humiliated her. Even in death."

"How would he do that?"

"He would've left her violated and discarded in the woods like an old inner tube, naked and twisted. I'd expect to find her panties still on but down around her ankles. For a woman, this would be the ultimate humiliation: found by strangers and gawked at, even photographed, dead in the woods with her legs spread and her pants down to her ankles."

Clay studied the photos from a standing position. He was having difficulty focusing on the awkward pose that death had selected for Carrie Lindsey. His mind kept substituting her face with that of the child he'd already buried.

"Now look at the morgue photos of her completely nude, front and back," Callie continued. "Except for that cut on the back of her head, there isn't a mark on her. There's no sign of violence, torture or cruelty. No indication that Carrie was killed by someone filled with hate and rage, as Harco seems to be."

"Are you telling me he didn't do it?"

"No. I'm trying to tell you that it's inconsistent with any psychological factors that would've caused him to do it."

Clay's jaw tightened. The volume of his voice began to rise. "That's psychological gobbledygook. Just say it. You don't believe he did it. Do you?"

"I'm not sure anymore."

Clay wheeled around abruptly, left the room and headed for the deck, stepping on some of the photos as he went. Callie reorganized all the photographs, replacing them in Harco's file. When she finished, she joined Clay on the deck. He stood at the railing, gazing into the darkness toward the river.

Coming up from behind, she put her arms around his waist and nestled her head against his back. "Was it the pictures?"

"I guess," he said, clearing his throat. "I get bent out of shape every time I try to look at them. It's a good thing you did. I would've overlooked all that completely."

"Are you beginning to have doubts again?"

"Maybe I am. I have no reason to. It's just that when I get upset, I'm ready to pull the trigger on anything that moves. Harco just seems such a likely target. And who'd really care if I was wrong?"

"Harco would," she replied.

"Why is it all of a sudden I'm taking your position, and you're taking mine?"

"Just lucky I guess."

Turning around to face her, Clay took her by both hands. "Look, I'm sorry for that outburst in there. I guess I'm not being as objective about Harco as I thought I was. Is it wrong for me to continue to think he's guilty?"

"Not at all. But there's something wrong with your wanting him to be guilty. Do you want him to be guilty?"

"I never thought of it that way, but maybe deep down inside I really do. I guess that would solve a lot of problems for a lot of people, including me."

"Only if he's convicted."

"What are you implying?"

"Nothing. I'm merely pointing out that if what you want is true, no one's problems would be solved unless Harco's convicted."

"You're right," Clay said.

"And, as I understand it, your job is to help him avoid a conviction. Right?"

"Right."

"So, everyday you're knowingly working against yourself just as hard as you can, aren't you?"

"Yeah."

"How long do you think you're going to last?"

"I've done okay so far."

"You weren't doing so red hot when I came out here a moment ago."

Clay sighed and turned away from her, staring out into the darkness.

"Don't you see what's happening? This thing's slowly eating away at you. You've done marvelously well so far, but no one can take this for long. I care for you. I don't want you to try to save Harco if you're going to destroy yourself in the process."

"What choice do I have?"

"You can quit," she said.

"I can't."

"Then somehow you've got to disassociate your personal feelings from what you've been asked to do. Or…"

"Or what?"

"Or prove to yourself that Harco's not guilty."

He turned back around. "You certainly don't expect much out of me, do you?"

"Well, your decision to have an independent psychological profile made of Harco was a good start."

"You're bragging now." He laughed.

"You've got that right. Now ask me for just a woman's viewpoint of what I've seen in your file."

"Shoot."

"I have no idea how Harco got his hands on Carrie Lindsey's doll, but odds are he didn't take it away from her."

"And why do you say that?"

"Because she'd already graduated from dolls and was obviously very interested in boys."

"How can you say—"

Callie held up her hand. "Hear me out, and try to be clinical for a moment. The pictures you've had a hard time looking at aren't of a child. They're of a nicely developing young girl. Physically mature for a thirteen-year-old. She'd already moved out of little girl's underclothes and into designer lingerie. She was shaving her legs and underarms, and when she died, she was wearing foundation makeup, blush, and eyeliner. I wouldn't expect her to be playing with dolls, much less carrying one around."

"How strongly do you feel about that?"

"Does the expression, 'she wouldn't be caught dead with one' mean anything to you?"

Clay shook his head in amazement, then after a slight pause, asked, "Would she have been attracted to Harco?"

"Not hardly. Even if he was handsome, to a thirteen-year-old girl someone over thirty's an old man. More than likely, she would've been infatuated with the high school boys who hung out at the corner market after school."

"You've certainly gleaned a lot from those photos. Maybe you should've been a lawyer."

"No thanks. Besides, this case didn't need another lawyer. All it needed was a woman."

CHAPTER 11

▼

The criminal motions calendar call was a zoo. All Clay's years of experience on the civil side of the docket hadn't prepared him for this. When civil matters were being argued, normally only attorneys occupied the courtroom, and they sedately used the time before and in between proceedings to socialize and exchange war stories about their cases or the various judges.

This was different. So different, in fact, that Clay felt out of place in a room where he made his living. The courtroom was humming with activity. Criminal defendants out on bond, their family members and their lawyers noisily filling the benches. In some instances, it was hard to distinguish among them.

Those who'd been denied bail or were unable to raise it sat on the front two rows, cuffed and conspicuous in their blue jumpsuits. Harco was among them. His bulbous head twitched nervously to a paranoid, offbeat rhythm. As his head moved about, his eyes frantically searched the crowded room. Not ready yet to satisfy Harco's need for contact, Clay kept someone directly in his line of sight. That was easy, because Harco had to remain stationary and could turn his head only over one shoulder or the other.

Clay figured he'd let Harco fret a bit longer, worrying if his lawyer was going to show up. Besides, he was unsure of what procedure to follow and wanted to observe unobtrusively for a while before anyone expected him to act, including his own client.

He hoped he'd see Solomon somewhere in the crowd, for moral support if nothing else. But Solomon had told him before that he hoped to keep his presence in the case from Rowland and Judge Armbrister until the last moment.

The wood on wood slap of the gavel cracked throughout the room, stifling all conversation in mid word, as Judge Armbrister entered. The resulting silence was then broken by the bailiff. "All rise. The Superior Court of Fulton County is now in session, the Honorable Jack Armbrister presiding. Be seated please."

When the noise of people taking their seats and some muffled comments had subsided, the judge greeted the throng with a rhetorical, "Good morning."

Like an elementary school class, a great number of them replied with, "Good morning, your Honor." That tickled Clay. He knew Armbrister didn't care if any of them had a good morning. As a matter-of-fact, he knew that in a few minutes Armbrister was going to make sure they didn't. As for the crowd, they were even less sincere than the judge.

Clay had momentarily been tempted to join in the chorus, but said, "Kiss my ass, your Honor," instead.

As the clerk called each case, a lawyer would break out of the crowd and take a seat at the left-side counsel table down front. He was either accompanied by his client or would be joined by him from among the defendants on the first two rows. The table on the right and the bench behind it were occupied by members of the District Attorney's office. Jason Rowland was nowhere in sight.

Clay was interested at first, but numerous motions were heard and ruled on, and it all became a blur of repetitive legal phrases, lawyer posturing, and gavel banging. One by one, little knots of interested parties left with their lawyers, until finally Clay sat exposed in the back of the room, plainly visible to Harco and, worst of all, to Judge Armbrister.

It soon became apparent that Harco's case had been saved to the last, and that it wouldn't be heard before lunch. Clay had been sitting in the courtroom for three hours, and there was never any sign of Rowland.

When they broke for lunch, Clay knew his suspicions were correct. Better than that, Rowland had to have known it all along, for he made his first appearance right on time, immediately after the recess. At that time, only Harco's motions remained to be argued. Judge Armbrister's reappearance in the courtroom wasn't so formal this time, there being no crowd to observe it.

"Keep your seats," the judge declared as he moved quickly to his bench. "Let's see. What do we have left? Oh yes, the Brewton motions. Mr. Rowland, are you ready?"

"Yes, your Honor."

"Are you, Mr. Delaney?" Then answering his own question, said, "Of course you are. These are your motions, aren't they?"

"Yes, your Honor."

"Mr. Delaney," Armbrister said, "why haven't you discussed a plea-bargain with Mr. Rowland?"

The only way Armbrister could've gotten that information was in some form of prohibited communication. Maybe not directly, but the judge and Rowland had been in contact about the case, perhaps through their staff. Rowland had given himself away by not showing up until the afternoon, and Armbrister by his poorly worded question.

"Who told you I haven't, your Honor?"

Rowland's face turned red, and the judge stammered and sputtered briefly. "I just assumed you didn't. I would've heard about it by now. I make it my business to know things like this."

"Then you must know that Mr. Rowland has decided not to bargain."

"Is that right, Mr. Rowland?" Armbrister asked.

"Well, your Honor, that may have been true early on, but that's not so any-more. We're willing to talk."

"What about you, Counselor? Are you willing to talk?"

"I'll need to consult with my client, your Honor," Clay replied.

"You do that. And if y'all can work it out, maybe we can save the taxpayers some money. If you can't, then we'll just have to use that money to introduce your client to Old Sparky. I'll be in my chambers. Y'all work it out now, you hear?" Armbrister abruptly left the bench.

Clay's eyes flashed across the front of the room in search of the court reporter. Not there. Armbrister's highly opinionated comments about Harco had gone unrecorded. Intentionally so, no doubt. He was one sly son of a bitch.

Rowland then hurriedly excused himself, leaving Clay, Harco, and one jail guard alone in the courtroom.

"You heard the man, Harco. What do you say?" Clay asked.

"That stuffed tomato thinks he's got my number. And that other little dandy just kisses his overripe ass."

"That's got nothing to do with it. Now's your chance to plead this case out. Don't blow it."

"But I didn't do it! Why should I go to jail for something I didn't do?"

"As strange as it may seem to you, that's hardly the point right now. Your case isn't going to be tried on what happened. It's going to be tried on what people say happened. And, whether you live or die is going to be decided by what a jury thinks happened. So, whether you did it is immaterial if you run a risk of going to the electric chair. And right now you're facing that risk."

"They'll want a lot of jail time."

"Probably life."

Harco pushed back from the counsel table. "I can't do it," he said. He got to his feet and moved around the table to face Clay. The guard at the door stood more erect and watched him closely.

"But there's always the possibility of parole."

"Not since the governor approved that life without parole law. Or don't you keep up with things like that?"

"I do, but we wouldn't agree to that. We'd agree only to a straight life sentence."

Harco shook his head. "Sometimes you amaze me, Mr. Delaney. I guess it's just because you're still cherry."

Clay ignored the criticism. He was interested in Harco's assessment. "How's that?"

"We don't agree to nothing with the one who gives the sentence. We agree with the D.A. to plead guilty in return for his recommendation of a certain sentence. The judge ain't no part of it. He can do as he pleases. Now, I grant you, most judges go along with what the D.A. wants. Otherwise, nobody'd ever cop a plea."

"So what's the difference here?"

Harco looked at the guard, then lowered his voice. "Armbrister," he said. "The word around the jail is he's been known to break with the D.A. on certain cases and give a stiffer sentence. Word also has it he has a wild hair up his ass about this case for some reason. And, as cozy as them two seemed to be out here a while ago, wouldn't surprise me none if they hadn't already worked it out."

For all Harco's faults, he knew his way around the criminal justice system. Clay had to give him that. It was bad enough just being a novice in the system, Clay thought, but being naive as well was treacherous.

"I'm going to need some help," Clay said as he rose to his feet. He excused himself and hurriedly left the courtroom, headed directly for the Public Defender's office on the fifth floor.

As usual, Solomon was at his desk, buried by his work and surrounded by barely sipped cups of cold coffee.

Clay used the opportunity to bring Solomon up to date on Callie's weekend observations about Harco, as well as Harco's thoughts about Armbrister.

"I'll have to hand it to your psychologist friend," Solomon said. "She cut right to the chase on this one. Who would've thought old Harco might be taking a bum rap?"

"What about his suspicion that Rowland and Armbrister are trying to ambush him on a plea?"

"Armbrister maybe, but not Rowland. He's a nut cutter of the first order, but you can trust him to do exactly what he says. Besides, he's not going to operate outside the law."

"I take it you don't feel the same way about Armbrister."

Solomon laughed. "That's one treacherous son of a bitch. Don't ever turn your back on him, even if you think you've got him by the short hairs."

"If they're not up to something, why's Rowland so agreeable about accepting a plea? He was dead set against it when we first met."

Solomon thought for a moment as he chewed on a cigar stump. He removed it from his mouth, and picked a tobacco speck off the tip of his tongue. "Armbrister probably had his clerk contact the D.A.'s office under the guise of setting the trial calendar. She must've asked them how long they expected Harco's case to last, and how sure they were that it'd be tried if reached. If they said the case was solid, then Armbrister would know Rowland wasn't bargaining. That would mean he was aiming for a conviction."

"So, how'd Armbrister get Rowland to change his mind? I didn't think judges were supposed to talk ex parte to D.A.s about a case."

"They're not, and they probably didn't. But Armbrister has a thousand ways of letting people know what he wants. He has more ways than that of putting pressure on them. Believe me. It didn't take long for Rowland to come around."

Seating arrangements in Solomon's office hadn't changed. Clay tried to make himself comfortable on the arm of the old loveseat. "If Armbrister's out to get Harco, why would he allow him to cop a plea?"

"For one thing, he knows how strongly Rowland feels about this case, and that he'd settle for nothing short of a life sentence. He must think that if he can force Harco to accept Rowland's deal, all he has to do is to convert it to life without parole."

"Can he do that?"

"He can do anything he can get away with. Since a life sentence is just what it says, he must have figured that the no parole modification wouldn't be viewed as such a deviation in the recommended sentence as to cause a reversal on appeal."

"Surely, Harco would appeal."

"Yeah, but that's just it. Anything can go wrong on appeal. There are so many hoops to jump through, if you miss one, it's over. If it's all handled properly, and there aren't any irregularities in the plea-bargaining and sentencing procedure, there's always the chance that, in the face of a guilty plea, the appellate court just might let it stand. In any event, Harco would have his work cut out for him. That's for damn sure."

Solomon leaned back in his chair, put both hands behind his head and stared at the ceiling.

"Is there anything we can do to prevent this?" Clay asked. "I've been telling Harco that he should let me work something out with the D.A. Now what'll I tell him?"

"The key is what he agrees to plead to. Life without parole was designed to be an alternative to the death penalty—a sop to throw to the anti-death penalty crowd.

To get life without parole, you've got to qualify for a death sentence."

"Doesn't Harco?"

"He does under the indictment. But that's not what he should plead to. The death sentence is reserved for murder or rape under aggravating circumstances. Rape is one of the aggravating circumstances of murder that can get him the chair."

"So what do you recommend?"

"Try and get Rowland to drop the rape charge, or—"

Clay interrupted him. "Get him to reduce the murder count to manslaughter and plead to both of them."

Solomon smiled and sat upright. "We just might make a criminal lawyer out of you, yet."

With time fast running out, Clay headed back to the courtroom. Rowland was already there. "Well?" he said.

"Hold your horses," Clay said. "We're not playing checkers here."

Clay leaned over and quietly explained the proposal to Harco, who then nodded his approval. Clay then put it to Rowland.

"Hell no," he said. "You're just trifling with me, Delaney. No way I'm going to ignore either the rape or the murder. The family of that little girl deserves satisfaction. The community demands it, and it's got to start with an admission from your client. I'm offering him a life sentence to plead guilty to the crimes committed. If that's not good enough for him, then he can chance a death sentence at trial. We've got him dead to rights, and if you want to play games, be my guest."

No amount of cajoling could budge Rowland from his stance, and Harco steadfastly refused to combine rape and murder in the bargain.

Notified of the impasse, Armbrister returned to the bench to rule on the motions. He sifted through the stack of pleadings in front of him without looking up. "Who's being so unreasonable in this matter, Mr. Delaney? You or your client? Or maybe the both of you."

"Neither, your Honor. I—"

"It doesn't matter. Bail won't be granted, and your motion for a continuance is denied. So are your motions to suppress evidence and the identification of the defendant by the witness, Jaynelle Eubanks. Is your client's refusal to plea-bargain on the indictment your final word on the matter?"

Clay looked down at Harco, then back toward the bench. "Yes, it is, your Honor. May I be heard on my motions?"

"No, you may not. I have your briefs."

"But, Judge—"

"Your motion to dismiss because of what you call prosecutorial misconduct I find particularly offensive, Mr. Delaney. This county's District Attorney's office is held in high esteem throughout the state."

"It's not a personal attack, your Honor. We've only pointed out that some of the procedures used in this case were constitutionally flawed, and—"

"I'm not going to hear your arguments, Counselor. I've already read them. That motion is also denied. Let's see. What's left?"

"That's it, your Honor."

"All right then. Y'all trade the names of your expert witnesses and their fields of expertise. I don't want to hear anyone complain about being surprised. Jury selection will commence next Monday morning."

When the gavel fell silent, Harco shuffled somberly away without bail, and Clay stood alone in the old, wood paneled courtroom. Only time would tell whether any of the rulings was prejudicial enough to assure a successful appeal. But, that was no consolation at this juncture. He'd have to defend the case with what he had. And that still wasn't much. Not much at all.

Christmas and the Final Four always moved interminably slowly toward Clay, while things like tax day and dentist's appointments rocketed in his direction. Harco's trial took its place in the latter category. He'd hardly put down his briefcase after the motions hearing when he was packing it for the trial. The week in between had gone by so speedily that Clay, at one time, lost track of what day it was. He hadn't gone to the office at all that week, but rather had closeted himself at home, cutoff from all distractions, to prepare his cross-examination of witnesses.

Since the State had to put up its evidence first, Clay didn't have to worry right away about who he might call as a witness. He could concentrate on what weak-nesses he could find and exploit in the testimony of those he expected Rowland to call.

He'd worry about the presentation of his case later. He could think of no one to call on Harco's behalf. Harco still wanted to testify, but Clay continued to fight him on that, and Harco was wavering. Clay knew that Rowland would like nothing better than to have Harco on cross-examination. It would be a turkey shoot—a prosecutor's dream come true. Hopefully, when the time came, he would've convinced Harco to stay off the stand, and out of Rowland's deadly sights.

With the weekend still left, Clay was so saturated with the facts of his case that he had to stop working. He could recite the facts in his sleep. He'd begun dreaming about the case at night. It was the same recurring dream. He was standing in front of the jury in Harco's defense, totally unprepared. He always woke up before he spoke, but he could feel the shame and embarrassment as if it were real. He used to have a similar dream about college and then law school where he found himself taking an exam in a course he knew absolutely nothing about. That dream went away after he had it so often he realized in the dream that it was only a dream. Maybe the same thing would happen to his new version.

The jangling of the kitchen phone startled him. He let the answering machine pick up the message. No need to have a new problem dropped in his lap on a Friday evening. Best way to avoid it was to avoid it. But, hearing Solomon's raspy voice, he picked up.

"I've got a lead on Lovie," Solomon said. He usually growled. He had to through his wet cigar butt.

"Lovie?"

"Lovie Brewton. Harco's long lost mother," Solomon replied. "Seems as if she's not so long lost after all. Goes by the name of Lovie Willis now."

"How on earth did you find her?"

"Well, we haven't exactly found her. We have an old address on her, in Lexington, Kentucky. The plates on Harco's car didn't match the car. So, we traced the vehicle I.D. The car was originally registered in her name some years ago. Looks like our boy wasn't shooting straight with you about not seeing his ma since he was a kid."

"Yeah? That's not surprising. He's not particularly addicted to the truth. If we do find her, what do we use her for?"

"Mitigation of sentence," Solomon said. "If the jury finds Harco guilty, they'll have to reassemble to decide if the death penalty is appropriate. We'll need someone to testify on his behalf during the sentencing phase. Someone who can testify about what a rotten childhood he had, and why he shouldn't die. What better person than old Lovie dovie? The State has the right to present his prior convictions during this phase to justify imposition of a death sentence. We'll need to show how he was driven to a life of crime."

"You don't really believe that, do you?"

"No. But I don't have to. I'm not the one who's going to decide if he dies."

"You have a phone number for her?" Clay asked.

"Nope. Someone's going to have to go check it out."

"Why don't we both fly up tomorrow and see what we can find? The break will do us good."

"They're not paying us enough to cover one ticket. Much less two."

"We can take my plane," Clay said. "I'll spring for the gas if the county won't pay it."

"You're on. I've always wanted to ride up front in one of those things."

After a brief struggle with the concrete, the red and white straight tail Beechcraft Bonanza broke free from the runway and lifted its nose cleanly into the cool morning air. As the sleek little plane climbed steadily into a clear sky above Atlanta, Clay scanned his instruments, then banked gently to his left until he was headed due north. He didn't have enough altitude yet to pick up any navigational aids out of Knoxville. He'd have to track outbound on the one in Norcross for a while. It was a straight shot to Knoxville and then to Lexington. With no headwind, it would take just under two and a half hours.

Clay could see the green peaks of the North Georgia mountains in the distance. They'd soon be rising beneath him. Stubborn patches of morning fog were clearly visible, clinging tenaciously to the bottoms and sides of some of the many valleys that dotted the approaching mountains.

Lulled by the soothing drone of the engine, Clay's thoughts began to wander. The lush green hillsides moving toward him were painfully reminiscent of another land, another time—the central provinces of South Vietnam. The sudden glint of sunlight reflecting on some water under the trees caused him to flinch momentarily. A little shock coursed through him before he realized that this was Georgia, and that wasn't a muzzle flash.

"You all right?" Solomon asked.

"Sure. I was just day dreaming. It's hard to fly without thinking about the war."

"You ever kill anyone over there, Clay?"

"Yeah," Clay said, shaking his head slowly. "But we were just hitting places on the ground. We knew people were there, but we were going so fast we rarely saw them. When we did, they were just figures without faces. You're not human unless you have a face."

It took a moment for Clay's comment to sink in. When it did, Clay and Solomon just sat in silence, looking at each other. They then turned away.

It wasn't long before they were out of Georgia. As the morning wore on, Tennessee and more than half of Kentucky had passed silently under their wing tips. The landing at Lexington was a good one. As a Navy carrier pilot, Clay had learned that there are only two kinds of landings: good ones and bad ones. The ones walked away from were good.

The address Solomon had was a four-room flat over a crumbling corner grocery store. They were disappointed but not surprised to find it vacant. The owner was the grocer, and he remembered renting to Lovie. She had moved there from Covington, Kentucky, he said. He also recalled the time when Harco arrived. After that, he heard many loud confrontations downstairs. Most if them were about Harco either being out of work or in jail.

Apparently, Lovie had confided that she and Harco had been separated for many years, but he'd found her in Covington. After a tumultuous few years there, she moved to Lexington. He had found her again. Fed up, she finally slipped away once more. The grocer didn't know where she went, but she had talked a lot about Atlanta.

While in Lexington, Clay called Tri-State Trucking, the company whose address he'd found among Harco's things in Montgomery. They remembered him as a fairly reliable driver from some years before, operating out of their terminal in Covington. However, he had quit without notice a few years back.

If Harco was still trying to stay up with Lovie, then the trail was leading them back to Atlanta. They decided to return.

Clay let Solomon handle the plane's controls on the flight back. He was like a little kid on a carnival ride, flying up and down. He was whooping and laughing almost all the way. Feeling overconfident as they approached Atlanta, he begged Clay to let him make the landing. Clay reluctantly agreed and talked him through it. At the last second, Clay had to take over to keep Solomon from crashing into the numbers that marked the runway direction. The landing was still hard enough to jar their teeth and send the navigation bag clear to the overhead.

After the plane was chocked and tied down and they were walking toward the hangar, Solomon asked with a broad grin, "How'd I do?"

"You made a good landing," Clay said, rubbing his back.

The name Franklin Willett meant nothing to Callie when Clay first mentioned it to her. But Willett's name had been given to Clay by Rowland as a psychological expert the State intended to call as a witness at trial, and Clay had asked Callie to take the lead in developing a file on him.

On learning that Willett headed up the University of Georgia's Psychology Department, Callie started calling around, seeking information on him. What she got was mostly redundant reputation, but rising consistently to the top was the same theme. Dr. Franklin Willett was honest, competent and highly regarded by his peers. That was all well and good, but Callie knew that was just background. That was the "what" part of the personal equation. She needed to know the "who" part. Who was Franklin Willett, the man, the psychologist, the professor?

It became obvious to Callie that she wasn't going to find the answers to those questions over the phone. So, if she couldn't find them in her back yard, she'd go to his—the University of Georgia in Athens.

Callie's first stop on arriving at the campus was the building that housed the Psychology Department. There she wandered around curiously until she located Dr. Willett's office. Making sure he wasn't in, she approached the secretary sitting closest to his door and introduced herself.

"Hi. I'm Callie Gallagher."

"How may I help you, Ms. Gallagher?" the woman replied pleasantly.

"I'm working with an attorney in Atlanta, and I'm trying to find out if any of the professors here offer their services as expert witnesses."

"Why, of course. We have several who do. There's Dr. Willett, the head of the department, and then there are Professors Levin and Greenway."

"The head of the department," Callie said. "That's impressive. But I'll bet he's too busy to take on new work."

"Not at all, and I have it on the best of authority."

"How so?"

"Because I'm his secretary," the lady half-whispered.

"Well, wouldn't you know it," Callie exclaimed, shaking her head. "Who would want anyone else if you can have the head of the department. Do you happen to have a current resume I could take back to Atlanta?"

"I do. I just updated it yesterday." The secretary reached into a bottom drawer of her desk.

Callie took the resume, and winked at Dr. Willett's secretary. "This is just what the doctor ordered. They'll be so pleased with this in Atlanta, I may even get a raise."

"Well, I hope so."

"Lord knows I need one."

Callie slipped outside and happily parked herself on a shaded bench. She started reviewing the professionally prepared three-page document. The listed honors were extensive and fully justified the kudos Callie had heard from everyone who knew anything about Dr. Willett. But nothing on the list of accolades was recent. The most current honor was at least ten years old; the same with his many papers and published articles. Everything was outdated. Noticeably current were the numerous consulting assignments listed in their own section of the resume. He'd served as a consultant or expert witness at least twenty-one times in the past three years, for lawyers and prosecutors all over the Southeast. That line of work was now clearly a major source of income for the good doctor.

Callie also surmised that, like the honors, the recommendations she was getting from others were historical, at best. She needed to know who Franklin Willett was now. She was already beginning to get a sense of who he'd been.

Her next stop was the University's Alumni Office. There, under the pretense of trying to locate old friends and colleagues, Callie was allowed access to an alumni database. Searching for the names and addresses of persons with post-graduate degrees in psychology that were awarded within the last five years, she found three that were still living in the State of Georgia.

One was now teaching under Dr. Willett at the University, one was in Savannah, and the other, surprisingly, was a young psychologist who had opened an office in the same building in Atlanta where Callie had her office.

She was reluctant to confront Willett's colleague, lest she lose the element of surprise. So, she called the one in Savannah. A recorded message indicated she would be away until Sunday. Callie decided to travel directly to Savannah and be there to interview her subject personally the following day. She could see the one in Atlanta when she returned.

First, she'd go to the University Library and see how many of Willett's published articles were physically available for her to review. Those not in the stacks would be on someone's computer system, somewhere.

While headed toward the library, Callie suddenly realized the hour. She remembered she was to have fixed dinner for Clay that evening, but it was already three o'clock. She still had some legwork to do, and then she was off to Savannah. She'd call. He'd understand. After all she was doing it for him.

Clay hurried home from Dekalb Peachtree Airport where he kept his plane. He was to have dinner at Callie's that evening, and he needed to shower and change. In the short time they'd known each other, all their activities together had been at his place. He had yet to visit hers. He was looking forward to a quiet dinner prepared by and cleaned up by someone other than himself.

With jury selection to start on Monday, this would be his last opportunity to relax before all the shooting started.

He was disappointed to find Callie's apologetic message on his answering machine. "Clay, I'm sorry, but we'd better cancel for tonight. It's three o'clock, Saturday, and I'm still over in Athens. I couldn't reach you this morning, but Solomon's wife said you two had gone to Lexington bright and early. Is that right? Still got loads to do running down leads on Franklin Willett. Looks like I may have to run down to Savannah before I'm finished. I may not be back till late Sunday night. I've been working on the questions I'd suggest you ask Rowland's psychological expert. They're rather generic, but when I learn more about Willett, I can tailor them more to fit him. I stuck a large manila envelope in your mailbox before I left. The questions are in it. Also in it are my suggested profiles of the best and the worst hypothetical jurors for a case like this. Any prospective juror who has four or more of the good characteristics I've listed would be acceptable. Anyone who has three or more of the poor characteristics is bad news. Talk to you later. Bye."

CHAPTER 12

▼

Solomon and Clay were the first ones in Judge Armbrister's courtroom on Monday morning. They wanted to make sure they got the counsel table of their choice. Clay believed that when you had a sympathetic-looking client, you wanted him sitting as close to the jury as possible throughout the proceedings. That closeness enabled the jury to observe him better, see his ups and downs and view him as a person, rather than as a named but unknown defendant.

In this instance they set up their files at the table on the right side of the room—the one that was the farthest from the jury box. They put Harco's chair on the far right side of the table, with theirs between him and the jury.

As soon as Judge Armbrister mounted the bench he spotted Solomon seated beside Clay at the counsel table. "I didn't know you were in this case, Counselor."

"Well, I am."

Armbrister folded his arms and glared at Solomon. "I won't allow you to participate in this trial, Mr. Solomon, unless you make a formal appearance as additional counsel of record for the defendant. Are you prepared to do that?"

Solomon shrugged nonchalantly. "I filed a notice of appearance with the clerk this morning, your Honor. It should be with all the other papers on the bench in front of you."

Armbrister scowled and fumbled with the papers on his bench. He continued to harp about Solomon's appearance as he looked, but never found the notice. "One would think that with all the work your office has to do, Mr. Solomon, you'd work full-time on the county's business and leave the case at hand to the one who was assigned to handle it."

"One would think that," Solomon said without looking up. He slowly finished arranging his books and papers on the counsel table, then whispered something to Clay.

The judge stared at the two defense lawyers talking quietly at the table in front of him, sighed heavily, then ordered that the defendant be brought in.

Clay had made arrangements to have some suitable clothes sent to the jail for Harco. Slacks and an open-neck long-sleeve shirt seemed best. Harco would look woefully out of place in a coat and tie. He'd also sent a modified golf glove for Harco's right hand. He figured if he covered up ESUK, then LTFC would be meaningless.

When a deputy led Harco into the courtroom, Clay was pleased to see the glove on. Harco had finally taken his advice. His satisfaction was short-lived, however. Judge Armbrister's first order of business, after he'd finished ranting about Solomon's presence, was the glove.

"Before we bring the jury panel in," he said, "I want to deal with the issue of proper attire in my courtroom." Armbrister picked up his gavel, and pointed it in the direction of Harco. "Mr. Delaney, the head jailer advises me that your client is wearing gloves."

Clay rose to his feet. "Only one glove, your Honor," he said. "And it's only a half glove at that. It covers just the upper part of his right hand."

"One glove or two. It doesn't matter to me. It's garb. It's paraphernalia. I won't allow garb or paraphernalia in my courtroom."

"Your Honor, may we have the court reporter present for this?" Clay asked.

Armbrister threw up his hands, still holding on to the gavel. "What do we need a court reporter for?"

"You're making a ruling that's affecting my client's rights, and I want it on the record."

"You and your precious record," Armbrister said shaking his head. "I don't see why you need a record when I'm only dealing with the proper and orderly operation of my court, and with the decorum I expect from the people before me."

Clay's volume increased, and he looked right into Armbrister's eyes. "I respectfully request a court reporter, nonetheless, your Honor."

"Request denied," Armbrister said as he hammered his gavel.

"Your Honor, the defendant is allowed to wear street clothes to trial instead of a jail uniform, so as not to prejudice him in the eyes of the jury. The half-glove serves a similar function in covering up an inscription that would only harm his right to a fair trial if displayed to the jury."

"I know what it covers up, Counselor. I guess he should've thought about that before he had himself 'inscribed,' as you put it. Request denied," the judge said, slamming the gavel again.

"But your Honor, not allowing him to conceal it is the same as injecting evidence of Mr. Brewton's character into the case."

Armbrister smiled. "He's allowed to do that."

Clay put both hands on the table in front of him and leaned forward. "Well, he's not introducing it. You are. And that's not allowed. At least not now."

"I don't want your client's right hand covered by a glove, Mr. Delaney. Tell him to take it off. Right now!" Armbrister's voice had become loud and agitated, and he pointed and shook the gavel at Harco.

Clay turned to his right toward Harco, asked him to remove the glove, then sat down beside him. In doing so, he noticed that there was a drawer in the center of their counsel table. He opened it and instructed Harco to put the glove inside. As Harco reached across Clay's lap with his left hand to place the glove in the drawer, Clay suddenly rose to his feet. "There's just one more thing, your Honor."

As he stood up, the tops of his thighs caught the drawer and slammed it shut, right on Harco's fingers. Harco let out a high-pitched screech and forcibly withdrew his hand. It was already spewing blood onto the top of the table.

"May Mr. Brewton wear a bandage on his left hand?" Clay said.

Harco howled, and Armbrister pounded his gavel until the handle cracked and the head of it fell off.

"You did that on purpose, Mr. Delaney," Armbrister said. "You've deliberately disobeyed my order. I'm going to hold you in contempt."

"If we had a record, your Honor, we could see exactly what your order was. But since we don't, you and I will both have to testify before the presiding judge to make one. Mr. Solomon will represent me," Clay said, then sat down.

Solomon sat in silence, his eyes widening and rolling slightly uphill. Harco was now merely whimpering. Rowland had yet to say a word.

Armbrister rose to his feet, and through gritted teeth said to the bailiff, "We'll take a twenty minute recess. Then bring the jury panel up."

Clay knew he'd won the prelims, but the main event hadn't even started.

After Armbrister left, Clay turned to Harco. "You'd better get that hand tended to. It looks like a nasty cut."

The striking of the jury was easier than Clay had anticipated. They were finished by two o'clock. Going against what appeared to be the obvious, Clay didn't use any of his peremptory strikes against women with small children.

Clay had listened intently to Callie. He'd almost convinced Solomon. When it was all said and done, he knew the jurors would be his strongest allies or his worst enemies. He just had to ease them past their inevitable perception of Harco and get them to focus on the crucial tidbits that Callie unearthed. That was all he had.

If he was successful, he just might have a shot at winning. If he failed, Harco would be convicted for sure. And worse than that, the death sentence would be a given. Solomon had summed it up quite nicely: "God help us if you're wrong, Clay. You know a lioness will kill a hyena if she can. Even if it's not threatening her cubs. She knows that sooner or later, it will."

If Clay lost the case, his jury choices would be the first of his errors that critics would point out.

The jury of eight women and four men retired for the day, and Clay went home. He was too drained to confront Harco about Lovie. He'd do that later. If she was the only thing he'd lied about, that would be wonderful.

After dinner, Clay went over his notes for the next day, then stepped out onto the deck. It was growing dark. A cool, fresh breeze was blowing in from the southwest, and the trees around him were swaying gently in the twilight. The smell of rain was in the air. He loved to be outside and experience the sights, sounds, and smells of an approaching storm, and feel the wind and early droplets on his face.

To his delight, also being borne on the wind of the impending rainsquall was the faint strain of the same piano music that had touched him so deeply some weeks before. Its impact on him this time was totally different. He felt mellow and content. He thought of Callie and smiled. He wished she could enjoy it with him. He slipped inside and called her from his kitchen phone.

"Step outside," he told her. "There's something you should hear."

She apparently did and returned to the phone. "Yeah. Sure sounds like rain to me. This your idea of a joke?"

Clay looked out and saw the rain now pouring down. "Never mind," he said, "I just waited too long to call. I'll talk to you later."

As the rain grew more intense, sporadic wind gusts threw it against the sliding glass door, creating a mystic cadence. Sometimes it would undulate, and other times it simply crashed against the glass. In between there was the staccato beat of rain on the wood floor of the deck. In the midst of it all, Clay was convinced that he occasionally heard the illusive sound of piano music being borne on the wind.

Sitting in his great room flipping through his trial notebook, Clay was distracted by the crack of lightning in the distance and the occasional flicker of his lights. He was going to have to reset the VCR, the answering machine, and every clock in the house. For an instant, he thought that some of the noise he was hearing was man-made. He got up, checked his doors, then dismissed the thought. He was tired. It was time to get some sleep.

As he began to undress, he suddenly had the sense that he was being watched through the broad expanse of his bedroom windows. Not being sure and concerned that he might simply be reacting to the eerie mood of a stormy night, he moved into his dressing room and out of clear view of his windows. There, he slowly removed his shirt and watched the expanse of glass through a dressing mirror.

Two successive flashes of lightning created a strobe effect, and a shape outside his window appeared to have changed positions. Clay was now sure that something or someone was moving outside his window. It was too large to be Fraidy. The other suspicious occurrences he'd experienced around his house flashed through his mind, and he knew instinctively that it was coming to a head.

His heart pounded as he tried to move nonchalantly across the room and turn out the light. He imagined that at any second the glass would explode, and his head would disappear in a hail of shotgun pellets. He had to move slowly and appear casually indifferent. With the light out, he quickly returned to his dressing room. While trying to acclimate his eyes to the darkness, he reached into one of his built-in drawers and submerged his hand in socks. Feeling along the bottom of the drawer, his hand stopped on the cold, blue steel of his nine-millimeter automatic. He knew the magazine was already in place. All he had to do was flip the safety with his right thumb and slide the receiver back, forcing a shell into the chamber. He did that easily and entirely by feel, never once taking his eyes off the silhouette of the window. The sound of the wind and rain completely masked the telltale click of metal on metal as the pistol cocked.

If he was ever to get to the bottom of the situation, Clay knew he couldn't simply wait. He had to go outside and confront whoever it was, head on. He moved barefoot and shirtless through the darkened house, his eyes still adjusting. He exited through the kitchen door, which put him on the opposite side of the house from his room and the deck. As he slipped into the yard, the wind-driven rain stung his bare skin, and the shock of the cold water made him shiver slightly.

He moved quietly around the side of the house, pausing at the corner. He sensed that someone was standing just around the corner, under the deck. Gripping the automatic tightly with both hands and holding it chest high, he swung quickly around the corner and extended his arms straight out. The muzzle of the pistol immediately came to rest against wet human flesh.

"Don't even think about moving," Clay said.

In the very dim light, he could make out the back of a human form huddled against the lower structure of his house. Through the gun barrel he could feel the body in front of him trembling, either from the cold or from fear. The hammer of the pistol was cocked precariously, poised to slam forward. The brass cartridge—just inches from the intruder's spine—awaited the command to explode and drive its blunt-nose slug through tissue and bone.

"Turn around. Slowly," Clay said.

Facing him in the darkness under the deck was a drenched and obviously terrified teenage girl. Clay lowered the pistol and carefully released the hammer, his hands beginning to shake for the first time. The two of them stood, staring at each other, shaking, with water running down their faces.

"Get inside," Clay finally said.

Once inside and with the lights on, the first thing he noticed about his young prowler was what remained of her lipstick. It was the same garish pink he'd seen in a tube when he'd first visited Harco's room in Midtown.

He retrieved two towels from the laundry room and handed one to her. He wiped his face and watched her start to dry her matted brown hair. She was in her early teens, and was cute but frail—almost bony. As she stood in the center of an ever-growing puddle in the middle of his kitchen floor, she reminded Clay of a hungry stray puppy let in out of the rain.

"Who are you and what are you doing here?" Clay asked gently.

"I'm Mattie Brewton. Harco's wife," she said shyly, not looking at Clay.

"Harco's wife? He never said anything about being married."

"Well, Harco says we're the same as married."

"How old are you?"

"Fourteen."

Clay shook his head. "Fourteen. I guess you're a Pascagoula special too."

"A what?"

"Nothing. It's just a term I heard Harco use once. I take it you've been here before."

"Here?"

"Around my house. Maybe even in my house."

She nodded and looked at the floor.

"How'd you know about me and where I lived?"

Mattie continued to look at the floor. "I visited Harco one Sunday at the jail. He told me not to come back, but he said you was going to defend him. I looked up your address in the phone book."

Clay walked over, put his hand under her chin, and raised her face toward his. "Where do you live?"

"I've been staying at our room. The one on Eleventh Street."

"But the manager said no one was living in there."

"I come and go through the back window. Harco never wanted anyone to see me."

Clay took the towel from her, and began gently dabbing water droplets on her face. "How'd you get way out here?"

"On the MARTA bus. The end of the line is only about eight blocks from here.

"I guess it's been pretty rough for you since Harco was arrested?"

"It was easy at first. I just sold a lot of the stuff he stole. But I didn't get too much for it. It's all gone now."

Clay caught her staring at a bowl of fruit on the countertop. "Listen, if you're hungry, I'll fix you a sandwich or something."

She nodded.

"Okay. Why don't we get something dry on, and then I'll feed you." He led her back to the guestroom, gave her several long shirts to select from, then changed clothes himself. By then the rain had stopped, so he called Callie, told her about Mattie, and asked her to come over with some clothes.

Later, back in the kitchen, Mattie wolfed down the sandwiches he prepared, and he placed a large glass of milk in front of her. "You do like milk, I take it?"

She looked at him and smiled self-consciously.

"Does Harco know you've been coming around here?"

"No. He'd be mad. He told me to stay out of sight. But I've been so lonely and afraid. I knew you were helping him, and I just felt like I wanted to be near you too. I hate that old room."

"Do you understand what's happened to Harco?"

"I think so. They say he killed that girl."

"Is there anything you can tell me about it?"

"No. 'Cept that when we came back from Montgomery, the man on the TV said she was missing from the day before."

Clay felt a chill go over him, and he tried to hide his excitement. "You heard this yourself? The man on TV?"

"Yeah."

"And you'd been in Montgomery with Harco?"

Mattie nodded.

"How long?"

"Couple days."

"Damn! Harco didn't put you up to this, did he?" Clay was up, pacing the room.

"No. He told me not to talk to anyone. Not even you. He'll be mad if he finds out. You won't tell him, will you?"

"Mattie, this is extremely important. I have some more questions to ask you, but I want to wait for that friend of mine who's bringing you something to wear. I want her to hear it, too."

Callie arrived, and after Mattie had changed clothes again, the three of them sat in the great room while Clay quizzed Mattie.

"He had me knock on people's doors to see if they was at home. If anyone came to the door, I'd pretend to be collecting for some kind of charity, or taking magazine orders."

"What was Harco doing all this time?" Clay said.

"Just cruising around. If no one was there, I'd signal him, and he'd come back and go inside. He was real good at gettin' inside."

"What did he do with all the stuff he took?"

"Well, when he had enough—and he wasn't greedy or nothing—we'd drive over to Montgomery that same day, and he'd sell it. What he didn't sell, he'd leave in a room over there and sell it later. Then after a few days of resting up, we'd do the same thing in Montgomery, then come right back over here to sell it. Harco was funny. If he broke into somebody's house, he wouldn't stay the night in the same town. He said it wasn't smart."

Clay studied Mattie for a moment. "Do you remember knocking on the door of a home on Sterling Close in Northside?"

"There's no way I could remember. I knocked on so many, and they was all alike to me."

"They found a red, white, and blue rag doll in Harco's car. Do you know anything about that?

"Yeah. I tried the front door of this one house, but no one answered. The garage was open, so I went in and knocked on the kitchen door. No one came to that door either, but I could hear someone inside so I left. On the way out of the garage, I saw some cardboard boxes filled with old clothes and toys. I saw my friend hiding in one of the boxes, so I—"

"Your friend?" Clay said.

A soft smile played around the corners of Mattie's mouth, and a far away look appeared on her face. She turned her head away from Clay, and looked through the sliding glass doors. Without taking her eyes off of the river, she answered softly. "That's what I called the rag doll. 'My friend.' She was going to help me whenever Harco made me feel bad." Mattie paused for a moment, then faced Clay once more. "Anyway, I saw her hiding, so I picked her up. When I got outside, Harco was gone. It was good that he was gone, because he never wanted me to take anything if someone was at home. He always said that might get us caught, and we'd go to jail."

"How'd you find him again?"

"He picked me up later. I was walking down the street."

Clay stroked his chin, and thought for a moment before speaking. "Did he know about the doll?"

Maggie's eyes widened, and her body stiffened. "No. I hid it behind me. Then when I got in the car, I put it under my seat. If he found out, he would've been bad to me. And he wouldn't buy me any candy."

"Do you like candy, Mattie?"

"Yeah. Harco always buys me candy when we finish, if I've been good."

"Did he buy you any candy that day—before you went to Montgomery?"

"Uh-huh."

"Do you remember where he bought it?"

"No. But we always stopped at convenience stores. He didn't ever want to be too far away from his car."

"Bingo," Clay shouted. He rose from his seat on the sofa, and began to pace. "I can't believe this. It's almost too good to be true. But why am I just learning about it? Hell, this is Harco's ticket home. What's wrong with him, anyway?"

Callie shook her head in bewilderment. After a brief pause, she said, "Aren't you the one who said you didn't want to have to prove that Harco's alibi was that he was in Montgomery committing another crime?"

"Well, that was different," Clay said, stopping in the middle of the room. "That was with Harco as my only witness and with nothing to back it up. Now I've got this very believable kid who can lay it all out. Callie, this is dynamite. We can win with this."

The storm that had roared up the valley of the Chattahoochee soon dissipated, and Callie left Clay's home with Mattie. The drive to Callie's house was short and quiet. Only the sound of Callie's tires clumping across the boards on the river bridge broke the uneasy silence.

While Mattie had voiced no objection, Callie sensed her reluctance to leave Clay. But taking her was the right decision. Clay had no way to care for her and wouldn't know how if he could. Callie certainly had no parenting experience, but at least she'd once been a teenage girl. It was also quite clear that Mattie was going to require some extraordinary support. Mattie was poised precariously on the narrow ledge of womanhood, yet she was still so emotionally tender—far more than her years would dictate. Her having lived a life on the run with a hardened criminal who'd ended up in jail for murder had to have taken a toll on her. Callie knew that even with her own professional training, she might not be able to deal with Mattie. But Clay had no chance at all.

"Mr. Delaney's nice, isn't he?" Mattie said suddenly, as the car eased to a stop in front of a wrought iron gate blocking their way.

"Yes, he is," Callie replied, as she lowered her window and pulled a rope dangling from a long wooden arm on her side of the driveway. The gate opened slowly, and Callie moved through. Then she closed the gate by pulling a similar rope on the other side of the gate.

The high beam of Callie's headlights revealed a long driveway, bounded on each side by a hedge-like border of old-growth azaleas. The alternating pink and white blossoms had already faded in the lateness of the spring and were fast losing their grip, forming, as they fell, a delicate carpet at the feet of their recent hosts.

The car's lights soon revealed a rambling frame house with a roofed veranda that wrapped around the front and both sides of the house. Light shinning through numerous dormer windows signaled the existence of a second story. Matching brick chimneys, towering high above the wooden shingles, flanked the house on both sides. A porch swing hung by chains from the ceiling of the veranda on the far right corner.

"This is really nice," Mattie said as they approached.

"I don't live here. My landlord does. I rent a little guest cottage in the rear."

Disappointment was evident in Mattie's "Oh," as they moved past the house and up to a much smaller house well behind it.

Mattie giggled when she saw where Callie lived. Callie knew why. Everyone's reaction was the same. Her house was a scaled-down version of the main house, including the color scheme, the veranda, and the two chimneys. One of the chimneys was fake, as was Callie's second story. When the two houses were compared, Callie's had the appearance of a matching dollhouse.

One significant difference between the two homes existed, however, and that was Callie's use of the many varieties of flowers she loved so much. Small white window boxes set against the gray sides of her cottage overflowed with a profusion of multicolored petals atop delicate stems. Equally colorful flowers and plants stood gracefully inside a white-picketed enclosure that formed Callie's miniature front yard.

Once inside the house, Mattie wandered around with uninhibited curiosity, inspecting and touching Callie's belongings. Callie watched closely but didn't say anything. She was uncomfortable enough just having a stranger in her house, but her knowledge of how Mattie had aided in Harco Brewton's burglaries heightened her anxiety. She tried to reassure herself of Mattie's child-like naivete, as well as her having been under Harco's dominant influence when those crimes were committed. But she still continued to watch Mattie closely.

A large family room with an open kitchen off to one side dominated the living space of the little cottage. It stretched from the front door to a bay window on the opposite side of the room. Bookcases built into the walls of the room, from the floor to the ceiling, were crammed with books of every kind imaginable. A few loose books and some magazines were stacked and strewn about in no discernable order.

Several soft chairs guarded by well-placed reading lamps seemed to beckon for occupants. Pressed flowers of several varieties, which had been matted but not framed, lay on top of an old piano. A cushioned seat filled the alcove that was formed by the bay window. On the seat was a small canvas depicting a mountain stream. The oil paint was still curing.

After thoroughly surveying the main living area, Mattie moved down a short hallway. When she reached the doorway to Callie's bedroom, she stood there, staring at Callie's four-poster bed. "Is this where you do it?"

"Do what?" Callie replied, knowing full well what she was being asked, but trying to evade the question by tossing it right back to Mattie.

"You know, do it—with Mr. Delaney."

"Mr. Delaney has never been here. We haven't known each other very long. I don't think he even knows where I live."

"You know where he lives."

"Yes, and I have visited with him some. He just hasn't had the chance to come over here, yet. I'm sure he will."

"I can see why you go over there. His house is so much nicer."

"Well, let me show you your room, and then I'll see if I can find you something of mine to sleep in."

The tiny house had only two bedrooms. Each bedroom had its own bath, so despite the close quarters, Callie was still assured of her privacy.

Mattie's bedroom contained Callie's childhood "cannonball" bed. It had been handmade just for her by Papa Gallagher. Large wooden knobs, like cannonballs, capped each of the bed's short corner posts. The deep luster of the old wood spoke of the care with which it had been cut, formed, and rubbed smooth by the rough hands of a gentle man.

Whenever Callie needed to feel close to him once more, or whenever she simply needed to be comforted or feel secure, she'd lie in her old bed for a while. Her tie to the past and her memory of her father were so strong that she felt enveloped by the same love that had fashioned the little bed for her so many years before. It was as if part of the old man's soul had fused with the grain of the wood as he labored over it, first in the barn, then beside the fireplace after the snow and the cold had driven him inside.

No one but Callie had ever slept in the old bed. But now she was offering it to Mattie. Maybe it would comfort and soothe her as well.

At the request of counsel, a deputy brought Harco to the courthouse an hour and a half early the next morning. Solomon and Clay were waiting for him in a conference room near Armbrister's courtroom.

"Why didn't you tell me you lived with Lovie in Kentucky?" Clay said.

Harco's eyes widened. "How'd you know about that?"

"You were driving her car, for Christ sake. You think no one was going to find that out?"

Harco picked at his moustache but was silent.

"You told me you hadn't seen her since you were a kid, and I fell for it. For a while there, I felt sorry for you." Clay tried to look into Harco's eyes, but he stared vacantly at the ceiling.

"What's the problem? She ain't got nothin' to do with this, anyway."

"That's where you're wrong," Solomon said. "If that jury in there finds you guilty, your mother's testimony could really make a difference during sentencing. Where is she?"

Harco shrugged, and continued to look away. "I don't know. Seems like I've been chasing after her my whole life. Leastways, ever since she left Pascagoula."

"How'd you find her the first time?" Clay asked. "Look at me, damn it."

Harco squirmed in his chair, and turned his head toward Clay. "I was working over the road for a few years for a truckin' outfit out of Laurel."

"Laurel?"

"Mississippi. On a trip through Kentucky, I ran into her at a truck stop in Covington. She was working behind the counter. I thought we could go back to being like old times. So, I signed on with a Kentucky outfit that had a terminal in Covington, and moved in with her."

"That didn't work out?" Clay said.

"It did for a while, 'cause I was on the road a lot." Harco paused and looked away again. "Then one day, I heard these truckers talkin' on the C.B. about gettin' some when they hit Covington." He paused again, cleared his throat, and continued slowly. "I didn't pay it no mind, until one of 'em let on that she wasn't called 'Lovie' for nothin'." Harco whirled angrily toward Clay. "Yeah. I lied to you, Mr. Delaney. Big deal."

"Okay. We've gone this far. Let's hear the rest of it," Clay said.

"Well, we had a big fight when I got home, and the next thing I knew she'd moved out in the middle of the night."

"How'd you locate her again?"

"Easy. All I had to do was keep my ears on." Harco shook his head. "It wasn't long before them bird dogs had done sniffed her out."

"And you moved back in with her in Lexington?"

"Yeah. Right or wrong, she's my momma."

"But that didn't work, I take it," Clay said.

"I quit truckin' to spend more time with her, but we fought a lot. Then one night when I was out, she slipped away again. Took off with some trucker, I think."

"And you've no idea where we might find her?" Solomon asked.

"Nope. I've looked in a whole bunch of cities. Figured Atlanta is just as good a place as any."

"I can understand why you wouldn't have said anything about your mother, but why in the hell didn't you tell me about Mattie?" Clay asked.

Harco's head snapped around. "They don't have her, do they?" he said nervously.

There was an odd urgency in Harco's question that Clay didn't comprehend. "No. But—"

"I told that little bitch to stay put." Harco's eyes narrowed, and his tone was vicious.

"Well, it's a good thing she didn't. She's your ticket out of here. She can put you in Montgomery the day Carrie Lindsey was killed."

"No way."

"What?" Clay said. He looked at Solomon then back at Harco. "I don't think you understand."

"I understand perfect."

Solomon shook his head. "This is the same alibi you were willing to buy from a three-time loser. What's the problem?"

"Nobody'll believe her. And even if they did, when this thing's all over, old Fancy Pants will have me right back in here for statutory rape, burglaries out the wazoo, contributing to the delinquency of a minor and God knows what else. Hell, I'll never get out of jail. No way I'm goin' to agree to something I know's goin' to send me to jail, just to try to stay out of jail. You all must think I'm fuckin' crazy."

"We're not just talking jail here," Clay said. "We're talking about the death penalty. She can save you from that. Doesn't that matter to you?"

"You ever been to jail, Mr. Delaney?"

"No."

"Then you don't really know what you're talking about. Maybe dying ain't so bad after all. It might just be better'n rottin' in prison. Specially for something you didn't do."

Clay looked at Solomon, who simply shrugged his shoulders. "It's his call."

Clay looked back at Harco, who was staring at the floor. For the first time since he met him, Clay felt sorry for Harco. The irony of Harco's plight began to dawn slowly on him. Perhaps Harco had already thought it through. He had an honest-to-goodness alibi. But he refused to let the one person who could prove it, testify about it. And his lawyer refused to let someone else lie about what was really true in the first place.

A sudden feeling of remorse flooded over Clay, as he recalled his earlier conviction that Harco was guilty, then his doubt about it, then his ambivalence. He was punishing himself for being so hasty, wondering if his attitude had prevented him from mounting the best defense available for Harco. Now he was ashamed that he might've let his personal feelings interfere with his professional judgment. He silently vowed to do what was necessary to set it straight.

A knock on the conference room door indicated that all the jurors were in the jury room. He placed his hand on Harco's shoulder—a gesture more conciliatory than friendly—and said, "Okay. We'll do it without her. Let's go." The three of them filed into the courtroom.

Jason Rowland sat at his table engrossed in his notes. As Clay passed behind his chair, he could stand it no longer, and out of frustration whispered to him, "He didn't do it, Jason."

By the time Rowland looked up and over his shoulder, Clay had already passed by and was taking his seat. When Rowland finally glanced over at the defense table, all he saw was Solomon flipping him the finger.

CHAPTER 13

▼

Jason Rowland's opening statement to the jury started out like an incoming artillery round, and it was right on target. Then round after round, explosions of graphic and heart rending details peppered the courtroom with searing pieces of the short life then death of Carrie Lindsey—at the hands of Harco Brewton. No one in the courtroom escaped the impact of Rowland's well chosen words. Those not hit directly were rocked by the concussion. The eyes of the jury were collectively riveted on Rowland, following his every movement. When he knew he had them totally in his control, he picked up the little rag doll. With the doll lying face up in his left palm, its head, arms, and legs dangled limply on each side of his hand. Then, he turned to face Harco for the first time.

"And when Harco Brewton had finished having his way with Carrie Lindsey, he zipped up his pants and walked away, leaving her body lying alone in the woods, as lifeless as this little doll. Her doll. The same one found hidden under the seat of his car at the time of his arrest.

"Harco Brewton is guilty. Guilty of the worst crimes that could possibly be committed against an innocent girl with a lifetime still ahead of her. He forcibly violated that innocence, then callously ended her life. Harco Brewton does not deserve to live."

When Rowland stopped talking, he stood in silence, staring at Harco. He'd been effective in shifting the jury's gaze from himself to Harco.

Harco hung his head. The timing was perfect. The effect Rowland created was so well devised the jury didn't even see him sit down. They were all still staring at the squirming Harco.

"Oh, he's good," Clay whispered to Solomon. "He already has half of them convinced."

"Anybody can be good if they have a good case. Let's wait and see how well he does when he's up to his lips in doo-doo."

Judge Armbrister cleared his throat. "Mr. Delaney?"

"Yes, your Honor," Clay said dutifully, unfolding slowly from behind the counsel table. He walked easily over to the jury rail and stood there, quietly facing them. Sensing that Rowland was way out in front of him, he scrapped the opening statement he'd so meticulously prepared.

"Some of you have already decided that Harco Brewton is guilty of the rape and murder of Carrie Lindsey. You've come to that conclusion because of what someone's just said to you. Someone you don't know. Someone you've never met. Someone you never saw in your life, before yesterday. Someone who isn't a witness to one single fact in this case.

"You've heard no testimony, looked at no physical evidence, and seen no photographs. Yet, you're already willing to say, 'He's guilty, and he should die.' If that's true of any of you, I'd like for you to go ahead and write 'Guilty' on a piece of paper, sign your name to it, place it in your seat, and go on home. You're no longer needed here. You'd only be bored if you stayed. While you're gone, the rest of us will be here struggling with the question of whether your children are now safe from the same person who killed Carrie Lindsey. Or, whether he is still out there somewhere, waiting for the opportunity to do it again.

"If Mr. Rowland and you are right, then everyone's problems are solved. But lock your door just in case you're wrong. Your problems will have just begun. Or on second thought, maybe you'd like to stay and see whether you should tell Mr. Rowland at the end of this case that he shouldn't stop looking for her killer—that he simply stopped looking a little too soon."

The first witness to take the stand was the Lindsey's next door neighbor, Roberta Felton. She told what she'd seen on the Wednesday morning before Carrie's Friday disappearance. She identified a photo of the rear of Harco's car as being the same as she'd seen parked in front of the Lindsey residence that morning. She was careful to point out the rusty top and the non-Georgia license tag. She was asked to describe the head of the man she saw in the car, and her description fit Harco perfectly.

Since he'd discovered Mattie Brewton, Clay knew he wouldn't contest Roberta Felton's testimony. But since he couldn't use Mattie as a witness, he decided to get as much mileage as he could out of Roberta. Consequently, when Clay cross-examined her, he didn't attempt to discredit her recollection. Instead, his questions seemed to lend support to her story and gave her a chance to repeat it.

"Ms. Felton, tell the jury when trash pickup day is in your neighborhood."

"Do you mean garbage pickup?"

"No ma'am. Household trash."

"Why, it's on Wednesday," she said.

"If you have trash to be disposed of, doesn't the county require you to place it at the curb in front of your house for pickup sometime during the day?"

"Why, yes."

"When you came out of your house that Wednesday morning, did you know whether Mr. Brewton had already gone through the Lindsey's trash?"

"Objection!" Rowland said as he rose. "The question assumes the existence of several facts which haven't been proved, your Honor."

"It certainly does, Mr. Rowland. But the phrasing of the question also suggests the presence of the defendant in front of the Lindsey house, as you're obviously trying to prove through this witness. Now do you really want me to sustain your objection and nullify a major piece of evidence in the State's case?"

"No, your Honor," Rowland replied.

"I thought not. Objection overruled," Armbrister announced, as he directed an arrogant smile toward Clay.

Clay smiled back.

"Would you answer the question, please ma'am," Clay said politely.

"I don't know."

"No more questions, your Honor."

Clay saw Rowland glance quickly around the courtroom, as if he were looking for someone to counter the point Clay had just made about the trash. But Rowland was on his own. All the witnesses, including Celeste Lindsey, had been sequestered. None of them were allowed in the courtroom when someone else was testifying.

Rowland rose from the counsel table. His slow approach to the witness and his lack of notes confirmed to Clay that he wasn't prepared to examine Roberta Felton on that subject. If that were the case, Clay thought, Rowland was about to ask questions that he didn't already know the answers to. That was a risk few lawyers were willing to take.

"Ms. Felton, did you see any trash in front of the Lindsey residence when you came out of your house that morning?"

"No. I did not."

Rowland smiled. "So, Mr. Brewton couldn't have been going through the Lindsey's trash that morning."

"I can't say that," Roberta replied. "The way his car was parked, it blocked my view of the place where the Lindseys normally put any trash. Besides, I was interested in the car and the man, not the trash. Now, later, when I came back from my hair appointment, I think I did see some boxes in front of their house."

A look of disgust came over Rowland's face, and he shook his head. "No further questions."

Clay smiled.

"You know Harco never went through any trash," Solomon whispered to Clay.

"I never said he did. All I did was ask her if she knew whether he had. Rowland and Armbrister took it from there, and between the three of them, they just may have proved that he did. You know, if Rowland's going to prove his entire case with circumstantial evidence, by golly he's just going to have to wade through a little of ours."

"The State calls Julie Felton," Rowland announced.

Julie Felton entered the rear of the courtroom with a book-bag slung over one shoulder. She wore a flowered sundress of soft yellows and white. Her blonde ponytail struggled to keep up with her as she bounced down the aisle. She was the same age as Carrie Lindsey. They'd been classmates. But to Clay's dismay, she wore no makeup and looked quite comfortable without it. Though the same age, it was obvious to Clay that Julie hadn't matured as rapidly as Carrie. In many ways, Julie was still a little girl. He knew her fresh, childish innocence would appeal to the jury.

Rowland kept Julie's story simple and direct. She and Carrie had pretty much grown up together. Classmates since kindergarten, they were close to the edge of finishing middle school when Carrie died. They had shared much together over their few years. They got bikes on the same Christmas, and both rode without training wheels on the same day the following summer. They made mud pies, had tea parties, played dolls, became Brownies, sold Girl Scout cookies, and went to summer camp.

Rowland didn't miss the opportunity to elicit from Julie Felton a recitation of all the wholesome things two young girls could do. When he finished, it didn't matter what she said. The jury was going to believe it. He then turned Julie's attention to the afternoon of Friday, April third. "Did you see Carrie after school on the day she disappeared?"

"Yes sir. We started walking home together."

"How long were you together?"

"I'm not sure. It's a long way. Maybe fifteen or twenty minutes."

"Had the two of you ever walked home together before?"

"Yes sir."

"Did anything different happen that afternoon? Something that hadn't happened on the other days you walked home?"

Julie nodded.

"Would you tell the jury about it?"

"This white car passed us going real slow. A little while later it passed us again, going in the opposite direction."

"Did the two of you say anything to each other about it?"

"Not until the third time it passed us. Then I said something to Carrie. She said she hadn't noticed it."

"How far did you walk together?"

"When we got to the street where the Zip 'N Mart is, she wanted us to go in and buy some candy."

"Did you?"

"I didn't. I wanted to go on home, so I left her on the corner."

"What was Carrie doing the last time you saw her?"

"Waving goodbye."

Rowland turned away from his young witness and walked over to his table. He turned around slowly to face her again. "Julie, do you have a favorite doll?"

"Yes sir."

"When you played dolls with Carrie, did you play with your favorite one?"

"Yes sir."

"Would you show the jury your favorite?"

Julie reached into her book-bag and pulled out a very worn blue and white Andy rag-doll and held it up to the jury. She then pulled it to her breast and held it there.

A reverent stillness settled over the room. The jury gazed sympathetically on the little witness. The only sound was the soft click-click of the old wall clock.

"I have nothing further for this witness," Rowland said.

Clay's mind raced. He instinctively knew it would be extremely dangerous to cross-examine Julie. He ran the risk of losing more than he could possibly expect to gain. As he quickly assessed her testimony, he recalled an admonition of Lane Morgan: "Listen to what a witness doesn't say, and use it to your advantage." She'd talked about a white car, but never mentioned the unmistakable rust, nor was she asked to identify any of the many photos of Harco's car that were in the courtroom. She'd talked about and showed her doll, but she didn't talk about Carrie's doll. She didn't say when she and Carrie last played dolls. But, most important, she never indicated that Carrie had her own doll with her on that Friday.

Since these were major points in his favor, Clay chanced losing them if he tried to take Juile any further. What's more, Rowland could be setting him up, so that the most damning evidence would come from the little girl while Clay was examining her. Discretion being the better part of valor, he decided to save those points to make during his closing argument to the jury.

Clay stood up and smiled at Julie. "Let's see, this should be your last week of school before summer. Is that right?"

"Yes sir."

"If you had to choose between staying here and answering a bunch of my dumb old questions or going back to school, which would you choose?"

"I'd go back to school."

When the jury's laughter subsided, Clay said, "I thought so. In that case, I have no questions for you, Julie. You may go."

"Let's recess for lunch," Armbrister said as he stood to leave.

The bailiff banged his own gavel and sounded out, "All rise. The court will stand in recess until one-thirty."

When Clay turned around, he spied Callie in the rear of the courtroom. He nodded to her to see him outside.

"How's Mattie doing?" he asked, once they were out of the courtroom.

"She's fine, I guess. But she's very lonely and insecure. I put her in my guestroom, but I found her asleep on the floor at the foot of my bed this morning. She talks about you a lot. I could tell she'd rather have stayed with you. But we're going shopping this afternoon. I need some food, and she needs a few clothes."

"Great. Can you get her down here right after lunch?"

"Is she going to testify?"

"No. I agreed with Harco not to call her as a witness. But I saw Jaynelle Eubanks in the witness room this morning. I expect Rowland to call Jaynelle next."

"Why do you need Mattie?"

"Because Jaynelle told us she saw Harco in her store with Carrie Lindsey. But it must've been Mattie she saw. All I want you to do is bring Mattie into the back of the courtroom when Jaynelle's on the stand. Then, take her back out when you know Jaynelle has seen her. And make sure Mattie wears that awful lipstick."

Clay sensed that Jaynelle was nervous. He knew that Rowland must've sensed it too, for he let her talk longer than usual about herself, her little girl, and her various jobs. When it was obvious that she'd settled down, Rowland led her into her story.

During all of the preliminary background testimony, Clay continually checked the back of the courtroom for Callie and Mattie. "Come on. Come on," he whispered to himself. "This is no time to have a flat, or God forbid, an accident. I need you, Callie. Come on."

Jaynelle started out a little shaky, but under Rowland's calm urging, she got stronger and stronger. Her identity of Harco in the courtroom was clear and convincing—as it should've been. She'd actually seen him in her store. And Harco Brewton was hard to forget. Unfortunately, the strength of her identification also carried over to the time she said she saw him. "On Friday, April third. In the afternoon."

Several of the jurors were visibly impressed by her placing Harco at the store on the afternoon Carrie disappeared. Others showed no emotion. But the entire jury—and the audience as well—reacted when Jaynelle testified that he was there in the company of Carrie Lindsey.

Rowland had laid no foundation for that part of Jaynelle's testimony. Any good trial lawyer would've objected at this point. But Clay knew that an objection could be construed by the jury as a yelp of pain from the defense, because a vital nerve had been struck. He also knew that Rowland could overcome that technicality and emphasize the correctness of Jaynelle's identification of Carrie at the same time. All he had to do was show her and the jury the morgue photos of Carrie lying naked on a stainless steel table, and then ask if that was the same person.

Rowland seemed poised for the objection, but it never came. Clay was not about to step on that mine. Rowland turned toward his adversary, looked him in the eyes, then nodded. Clay held Rowland's gaze for an instant, then nodded back.

"She's with you," Rowland said as he passed the witness to Clay.

Clay planned to do nothing to make the jury think he disputed Harco's presence at the Zip 'N Mart. But he desperately needed to create doubt about when he was there and whom he was with. If he could create the doubt in Jaynelle's mind, he felt she was honest enough to admit it. If he was unable to do that, maybe the jury would follow his logic anyway. In any event, he knew he couldn't alienate Jaynelle in the process, or she'd become defensive and resist any concession whatsoever. Nor could he attack her in the eyes of the jury. They would silently defend her.

"Ms. Eubanks," Clay said, "is it fair for the jury to assume from what you've said that you saw Mr. Brewton in your store only one time?"

"Yes."

"And it's that one time that you've been talking about this afternoon?"

"Yes, it is."

"The first time anyone contacted you and asked you to recall if Mr. Brewton had ever been in your store was on April twenty-third, wasn't it?"

"I don't remember the exact date, but it was about two weeks later, yes."

"And you told them he'd been in your store about two weeks earlier?"

"Well, yes."

"Were you working at the market on Wednesday, April first?"

"Yes sir."

"From seven a.m. to four p.m.?"

"Those are my normal hours."

"How far is Sterling Close from your store?"

"About four or five blocks."

"Ms. Eubanks, this jury needs to know how you're able to say Mr. Brewton was in your store on Friday, rather than on Wednesday. Would you please tell them."

Jaynelle hesitated and looked at Harco. "I recognize him," she said. Then she smiled. "And besides, he's easy to remember."

"I'll grant you that, Ms. Eubanks, but I'm not questioning whether he was there, I'm asking you to reflect on when he was there."

"I just recognize him. That's all." She folded her arms and sat back in the witness chair.

"Well, let's come at it this way," Clay said calmly. "Quite a lot of your store's afternoon business came from the students at nearby Riverforks High School, did it not?"

"Yes. It did."

"As a matter-of-fact, your Zip 'N Mart location was a regular afternoon hangout for the high school crowd, wasn't it?"

"Yes."

"Over the time that you worked there, didn't you come to recognize quite a few of the students?"

"Oh, yes."

Clay walked over to his counsel table and held out his hand toward Solomon. Solomon handed him a large book with a hard cover. Without looking at the book, Clay approached the witness box and laid it on the railing in front of Jaynelle. "Let me show you a copy of the Riverforks High School annual that just came out last week. It contains hundreds of pictures of the students there. Are you willing to swear to this jury that any one of them was in your store on that Friday rather than on the preceding Wednesday?"

Jaynelle stared at the book in front of her but didn't pick it up. "No, I'm not."

"But you're willing to swear that about Mr. Brewton?"

Jaynelle hesitated for a moment. "It's just something I remember." Then after looking over at Rowland, she added, "Besides, he was with the little girl."

Rowland nodded and smiled.

"Yes ma'am. Let's talk about her just a moment. I'm sure the jury wants to hear everything you can recall about that."

Rowland rose quickly to his feet. "Objection, your Honor! Mr. Delaney can't tell this witness what the jury does or doesn't want to hear."

"Don't presume to speak for the jury, Counselor," Judge Armbrister said.

Just then, one of the female jurors on the back row spoke up. "I don't know about the rest of us, but I certainly want to hear it." The others nodded their agreement.

Armbrister turned red. He looked over at the outspoken juror and said, "Thank you, madam. Please continue, Mr. Delaney."

Rowland sat down. Solomon smiled.

"I take it you never knew Carrie Lindsey or her family."

"That's right."

"And you'd never seen her in your store before?"

"Never."

"Nor had you ever seen a photograph of her taken while she was alive."

"True."

"As a matter-of-fact, the only picture you ever saw of her was taken in the morgue almost a week after she died, wasn't it, Ms. Eubanks?"

"Yes, that's right."

"And it was from that morgue photo that you concluded that the strange girl you'd seen in your store some two weeks earlier with Harco Brewton, was Carrie Lindsey?"

"Yes."

"Ms. Eubanks, have you ever taken the time to question the accuracy of your identification of Carrie Lindsey."

"No."

"Have you ever stopped and wondered if you were correct?"

"No."

"Can the jury assume that you've never once concerned yourself with what could happen to Harco Brewton, if what you told them was wrong?"

Jaynelle didn't answer. She just stared at Clay until he felt she was staring right through him. He was a little taken aback and couldn't figure out what was going on with her.

"Ms. Eubanks?" he said.

When Jaynelle turned white, Clay knew that Callie and Mattie had arrived. All eyes in the courtroom were focused on Jaynelle as she struggled to maintain her composure. Clay never turned, but he knew when Mattie was gone by the look on Jaynelle's face.

"What?" she said, seeming to return to a rational state.

"I guess what I'm asking you is whether you're willing to admit the existence of some doubt in your own mind, and the possibility that the person you saw wasn't Carrie Lindsey?"

Jaynelle again stared at him, then finally stammered, "I thought I was right. I'm not trying to lie, but I'm not so sure anymore."

An undercurrent of hushed comments flashed through the room, and Armbrister banged for quiet. Then addressing Jaynelle, he said, "Your testimony about what you saw was your best recollection, wasn't it, ma'am?"

"Yes, your Honor."

"Well then, there's no requirement that you be positive about everything. You just tell it the best way you know how."

"And the best way you know how," Clay added, wresting the witness away from Armbrister, "is that you saw Mr. Brewton with someone you think was Carrie Lindsey, but you just can't be sure."

"Yes sir."

"And the same thing is true for when you saw him? You think it was Friday, but you just can't be sure?"

"Yes sir."

"Thank you for your candor, Ms. Eubanks. That's all I have, your Honor," Clay said, returning to his seat.

Rowland acted as if he hadn't been harmed by Clay's cross-examination of Jaynelle. Clay assumed he was too gun shy to try to rehabilitate her, and would be afraid her testimony just might get worse. Clay was right. Smiling broadly, Rowland simply thanked Jaynelle and excused her.

He then called in quick succession the two Riverforks teenagers who had found Carrie's body. Their story was simple and similar. They called the police after coming across Carrie lying behind some bushes on a dirt road that ran along the river. The spot was near the Indian Trace Dam, less than three miles from the corner market. They identified the spot and Carrie's body from the enlarged crime scene photos that Rowland introduced into evidence.

Clay had no cross-examination for the first teen, but he established through the second that the place along the river was well known for high school kids to park.

Continuing with his methodical and orderly presentation, Rowland put up a pathologist from the medical examiner's office. Through him, he established the fact of the rape and the cause of death—a single blow to the back of the head. The morgue photographs were also identified and introduced.

The crime scene photos had caused little stir among the jurors. The morgue shots were starkly different, however, and one mother hung her head, seemingly in prayer, after she had passed them on. Rowland asked no questions while the photos were moving through the jury box. Doing that kept the jurors from being distracted from the full effect of the little naked body laid out on cold steel.

The majority of the photos had no bearing on the State's evidence and weren't necessary to prove either the rape or the murder. Clay presumed that Rowland was simply using them to touch the jurors and incite them against Harco. It was difficult, but he didn't object.

The last witness of the day was the homicide detective, Lt. Pete Figuroa. Lt. Figuroa was very professional and obviously tuned in to all the details of the Lindsey investigation. He'd interviewed most of the witnesses and ultimately made the Brewton arrest.

He was very believable, and he believed what he was saying. It was easy to see he'd impressed the jury with his thoroughness and the easy manner in which he presented the facts to them. The first thing he did was describe Harco's car and identify a number of eight by ten color photographs of it—inside and out. He then identified Carrie's rag-doll and told of personally finding it stuffed under Harco's right front seat.

Rowland had saved the porn magazine for last, and Detective Figuroa testified he found it in Harco's back seat. The jury didn't react at all, until Rowland brought him over to the jury rail and had him flip the pages. Every woman on the jury flinched when they saw how the breasts and crotches of the models had been ripped and slashed. When Rowland sat down, some of the women still shook their heads.

Clay confined his inquiry to the rag-doll. He asked the Lieutenant to hand the doll to the jury and allow it to move among them. When it had passed all around, he then asked if that was the condition in which it was found. Lt. Figuroa replied that it was actually wet when found, but it had dried somewhat since. Clay then got Figuroa to tell the jury that the floorboard of Harco's car was almost rusted out, and that the entire carpet was also wet when he found the doll.

Even the jurors seemed puzzled by that line of questioning, but Clay felt comfortable that they wouldn't forget anything that had to do with the doll. It seemed so central to the case. He knew he had to just keep on making little dots.

When Clay finished, they adjourned. As they were packing to leave, Solomon turned and said, "That Mattie move was brilliant. Rowland turned as white as Jaynelle, but for a different reason. He still doesn't know what happened."

"It wasn't as brilliant as Callie's timing. I tell you, Herb, she's something else. If Harco dodges this bullet, he'll have Callie to thank, not us."

The red call-light on Clay's home phone answering machine beckoned to him as soon as he got home that night. The allure of the little colored bulb never ceased to amaze him. Actually, it really wasn't the light that tempted him, it was the power of the unanswered phone that held sway over him and all mankind. At least he was in good company. Clay hated phones, but sooner or later he had to answer the call. His brother-in-law could be dead, or worse, just hurt. He could've won some money. He might owe some. It might be an old tailhook buddy passing through town looking for some action. His curiosity got the best of him, and he pushed the button.

It was Callie. "Clay, please call me as soon as you come in." There was an odd urgency woven through her message. Something he'd never sensed in her before. He called.

"That slimeball bastard," she said on the other end.

"Who?" Clay asked.

"Harco! No wonder he didn't want Mattie to testify."

"Callie, what are you talking about? And calm down, please."

"I bought Mattie some clothes today."

"And?"

"And she tried them on at the store."

"So?"

"So, when we got home, she modeled some of them for me. She was so excited, Clay."

"Callie, what's the problem?"

"I didn't help her at the store. There wasn't enough room in the booth. But I helped her here tonight."

"Are you going to tell me what's wrong?"

"Clay, she's been terribly abused."

"How do you know that?"

"Her little body is horribly scarred. Her breasts. Her vulva. They look like they've been intentionally sliced in places."

"Did she say Harco did it?"

"She wouldn't talk about it."

"How do you know he was the one?"

"She also has scars from cigarette burns all over her tummy and on her breasts. Who the hell else could've done it?"

"Where is she now?

"Taking a bath. I'm going to feed her and put her down for the night. Clay, we've got to tell someone about this. This is criminal."

"Hold on now. First, we only suspect Harco at this point. Second, as much as I detest him, he's my client, and I can't do anything that would jeopardize his chances at trial. And reporting it certainly would do that. Third, his relationship to Mattie is a client secret he wouldn't want revealed. He's already told us that, as well as what he thinks could happen to him if we do. He knew what he was talking about."

"He's not my client, by God!"

"In a way he is. When you agreed to help me with his case, and I allowed you access to his file and then later to Mattie, you took on the same obligation as I did. And that wasn't to reveal his confidences or secrets to anyone."

"Damn!"

"I even went an extra step and paid you a buck to consult with me. That was to assure the semblance of a professional relationship and keep Rowland from calling you as a witness against Harco. But, even without the dollar, you would've been bound to silence once you began to help me with his defense."

"Damn!"

"You already said that. Listen, I'll go by the jail after dinner and confront Harco with this. I need to know more about it. I'm getting sick and tired of learning bad stuff about him the hard way. And this is bad. You're right—he is a slimeball bastard."

Clay was tired of dealing with Harco one on one. He asked Solomon to meet him at the jail. There the two of them waited with finger thumping impatience in the small visitation room.

"I'm afraid to go back in the courtroom with another unknown hanging over my head," Clay said. "I don't think Harco understands the danger of us not knowing as much as we possibly can about him. We'll get blindsided by Rowland sooner or later, sure as hell."

Solomon nodded his agreement. "He doesn't trust us. Most of them don't. And they all think they're smarter than their lawyers and the D.A. combined. They tell us what they want us to know and think no one will ever figure out the rest. 'You'll burn, baby, burn' is what I tell 'em."

Harco slipped quietly into the room, cowed somewhat by the presence of both Solomon and Clay. The three sat in strained silence for a moment.

Clay finally spoke. "Harco, we've agreed with you not to use Mattie. We understand your concerns about what could happen to you if Rowland learns about her. But you can't leave us hanging out there, either."

"Like what?" Harco asked.

"Well, we're learning that Mattie's been physically abused and that possibly you were responsible."

"Did she say that?"

"No. But you need to talk to us about it. We're your lawyers. If there's something that important in your background, we need to know about it. You can't let us stumble on it. If we can, there's always the possibility that Rowland can. In other words, what we don't know can hurt you. We don't know what to be on the lookout for."

Harco sat without speaking. His eyes flitted from Clay to Solomon and back to Clay. Then back around again. "What kind of stuff do you want to know?"

"Well, for starters, who else knows about you and Mattie?" Clay asked.

"No one that I know of."

"What about the manager of the rooming house on Eleventh Street?"

"I always let Mattie in the back window."

"And the manager in Montgomery?"

"She was always at work, and that old man of hers slept all day."

"Did you ever hurt Mattie?" Clay asked, looking Harco straight in the eyes.

"This is one of those things you guys can't ever tell on me, isn't it?"

"Yes," Clay answered.

"Unfortunately," Solomon added wryly.

Harco glanced over at Solomon then quickly back to Clay.

"Did you ever hurt her?" Clay asked again.

"Only when she was bad."

"Bad?"

"Yeah. You know. When she wouldn't do what I told her to."

"You tortured her," Solomon said.

"No. I punished her," Harco rebounded with a grin. "All bitches need punishing. Including that Lindsey kid."

Clay and Solomon looked at each other and shook their heads. Finally, Clay said, "Did you punish Carrie Lindsey?"

"No! I already told you that."

"How do we know you're telling us the truth?"

"You heard what Mattie said. Mattie doesn't lie—even when she's being bad. Besides, I'll tell you about a lot of others I punished. If I tell you about them, what reason would I have not to tell you the truth about the Lindsey kid?"

"Tell us," Solomon said.

"You realize I ain't ever told anybody about this. And the only reason I'm telling you is because you're my lawyers. And you say you need to know stuff like this to defend me. Okay?"

"Okay," Solomon said. Clay simply nodded.

"And you can't ever tell anybody, either. Right?"

"Right," Clay replied with some disgust.

Harco stood up and turned sideways, rolling up the left sleeve of his jumpsuit to reveal the names "Laura, Maud, Samantha, Amanda" tattooed on his left forearm.

"That there is a walkin', talkin' record of all the punishment I ever dished out," he said. "Right under everybody's nose."

"You hurt all those women?" Clay asked.

"More than hurt, Mr. Delaney. I snuffed 'em."

Clay felt as if his vocal cords had been hot glued in place. He tried to clear his throat.

"You telling us you killed all the women whose names are tattooed on your arm?" Solomon asked.

"Those are not women's names. Those are the names of places."

"Places?" Clay finally stammered.

"Yeah. Those are places along my old truckin' route where I killed 'em. Neat, huh? So, you see," Harco explained, "if I'd killed Carrie Lindsey, I would've had plenty of time to have 'Atlanta' tattooed on my arm. Besides, I generally have it done in advance."

Silence fell over the small room. Neither Clay nor Solomon could break through their own shock.

"Listen. You guys wanted to know all this shit," Harco said. "It's not going to change anything is it? I didn't kill the Lindsey girl. I swear."

"No. It's not going to change anything," Solomon replied quietly.

"Good!" Harco said, suddenly becoming indignant. "You know, it kind of galls me that I'm on trial for something I didn't do. Just goes to show you what kind of justice we have in this country."

"Tell me about it," Solomon said. "Come on, Delaney. I've had all the shit I can handle in one night."

Solomon led the way out of the jail, as Clay followed numbly behind.

Harco's confession of guilt just to prove his innocence was more appalling than Clay ever dreamed was possible. He wished he'd never asked. It would've been better, he thought, to go through life always wondering if his client was guilty of one murder, than to know for sure he was guilty of four. Clay Delaney's heart wasn't designed to bear that much weight.

He tried to get Harco's statements out of his mind, but couldn't. The longer he thought about them, the more dejected he became. He'd never known depression. Intense sadness, yes, but not depression. Now, though, dejection was progressing toward despondency. Whatever his feelings were, he knew they were different from anything he'd known before.

He needed Callie, but he felt it would be selfish to wake her. He tried to sleep, but couldn't. He turned on a light and tried to read, but found himself staring at the same two pages. Late-night TV wasn't even a remotely possible distraction. There wasn't much of interest in the fridge. With the trial hanging over him, grocery shopping hadn't even been on his priority list.

After wandering around his great room, he ended up fumbling aimlessly through the magazine rack. Maybe something with pictures would help. Instead, he spied an old, coverless road atlas, half slid to the bottom of the rack and badly crumpled. He recalled Harco's words. "Those are places along my old truckin' route where I killed 'em." Overwhelmed by a need to know and an aversion to finding out the truth, Clay opened the tired old atlas.

Turning to Mississippi, he searched along Interstate fifty-nine from Laurel down to Hattiesburg and on to I-ten, then back up all the way to Meridian. Nothing. He then divided Mississippi into quadrants with a pencil and carefully scrutinized each section slowly and methodically. Nothing. Then he went back over it again, until he would stake his life on the fact that those places weren't on his map of Mississippi.

His eyes began to hurt from the strain. He moved to the kitchen table for more light and put on a pot of coffee. He wasn't going to stop until he found them all. When it came to Harco Brewton, he swore to himself he'd never be in the dark again. He was going to know every goddamn thing one human being could know about another. And it was going to start right there.

Clay skipped Alabama, Georgia, and Tennessee and went straight to Kentucky. He'd go back to them later, if necessary. By the time he'd finished with Kentucky, he was on his second pot of coffee. His eyes no longer burned—they stung. And he still hadn't found even one of the towns with female names that were embedded in Harco's arm and now in his own brain.

Rather than waste time by guessing, he called the night dispatcher at Tri-State Trucking Company in Lexington, Kentucky. "Tri-State" meant it operated in three states, and he presumed one was Kentucky. All he wanted to know was the other two.

"The Lexington terminal normally handled Kentucky and Indiana, while the one at Covington served only Ohio," the voice on the phone said. Clay went back to the map.

Harco operated out of Covington. His route would've been throughout Ohio. Clay resumed his relentless search. He covered the entire north half of the state from Toledo, Cleveland and the shores of Lake Erie, south to Columbus. Nothing.

The southern half of Ohio was just as big and was going to be equally as difficult to search. Had he made a mistake? Was he looking at the wrong states? Had Harco lied again?

Bingo. There, just to the southeast of Columbus, off Highway twenty-two, he saw the town of Amanda. He was on the right track, and on the right map.

Moving west toward Springfield and Dayton, he next spotted Laura just off State Road 571, northwest of Dayton. His eyes followed I-seventy-five southward, and he quickly spied Maud just off the Interstate, slightly to the north of Cincinnati.

He was on a roll. Harco was right. The son of a bitch couldn't have made that up. It had taken Clay almost all night to find them, but there they were. They were real places. Any murders committed there would be easy to determine. All he needed now was Samantha, and his all-nighter would've been worth it. He knew it had to be in the same part of Ohio, and he was determined to find it.

Looking up from the table, he noticed that the darkness outside had taken on a lighter shade. He needed something to wake him up, but he was coffeed out. Maybe some fresh air would do.

The air on the deck was cool and still. He took a few deep breaths, stretched, and tried to focus on the river. He could hear it, but not yet see it.

It's amazing, he thought, how your other senses sharpen themselves when one of their number is unable to function, and how the brain seems to handle information faster when input from the eyes doesn't have to be processed. Clay always found it difficult to think with his eyes closed. He tended to fall asleep. He seldom had the occasion to think in the dark with his eyes open, but he was doing it now, and doing it very well it seemed.

His search for Samantha had caused him to recall all the Samanthas of his life: a storybook character from a fifth grade reader, a cat owned by his Aunt Mable, and the valedictorian of his high school class, whom everyone called "Sam." And one other—somewhere, long ago, in his distant past. It was dark out, and raining. It was green and white. It was a sign. A road sign? Yes. It read, "Washington Court House twenty-seven miles, Samantha six miles."

Was this Samantha, Ohio? He'd been in Ohio only once. When Chelsea—

"Oh, no," Clay cried urgently, as he raced for the kitchen. "Please, God. No. Oh, please God—please."

Exploding in his ears as he approached the atlas lying open on the table, were those long forgotten words of a lifetime ago. "This is Sergeant Kauffman—We found her. An old vagrant stumbled on her in some woods near a small town above Hillsboro."

"Above Hillsboro," he'd said. It was somewhere to the east of Cincinnati. There it is on Route fifty. And six miles above Hillsboro is the town of…. "Oh, dear God. Not my Chelsea—not my little girl."

When dawn broke over the river that morning, the heart of Clay Delaney broke with it.

CHAPTER 14

▼

When Lt. Karl Kauffman walked into the Highland County Sheriff's office in Hillsboro, Ohio, he was greeted by the night-duty officer who was just getting off work. "Karl, you remember that kid whose body we found up in Samantha about six years ago?" he said.

"Yeah. Why?"

"Well, some guy from Atlanta called early this morning. Said he was her father. Wanted us to fax the investigative file and autopsy report to him right away."

"Oh, yeah. The lawyer. Delaney, I think was his name. What'd you tell him?"

"I told him it was up to you. It was still your case. I put the file on your desk."

"I wonder why he's so interested after all these years?

It just goes to show you, you never know about people."

Callie dressed and left her house as soon as she got Clay's call. Even in adversity she found him stable, even tempered, and deliberate. This had been borne out that day on the river when they first met and hadn't changed since. Even when opening up to her about the pain and sadness in his life, he always seemed to be in control and never maudlin. His call that morning was different, though. There was anguish in his voice and unquestionable helplessness in his plea for her to come to him.

The two of them sat sipping coffee at Clay's kitchen table as he told her of his meeting with Harco, what Harco had revealed, and what his search of the atlas had confirmed. Clay had done most of his crying before Callie arrived. But the last tear left in his body made a slow and lonely trek down his cheek as he told her of recalling the road sign in front of the Hillsboro hospital.

Shock and dismay had short-circuited Callie's ability either to cry or talk. All she could do was put her arms around the gentle man and hold him close to her. She hoped futilely to relieve him of his grief by absorbing it and making it her own. An instinct of the ages, laying dormant in her genes, awoke within her and matured in an instant, as she sought to comfort and protect Clay as if he'd been borne of her body.

Callie's emotions began slowly to rotate from compassion to anger, as Clay's mini-lecture on not revealing a client's confidence returned painfully to her memory. The knowledge of Harco's brutality to the child of the man who was desperately trying to save his life was locked in secrecy, a secrecy maintained solely for the benefit of the brute. Clay didn't have to lecture her this time. She already knew the root of the helplessness that was overwhelming him. He'd finally learned the identity of the man who'd savagely torn his child from his life, and he was powerless to do anything about it. But even worse, he was bound to help save the life of the same man.

"Surely, they won't make you continue with the case," Callie said quietly, as she finally released Clay from the protection of her arms.

"I'd certainly hope not, but I don't know exactly what I'm going to say. I can't tell them the real reason."

"Not even the judge?"

"Not even him. And that's what worries me. But I'll be at his office when he gets there this morning. I'd better get dressed. Would you please call Solomon? Tell him what I'm up to, and that I'll catch up with him later."

Clay sat drained and hollow-eyed in Jack Armbrister's reception room, waiting for "his Honor" to arrive. He'd tried unsuccessfully to reach Rowland, but the D.A.'s office hadn't opened yet, and prosecutors' home phones were unlisted. He knew Armbrister would be reluctant to give him an audience without Rowland. Something told him it wouldn't work that way if Rowland needed to be heard.

He couldn't settle on what he should say to the judge. Everything he thought of sounded like a weak excuse instead of a good reason. He was tired, and not thinking clearly. But it would come to him. It had to.

Armbrister arrived before his secretary and was surprised by Clay's presence in his anteroom. His superficial, "How do you do?" was curt and rhetorical. When he learned that Clay wanted to see him, he seemed agitated and put out. When advised that Rowland was unaware of the request, he flatly refused. He required that Rowland be present in person or on a conference call.

"I don't care how important it is," he remarked.

After forty-five minutes of stewing, fretting and pacing, Clay finally reached Rowland by phone, and he agreed to be patched into the judge's chambers.

When Clay entered, Armbrister was still in his street clothes. He stood near the butler's table, pouring coffee out of a carafe. When he finished, he took a seat on the end of the sofa near a telephone. Clay stayed on his feet.

"You want to what?" Armbrister roared when he heard Clay's request. "Did I hear you right? You want to withdraw?"

"Yes sir," Clay said politely.

"Other than wanting to throw your client to the wolves, what possible reason could you have to walk out on him at this point?"

"I'm not at liberty to tell you specifically, but I can say that we have irreconcilable differences, and it's in both our best interests that I withdraw."

"What's in your best interest is of no concern to me, Counselor. What's in your client's interest, is. Pray tell who would take over the case if I were to allow you to withdraw?"

"I presume Mr. Solomon would, your Honor."

"Have you discussed this with Mr. Solomon?"

"No. I have not."

"Have you even discussed this with your client?"

"No sir. He doesn't know why I need to withdraw."

"It's in his best interest that you withdraw, and not only does he not know you're here, if he did know, he wouldn't know why. Is that what you're telling me?"

"Yes sir. I know it sounds strange, your Honor, but believe me, it's the best thing for all concerned. There are extremely critical reasons why I shouldn't go forward with his defense."

"Are you going to tell me what they are?"

"No sir. They're confidential, and I can't. I'm sorry."

Armbrister placed his cup on the table in front of him and got to his feet. "Not half as sorry as I am, Counselor," he said as he crossed the room to where his robe hung on a coat rack in the corner. He continued to address Clay as he removed his suit coat and slipped into his robe. "This is the most despicable display of unprofessional conduct I've ever encountered. You tried to get out of this case to start with. I had to lecture you about your duty and obligation to the indigent. I should've known then you didn't have the heart for it. You've mucked it up from day one. You struck a jury that would convict eleven of the twelve apostles. You're ill prepared. You've conceded half your case away. You've let in evidence a first-year law student would've kept out. You've let Mr. Rowland run roughshod over you. It's as if you never intended to provide a proper defense for your client, and now—now, when he's on the ropes, you want to walk away from him."

Armbrister stopped talking as he located the two ends of the zipper on the front of his robe. He closed the zipper with one swift movement, and turned back toward Clay. "It's as if you set him up. You did. You set him up, and now it's time for the knockout. Everyone knows about you, Delaney. We know you're incapable of being objective in a case like this. You're just using this assignment to get even."

As Armbrister carried on, his volume progressively increased, and his face became red and apoplectic. He rattled on and on while Clay continued trying unsuccessfully to interrupt.

Finally seizing a pause in Armbrister's tirade, Clay said, "I'm sorry you feel the way you do, Judge, but what you say is simply not so, I—"

"Are you calling me a liar?"

"No, your Honor, we obviously have a difference of opinion about my handling of this case as well as my motives."

Armbrister moved over to his desk and sat down. He straightened up some papers in the center of the desk, then looked up. His face had become cold and grim, and his eyes narrowed. "I'll tell you how big a difference we have, Mr. Delaney. You are not going to withdraw from this case. No way. And when it's over and you've finished sacrificing your client to that jury out there," he said, pointing toward the door, "I'm going to see to it that a complaint is filed against you with the State Bar Disciplinary Committee."

"Do what you feel you must, your Honor, but I'm begging you. Please don't require me to finish this case."

A crooked smile eased across Armbrister's face. "I never thought I'd ever see a high and mighty, silk-stocking lawyer crawl. How does it feel to be down here in the dirt with the rest of us? You high-toned types think you're so much better than the rest of us. Too good to do the dirty work of the law. Not enough money in it for you. You be sure and tell all those important partners of yours you begged Jack Armbrister for a favor, and he turned you down. And better than that, he's going to personally testify against you at your disbarment hearing. You be sure and tell them that too, now, you hear?"

"I'll be sure and tell them, your honor," Clay said stiffly, as he turned and left Armbrister's chambers.

When he was just outside the door, he stopped and waited for the green light on the secretary's phone display to go out. When it did, Clay quietly stepped back into Armbrister's chambers and shut the door.

Armbrister's head jerked back and his mouth flew open when he looked up and saw Clay leaning over the front of his desk.

"Now, you listen to me, you little piece of judicial snot," Clay said calmly. "I've taken all the shit I'm ever going to take from you in one lifetime. I don't know where I went wrong with you, but that doesn't matter anymore. Regardless of the outcome of this case, if you initiate disbarment charges against me or testify against me on any charges, you be sure and tell your next of kin that I'm the one who's going to double clutch a dual-wheeled truck up your cracker ass. You be sure and tell them that, 'now, you hear?'" Clay turned and walked to the door, where he wheeled around to face the stunned Armbrister. "And, oh, by the way," he said, "Fuck you!"

By the time the trial was ready to resume, Solomon was aware of everything that had happened. He offered to examine the next several witnesses to give Clay some momentary relief, but Clay refused. He even offered to change seats so Clay wouldn't have to sit next to Harco. Again Clay declined. Solomon knew he couldn't console Clay. No one could. So, he did the next best thing. He offered advice.

"Whatever it is you're thinking about doing to Harco," he said, "he isn't worth it. You can't touch him. As long as you, Callie, and me are the only ones who know what he's done, he's safe from prosecution. If one of us blows the whistle, it can never be used, and he'll walk, no matter what. If you sabotage this case, he'll eventually walk—for that very reason—and you'll go down. If you harm him physically, he may go down, but you'll go with him. It doesn't matter how you do it, he'll take you down. And it just isn't worth it."

Clay's response was simply a look of cold blue.

"You remember what I told you the first day you ever set foot in my office?" Solomon asked. "It still goes. Our obligation is to protect the system and keep it safe. No matter what. That hasn't changed."

Clay's look was enough to chill the soul. When Harco entered the courtroom every nerve ending in his body came alive simultaneously, and he turned to face the killer of his child for the first time. If he'd been an animal, he would've snarled. As Harco moved toward them with his cocky, rolling gait, Solomon put his hand on Clay's shoulder. The pressure increased proportionately as Harco neared and passed them without speaking to take his seat.

Before Clay could focus on his hatred for the oblivious Harco, Armbrister arrived.

"Are you ready, Mr. Rowland?" he asked.

"Ready, your Honor."

"Are you ready, Mr. Delaney," he asked, as if their encounter had never taken place.

"More than you know, your Honor."

"I'm sorry. What did you say?" Armbrister inquired.

"He said, 'More than ready to go,' your Honor," Solomon interjected.

Armbrister just grunted.

"Straighten up," Solomon whispered to Clay, as he pretended to fuss with the papers on their table.

"Bring the jury in," the judge ordered.

Like a well-trained and seasoned combat pilot, Clay snapped mentally to attention at the judge's order. He had learned that you never grieved for a lost wingman while you were still in the air. You waited until you were on the ground, or else you'd soon join him. His anger at Harco didn't subside, it simply moved over so he would have enough room to function again. He was scarred from too many battles to lose control now. Something deep inside him rose to the fore and took over. His need and will to maintain control and survive had never succumbed to fear. It wasn't going to give in to grief or anger now. He would deal with Harco later, and make his mother proud in the process.

"The State calls Marcus Bowman," Rowland announced.

"Who's that?" Clay asked Harco.

"My old jail buddy from Montgomery."

"The friend you tried to talk into faking the alibi?"

"Yeah."

"Great. You know, Harco, Solomon and I would have a great case if it wasn't for you."

"Sorry," Harco said apologetically, missing the point entirely.

The testimony Rowland elicited from Marcus Bowman was much as Harco had described it. They'd known each other before. They ended up in the Fulton County Detention Center at the same time. They talked about why they were in jail, and Harco asked Marcus if he'd provide an alibi for him by saying he was in Montgomery on April third.

"Were you in Montgomery on the afternoon of April third?" Rowland asked.

"No, I wasn't," Marcus replied.

"Was Harco Brewton in Montgomery on the afternoon of April third?"

"Objection," Clay stated, rising quickly to his feet. "The witness isn't competent to testify to where Mr. Brewton wasn't on April third, until he can testify to where he was. Otherwise no foundation has been laid for his conclusion. If he's going to testify he knows where Mr. Brewton was, he could only do that if they were together. If they were together, he's giving Mr. Brewton an alibi, unless, of course, Mr. Bowman is saying he was an accomplice to rape and murder."

Bowman turned pale. "I didn't do anything like that."

Rowland looked baffled and turned to the judge for help. Armbrister seemed puzzled and didn't speak. Rowland then realized the jury was staring at him and his witness and said, "I withdraw the question. Mr. Bowman, were you with the defendant at anytime on April third?"

"No," Marcus said emphatically.

"So, you couldn't have provided him with an alibi."

"That's right."

"That's all I have." Rowland sat down.

Clay stood up and stepped behind Harco's chair. Then, with considerable inner turmoil, he lightly placed both hands on Harco's shoulders in what appeared to be a protective gesture, and asked, "When you and Mr. Brewton were in jail discussing whether or not you'd come to court to testify that you knew he was in Montgomery on April third, didn't you agree to do it?"

"Yes."

"But at the time you didn't know where he was, did you?"

"No."

"Nevertheless, you were willing to come into this courtroom, swear to tell the truth, then lie to this very jury, weren't you?"

Marcus hesitated, looking around for some support, but finding none.

"You were willing to lie to these same ladies and gentlemen, weren't you?" Clay insisted.

Marcus looked down. "Yes sir."

"The jury can't hear you, Mr. Bowman."

Marcus raised his head, cleared his voice, and repeated his answer.

"Why were you willing to lie?"

"Because we were friends."

"Are you still friends?"

"I guess."

"Tell the jury who called you as a witness in this case, Mr. Bowman."

"Mr. Rowland did."

"Mr. Rowland, the district attorney?"

"Yes sir."

"That man over there with the suspenders that match his socks?" Clay asked, pointing.

Marcus nodded.

Clay could see the jurors on the front row trying to look under Rowland's table, and Rowland self-consciously pulling his feet up under his chair.

He pointed at Harco. "Did this man right here call you to testify in this case?"

"No."

"Did I?"

"No sir."

"So, regardless of what Mr. Brewton first asked you to do, he ended up not doing it. Isn't that so?"

"I guess."

"You guess! Didn't he come to you after you agreed to do it, and tell you he'd changed his mind?"

"Yes sir."

"And after that, you contacted Mr. Rowland and told him about your conversation with your friend."

"Yes sir," Marcus responded quietly.

"Why did you do that?"

"Because I thought it was my duty."

"You thought it was your duty to tell Mr. Rowland that your friend had decided you shouldn't come into court and lie?"

"Well, I..."

Clay waited patiently. Finally, he said, "It's okay if you can't answer the question Mr. Bowman."

"Objection," Rowland exclaimed. "Mr. Delaney shouldn't be lecturing the witness on his obligations."

Before responding, Armbrister looked over toward his vocal juror. Before he could react, Clay said, "Mr. Rowland's right, your Honor. I withdraw my comment and request the court to instruct the witness the same way you instructed Ms. Jaynelle Eubanks: to simply answer the question the best way he knows how."

"Do that, Mr. Bowman," the judge instructed.

"Well, I uh—I uh—thought I should tell the D.A. that Harco was trying to prove he was in Montgomery when the little girl was killed."

"What's so unusual about that, Mr. Bowman?"

"Well, because Harco ain't got nothing to do with Montgomery."

Clay moved out from behind Harco and advanced on the witness. "Are you telling this jury that you're unaware that Harco Brewton lives in Montgomery?"

Rowland vaulted out of his chair. "Objection! Objection! There's absolutely no foundation for that question. Mr. Delaney can't prove with a mere question what he can't prove by the answer. There's no evidence in this case, and never will be I might add, that Harco Brewton lives in Montgomery. Mr. Delaney's question insinuates that, and I move it be struck and the jury instructed to disregard it, your Honor."

"What do you have to say about that, Mr. Delaney?" Armbrister said over the top of his glasses.

"I can connect it up later, your Honor."

"This I gotta see," Rowland quipped.

"You'd better," Armbrister declared. "I'll allow the question only if you can establish the fact, Mr. Delaney. If you can't, I'll strike the question and the answer and hold you in contempt. The objection is conditionally overruled."

"Mr. Bowman," Clay said, "my question was: are you telling this jury that you're unaware that Harco Brewton lives in Montgomery?"

"I didn't know that."

"If it turns out that Mr. Brewton lives in Montgomery, would you agree that there should be nothing unusual about his trying to prove he was there when he's charged with committing a crime somewhere else?"

"No sir, that wouldn't be unusual."

"Thank you, Mr. Bowman. I have nothing further."

The judge let the jury take a short recess.

Clay turned to Solomon and remarked, "The best advice my daddy ever gave me was 'never pass up an opportunity to go to the bathroom.' Let's go."

The two of them went out and down the hall to the men's room. Apparently, Rowland's father had given him similar advice, for he was already facing the wall when they arrived. Solomon, not one to ever miss an opportunity, moved over to stand beside Rowland.

"I see you've still got it in your hand," he said.

"What?" came the perplexed response.

"Oh, nothing," Solomon replied, attending to the business of the moment.

Ushering Solomon out of Rowland's presence, Clay said, "Leave him alone, Herb, you'll just challenge him. He's not exactly chopped liver, you know."

"I know, Clay, but sometimes I just can't help myself. He was caught in that courtroom with his dick in his hand. He can stand being cut down a notch or two."

"Maybe so, but can it wait till this is over?"

"I'll try. I won't promise, but I'll try."

The two men left the bathroom and walked down the corridor together. When they reached the courtroom, Solomon went inside, but Clay stayed in the hall. He'd seen Callie approaching.

"Hi," he said as she reached the double doors. "I was hoping you'd come." He hugged her, inhaled her perfume, and absorbed her warmth. "We're due back in. I'll bring you up to date later."

As they embraced, Rowland appeared and waited politely to one side. Clay realized that they were blocking the door and pulled away from her. He introduced Rowland to Callie, and they all entered the courtroom after exchanging some pleasantries.

Waiting just inside the courtroom door was a young runner from Clay's office. "Mr. Delaney," he said, "your secretary asked me to deliver this fax to you. She didn't know whether it was important or not."

Clay reached for the papers and immediately saw the form legend at the top: "Sheriff's Office, Highland County, Ohio."

"No. This is personal," he stated, "but I'll take it. Thank her for me, will you?" He then folded the papers and stuck them in the inner breast-pocket of his coat.

When the jury was back in the box, Rowland called his next witness.

Slade Woolman was a lanky, raw-boned Texan, pockmarked and prison savvy. He'd spent most of his adult life behind bars for burglary, armed robbery, auto theft, forgery, and a host of other similar crimes. The homemade, self-inflicted tattoo on his left forearm inartfully spelled "Mother," and bore witness in Clay's mind to his penchant for shortcuts. He kept it prominently displayed toward the jury.

Clay wondered why Rowland would use him as a witness. He could be so easily discredited by simply showing his life of crime. But Woolman was the jail-house lawyer who'd advised Harco to go on TV, so Clay settled back and listened to what he had to say.

Rowland very cleverly brought out almost all of Woolman's shady past during his direct examination of him. This was to deprive Clay of the opportunity of surprising the jury with it. Once that was out of the way, Woolman began to describe his conversations with Harco.

It quickly became apparent why Rowland needed that information. Their conversations had to do with Harco's account of his childhood. That was the background information necessary to lay the foundation for any opinion Rowland's psychological expert would give.

Slade Woolman had a great memory. He recounted every bad thing Harco had ever told Clay about his childhood, and then some. And Woolman never missed an opportunity to pepper his testimony with Harco's statements indicating his disdain for women. Throughout the course of it, Clay kept checking with Harco to see if what Woolman was saying was correct. It was. But Clay knew Woolman had suddenly shifted from truth to fiction when he said Harco had confided in him that he'd raped and murdered Carrie Lindsey. Harco stiffened.

The jury openly reacted to the supposed jailhouse confession.

"That son of a bitch," Solomon said.

"Who? Woolman?" Clay whispered.

"No. Damn it, Rowland! I expected Woolman to do it. You'd think Rowland would have a little more class."

Slade Woolman's recitation of the confession was the high point of his testimony, and Rowland ended it there. He smiled as he passed the witness to Clay.

"Mr. Woolman," Clay started out, "do you come here as Harco Brewton's friend?"

"Wouldn't say that. We just recently met."

"Well then, do you come here as his enemy?"

"Naw. I ain't his enemy. I ain't nobody's enemy," he said, grinning broadly to the jury.

"Let's see now. You're not his friend. You're not his enemy. You just met him in jail, and in one day he tells you his whole life story, then confesses to a crime that could send him to the electric chair. You must be his priest and Father Confessor."

"Of course not," Woolman shot back.

"Of course not," Clay said. "Everybody in this room and the Georgia prison system knows better than that."

Woolman turned red, but remained quiet.

"Then, just what are you, Mr. Woolman? Would you tell the jury, please sir."

Woolman glared at Clay, recovered enough to try to act polite, and said, "I'm just a concerned citizen."

"A concerned citizen? With your record, are you allowed to vote?"

"No," Woolman said.

"To sit on a jury?"

"No."

"To hold public office?"

"No."

"To join the armed forces?"

"No."

"To even carry a firearm?"

"No."

"As a matter-of-fact, you can't even walk the streets, can you?"

"Well, not right now."

"But you'd like to wouldn't you?"

"Sure. Who wouldn't?"

"Tell the jury what you're presently in jail for."

"Assault with a deadly weapon."

"And?"

"Possession of a firearm."

"By a convicted felon," Clay added. "The one you weren't supposed to be carrying in the first place, isn't that right?"

"Yes, sir."

"Now, Mr. Woolman, what you really are is a concerned criminal, aren't you, sir?"

"I suppose."

"And you're concerned about when you're going to be back out on the street, aren't you?"

"There ain't nothing wrong with that."

"Did Mr. Rowland promise to have you back out on the street if you came in here and testified against Harco Brewton?"

"No, sir," Woolman said loudly.

Clay sensed he'd been prepared for that question. "Did Mr. Rowland or anybody make you any promise of leniency, if you testified?"

"No!"

Clay was puzzled. Woolman couldn't lie about this right in front of Rowland and his staff. What he was saying must be so. Damn. Just then he heard, "Psssst, psssst." Solomon motioned with his head for Clay to come over to the table.

"You're asking him the wrong question. Ask him if he expects some sort of consideration from the D.A. for doing him a favor. They never promise them anymore. They just hint."

Clay turned back around to face the witness. "Excuse me, Mr. Woolman. Mr. Solomon tells me I'm asking you the wrong question. Didn't Mr. Rowland or someone from his office place you in Mr. Brewton's cell and ask you to find out what you could from him?"

"Well, he asked me to keep my ears open."

"No sir. My question was, didn't he purposely put you in the cell with Mr. Brewton with instructions to pump him for information?"

"Yes."

"You don't strike me as the kind of person who just gets ordered about, Mr. Woolman. Am I right?"

"You're close."

"You had to agree to do this, didn't you? I mean, it was a favor to Mr. Rowland, wasn't it?"

"I guess so."

"And, as a favor, you expected to get something in return, didn't you?"

"Well, you know how it is. You scratch my back, and I'll scratch yours."

"Isn't freedom the thing that you want most?"

"I'd say so. Yeah."

"Did you think you had a better chance of getting it if you pleased Mr. Rowland than if you disappointed him?"

"Well, yeah."

"Didn't you simply make up Mr. Brewton's confession to make Mr. Rowland really happy and increase your chances of walking, Mr. Woolman?"

"No."

With that Clay turned to Armbrister and said, "May we have this witness sworn, your Honor?"

Rowland, taken completely by surprise, stood up and said, "But he's already been sworn."

"Well, it's obviously worn off, and I think he should be sworn again," Clay said.

"Objection!" Rowland said. "That's totally uncalled for. Mr. Delaney can't comment on the witness like that. I want that struck and Mr. Delaney admonished, your Honor."

"Objection sustained," Armbrister announced. "The jury will disregard Mr. Delaney's comments on the credibility of the witness. Mr. Delaney, save that for your closing argument."

"Yes, your Honor. I most certainly will. Mr. Woolman, do you expect the jury to believe that Harco Brewton confessed his sins to a stranger?"

"Yes."

"Why should they believe it?"

"Because it's true."

"Do honest people tell the truth?"

"Yes, they do."

"What about dishonest people? Do they tell the truth?"

"Sometimes."

"Would you be honest with this jury and tell them whether you are an honest or a dishonest person."

Woolman hesitated.

"Look them in the eye, Mr. Woolman, and tell them."

Woolman continued staring blankly at Clay.

"Okay. Let's do it the hard way. Are you a burglar?"

"Yes."

"Are you a thief?"

"Yes."

"A robber?"

"Yes."

"A forger?"

"Yes, Yes."

"Now tell them. Are you an honest or a dishonest person?"

"Dishonest, Mr. Delaney. Dishonest!"

"And you only tell the truth sometimes? Isn't that right?"

Woolman didn't answer.

Clay waited a bit then continued, "If we had to bet someone's life on whether this was one of those times, would that be a safe bet, Mr. Woolman?"

Woolman sat there in cold silence.

"I have nothing else for this witness," Clay said, as he walked away to take his seat.

"But he didn't answer the last two questions," Rowland said.

"Yes he did. Loud and clear."

Armbrister took long lunch recesses, which made Clay happy. He rarely ate lunch when he was on trial, so he used the time to get honed for the afternoon. This time, however, Callie cornered him. "Take me to lunch."

Clay protested but lost, mainly because she said she had some information on the State's psychology expert, Dr. Franklin Willett. Clay realized that he had to hear it now. He suspected Dr. Willett would be Rowland's next witness.

They found a table at a nearby delicatessen, and Callie told Clay everything she'd learned about Dr. Willett, not only from his writings but also from practicing psychologists who'd studied under him. Callie had even read and summarized some of his former students' old classroom notes.

"Apparently, he loves the psychology of the criminal mind," she said, "and refers to it often in his lectures. It's common knowledge that his advanced psychology courses invariably have a criminal psych question on the final exam."

"Does he have a pet theme or thesis that dominates his thinking in that area?"

She flipped open a notebook lying on the table in front of her. "Yes. His theory of the 'environmental imperative' is that a poor environment reasonably predicts future criminal behavior."

Delany pecked halfheartedly at his sandwich. "Anything else?"

"Yes," Callie said, referring again to her notes. "He teaches that if you expose criminal behavior to what he terms 'ultra violent light,' the emotions that precipitated the crime will shine through like fingerprints."

"That's good work," Clay said. "Thank you."

She held up her hand. "Wait. There's more. I've noticed that he hasn't written anything in years. He seems to have lost his research discipline. The word is that all his lectures are canned and predictable. It appears that since he's become the tenured head of the department, he no longer has the stomach for hard work or long hours."

"Were you able to find out anything about his work as a consultant in legal matters?"

"Only that he does a lot of it nowadays, both civil and criminal. From what I gather, though, he rides out on his reputation and stays in the saddle by simply dodging bullets. They say he's well spoken and very distinguished looking."

Clay got to his feet. "That it?"

"Not quite. You should know that he's generally regarded as intellectually honest." Callie smiled. "Oh, yes. He likes roses."

Clay thanked her, wiped some crumbs from the corner of his mouth, kissed her on the cheek and said he had to get to a phone, and would see her in the courtroom. At the deli door he turned around, rubbed his thumb and index finger together, pointed to the cash register and smiled. Callie nodded, returned the smile and gave him a "shoo" sign with the back of her hand.

Clay called Lane Morgan. He didn't want to talk law. He wanted to talk roses. He wanted a common denominator to keep in his pocket should he ever need it when examining Dr. Willett. Morgan couldn't supply it, but his wife Catherine could, and did. Satisfied, Clay went back to work.

Since he'd learned the vicious truth about Harco, Clay spent no time at all with him. Though they sat side by side, the only interaction between them was when Clay needed to check on the accuracy of one of Rowland's witnesses. Those too few times were still too much for Clay, but they were enough to give the appearance that nothing was amiss. Not even Harco suspected anything. The strain of controlling his hatred and revulsion and maintaining his composure was slowly taking its toll on Clay. He had to stay in constant mental motion to keep his feelings at bay. Whenever he slowed for just an instant, anger began to nibble around the edges of his mind. He never looked up from his notes when Harco returned from lunch.

Clay was right about Rowland's order of witnesses. There'd been a very logical pattern to his presentation thus far. Every material moment in time was recorded by testimonial snapshots that Rowland was pasting in the jury's mental scrapbook. Once all the pages were complete, the jury could review it from front to back or back to front, and understand it. There was a simple thoroughness that Clay appreciated, and feared.

The only possible remaining witnesses had to be Dr. Willett and Celeste Lindsey. Clay figured Willett would be next. He'd provide motive to tie Harco emotionally to the crime. Carrie's mother would come on last for sympathy and effect.

If anything, Callie's sources had understated Willett's manner and demeanor. There was an aura of competence that swirled around him, and was complemented by his frank speech and gray-haired handsomeness. When it all connected, it sent a clear message of trustworthiness: the most desired quality in any witness.

Clay had been hoping for a hired gun: someone whose opinion was headed for a predestined result, irrespective of the facts. Many times an alert jury would pick up on the illogic required to get there, and would see right through the expert for hire. Clay also knew that the sad truth about any trial was that even an honest witness could get to the same result through the use of different facts. Or, simply through a legitimate difference of well-intended opinions.

Clay attempted to concede Dr. Willett's expertise in psychology in order to keep Rowland from examining him about his education, teaching experiences, honors and awards. But Rowland wasn't buying any concessions now. It was a slick move by Clay in trying to finesse testimony about Willet's distinguished career, but it was equally slick of Rowland to turn him down. The jurors heard it all and were impressed. So was Clay.

With Willett's expertise established, Rowland adroitly fed him all the sordid facts that Woolman had established about Harco's formative years, and asked Willett to assume they were true. He then asked Willett if he would show to the jury, then comment on, statements made by Harco on a video of the TV interview he'd given some weeks before.

The courtroom lights dimmed, and a grinning, larger-than-life Harco suddenly appeared before the jury. The chipped white painted bars of the jail made a perfect backdrop for his face and his attitude. The next five minutes was a sneering diatribe of women in general, as Harco unconvincingly denied the off-camera newscaster's questions about his involvement in the rape and murder of Carrie Lindsey. This showing, however, didn't enjoy the benefit of a censor's bleep.

The jury was transfixed by the video, but no more so than Clay. He sat in the darkness, half dreaming that Harco's face was centered in the electronic gunsight of a Heads Up Display. One twenty millimeter cannon round, he thought, would turn his head into a fine, red mist. One full burst and they would find just enough of Harco to bait a hook. Wouldn't that be the ticket, Clay thought, to take Harco fishing. Probably the only thing that would take him would be a carp. They'd eat anything.

Clay snapped out of his morbid daydream with the return of light to the room. With the TV off, all eyes were turned to Harco. Like most bugs, he didn't do well in bright light. His reaction to scrutiny was always the same: a hung head and a tucked tail—what Clay's dad had always referred to as a suck-egg dog. Much as he wanted to see Harco suffer in the spotlight, Clay was still locked in deadly combat with Rowland. So he did the only thing he could: he spilled his glass of water. The moving of papers and the sopping broke the tension and diverted the jury's gaze to Solomon and himself.

Rowland was soon interrogating Willett again, this time soliciting his comments on Harco's psyche and his underlying motivation to kill Carrie Lindsey. Rowland had positioned himself so that the jury could not see him and Willett at the same time. This allowed the jury to focus entirely on Willett, who seemed to be carrying on a conversation with them.

"From everything we know about Harco Brewton's background and from what we can see on the videotape," Willett said, "he's a classic misogynist."

Several jurors nodded their agreement.

"What in particular has brought you to that conclusion, Doctor?"

"Well, for one thing, his background reads like a textbook on the subject. He had a childhood devoid of any parental love and tenderness. He was sexually exploited by his aunt and abandoned by his mother at a tender age and had to make it on his own."

"What else?"

"His background alone is sufficient to support my diagnosis. But the video we just saw is like an office visit. It's real-time information. On it, we could see and hear Mr. Brewton's resentment for his mother modulate rather quickly into hatred for women in general."

"Can you give us some idea of the intensity of that hatred, Dr. Willett?"

"From what I saw, it's the kind of hatred that easily transforms into rage—the kind of rage that requires a victim for relief."

Clay sat up straight in his chair and made a note.

"Are you telling us that Harco Brewton hates his mother?"

"No. I'm not saying that at all. He's emotionally incapable of consciously hating her. But he does harbor significant resentment, and that explains why he's moved to take out his strongest feelings on women as a gender. To his subconscious, the group manifests all that's wrong with one of its number. Since he can't bring himself to hate the one, he turns those feelings against the group from which she came."

"Earlier you described his rage as the kind that needs a victim for relief. Would you explain that."

"Certainly. His way of dealing with the rage that builds up within him would be through physical harm. Symbolically, it would take the form of sexual violation. This is a classic reaction to the level of strength of his feelings—a level that was quite evident on the tape. Such sexual violation would be his way of regaining control, getting even, or punishing, and releasing the pressure of such a large emotional boil."

Clay wrote rapidly for a moment, then leaned back.

"Doctor Willett," Rowland continued, "is it your opinion that Harco Brewton had ample motive to rape and kill a young girl like Carrie Lindsey?"

"Yes. There's absolutely no question in my mind about it."

When Rowland finished with him, Dr. Willett owned the courtroom. Everything he said had been absorbed and accepted by anyone who heard it—including Clay—because it was so obviously true. It just wasn't complete. Dr. Willett had ended where Callie had started. No question that Harco was motivated to murder women. The ultimate issue, however, was whether he'd murdered this one.

Clay knew that cross-examining Willett was going to be like walking through a minefield. He had Harco pegged just right. A lot depended on whether Willett had been asked simply to supply Rowland with evidence of motive, or whether he'd been asked to go further and try to tie Harco specifically to the crime. He'd seen no indication of the latter in Willett's testimony, and Harco had already been tied to the crime in so many other ways before Willett ever came along. If he was wrong, he'd play hell getting any concessions out of Willett. But if he was right, he could use Willett's own credibility to prove Callie's point.

Lane Morgan had taught him that the best way to prove a point was out of the mouth of the other guy's witness, especially if the witness was as effective as Willett. But the principle wasn't reserved for lawyers. "Use their own strength to defeat them," he could hear his Navy preflight drill instructor say, as he introduced his class to judo.

The thing Clay loved about the courtroom was its humanity. It was life in microcosm. It was a place of human conflict, and a place that lent itself perfectly to the application of simple precepts of everyday living from the real world just outside the double doors. The lawyer who forgot that, more often than not, was called the appellant.

Rowland was interested in seeing how Delaney would handle Dr. Willett. To his credit, he was beginning to enjoy watching Delaney ply his craft. True, he didn't always understand where Clay was going with a witness, or what he had in mind, but he had to admit that the case had taken a few unusual turns because of Delaney's unique approach. He was slowly beginning to believe that Armbrister's accusations might very well be a bum rap.

"I now know why your students hold you in such high regard, Dr. Willett," Clay said. "Your skill as a teacher is quite evident."

"Why, thank you," Willett replied.

Rowland stiffened. As before, he had no idea where Delaney was going, but he didn't like it already. He could see Willett relaxing. That wasn't good. He had told him to stay on guard and not let Delaney lead him down a blind alley. "Beware of Irishmen bearing gifts," he doodled on his legal pad.

"Do you enjoy teaching?" Clay asked.

"Yes, I really do."

"In a way, have you been teaching us today?"

"Now that you put it that way, I guess I have been," Willett said with a smile.

"Would it be safe for me to presume that the reason you became a teacher was to impart knowledge to others?"

"That was the main reason, yes."

"In your mind, is there a relationship between knowledge and accuracy, Dr. Willett?"

"Yes, there's a direct relationship. Information that lacks accuracy isn't knowledge at all."

"Like two times two equals five?"

"Right."

"You'd never teach that."

"Of course not."

"Do you attribute some measure of your success as a teacher to your personal desire to be accurate?"

"Yes, I do."

"Dr. Willett, would you please tell the jury what 'environmental imperative' means?"

Willett turned and looked at Rowland, who simply shrugged his shoulders. He then turned his face back toward Clay. "I see you've been talking to some of my students,"

"Yes, very accurately trained ones, I might add."

"Is this going to be a case of the student teaching the teacher, Mr. Delaney?"

"No sir. It's a case of reverence and respect for one's mentor."

Willett thought for a moment, then said, "Environmental imperative. Let's see. That's my way of expressing the theory that certain characteristics of one's early childhood environment directly impact one's social behavior in later years."

Rowland began to take notes for the first time.

"By social behavior, aren't you specifically referring to antisocial or criminal behavior?"

"Yes, I am."

"And you've applied that theory here in this courtroom today—when you analyzed the childhood of Mr. Brewton?"

"That's correct."

"The first premise of that theory is that Mr. Brewton's relationship—or lack of relationship—with his mother made him prone to certain criminal behavior in his future?"

"That's true."

"And once you'd theorized that, you concluded from his actual statements on TV that his anger had gotten to the boiling point. Is that a fair summary of your analysis?"

"Very fair, Mr. Delaney."

"Then, Dr. Willett, you went one step further and told us that physical harm coupled with sexual violation of women was Mr. Brewton's way of dealing with his pent up rage. Is that correct?"

"Yes, it is."

Rowland was at a loss to understand where Delaney was taking the witness. Everything Willett had said in response to Delaney's questions seemed to dig Harco a deeper hole.

Idly toying with the porn magazine that Detective Figuroa had identified and left laying on the clerk's desk, Clay said, "Would you please tell the jury what objective evidence you relied on for that last conclusion."

Willett smiled and relaxed even more. "The objective evidence, Mr. Delaney, is that magazine in your hand."

Rowland smiled. He knew Clay would step on a mine sooner or later.

"This magazine?" Clay said.

"Yes."

"Would you explain to the jury what you're talking about?" Clay handed the magazine to Willett.

"Firstly," Willett said, switching back into his teaching voice.

Before he could continue, Rowland stood up. "May he step down in front of the jury, your Honor?" he said, trying to interfere and make Willett's testimony more dramatic for his side of the case.

"You may step down, Professor," Armbrister responded magnanimously.

Willett stepped up to the jury rail, held the open magazine up to the jury, apologized profusely for its contents, then said, "The first indication that Mr. Brewton is relating to his mother is the fact that he has blackened the faces of all the…the models. As I've said before, he couldn't face her. To do that would be to admit his extreme anger at her, which he's emotionally incapable of doing. But objective proof of his need for violence and sexual spoliation is found in the slashing of all the female private parts—clearly indicating that he needs this form of release, and clearly substantiating a personal motive to rape and kill the likes of little Carrie Lindsey."

"What you've just pointed out to the jury isn't theory, is it, Dr. Willett? It's more like physical evidence left behind by Harco Brewton, isn't it?"

"Most certainly."

"We could almost view them as we would fingerprints, couldn't we?"

"Yes, we could," Willett agreed.

"As a matter-of-fact, we could consider these 'emotional fingerprints,' couldn't we?"

"My, my. You have done your homework, Mr. Delaney. Yes, these are emotional fingerprints. No question about it."

While standing beside Willett, Clay shuffled through his papers until he came to a document labeled "Autopsy," and fumbled with it long enough for Willett to see the legend. "Dr. Willett," Clay said, "if you don't mind, would you please return to the witness stand?"

Willett complied, and Clay studied the report in front of him. Rowland strained to see what it was, but couldn't.

"Am I correct in assuming that the kind of fingerprints Mr. Brewton would leave behind on a victim of his rage would be…" Clay flipped the first page of the report over and read, "Facial features totally blackened by what appears to be a mud mixture."

"Oh, yes," Willett replied quickly.

Rowland began frantically searching for a file folder as Clay continued. Solomon looked puzzled and did the same.

"Left nipple severed from breast—not recovered for analysis."

"Definitely," Willett replied.

"Four longitudinal incisions and three lateral incisions across right breast, ranging from ten to twelve centimeters in length."

"Yes."

"Vaginal wall perforated by sharp instrument on both left and right sides."

"Yes."

"Remnants of what appeared to be an oak stick broken off and lodged in posterior wall of vagina."

"That's it exactly," Willett stated loudly.

Rowland located his folder containing the report of the Lindsey autopsy. He leafed quickly through it, then laid it on the table. He didn't know whose autopsy Delaney had just read to Dr. Willett, but he knew it wasn't Carrie Lindsey's.

Clay wiped his eyes, cleared his throat, and continued. "Are you saying that the very same compelling emotions that would drive Mr. Brewton to kill a female victim would also drive him to sexually mutilate her as well?"

"Yes, I am."

"It's all part of the relief he needs, and the two are so bound together that he couldn't separate them, could he?"

"No, he couldn't."

"From what you've told us then, the sexual mutilation is an integral part of his need to punish his own mother vicariously for what she did to him. And without it he'd have no motive to kill, would he?"

"I'd think not."

"Dr. Willett, would you please step back down in front of the jury rail?"

When Willett was back down front, Clay handed him all the photographs. "These are all the crime scene and autopsy photos of Carrie Lindsey. Would you please study them and then point out to the jury any emotional fingerprints that belong to Harco Brewton."

The jury watched with anticipation and waited expectantly.

Willett flipped quickly through the photos. A strange look came over his face. He went through them again, slowly, one at a time. He backed up two or three photos, then continued forward. When he finished he handed them slowly back to Clay. "I don't see any," he said softly.

"I didn't hear you," Clay said. "Would you repeat your answer please."

"I don't see any," Willett said much louder.

The jury had heard him, but they were busy poring over the photos that were now being passed around the jury box.

Clay let them finish looking, then, without allowing Willett to retreat to the relative safety of the witness stand, said, "Now, Dr. Willett, would you put your professional reputation behind the conclusion that Harco Brewton killed Carrie Lindsey?"

Willett hesitated, looked around, then replied, "It's still possible, of course."

"All things are possible," Clay responded, "but are you willing to stake your entire career on a mere possibility?"

"I'd rather not."

"I gather, then, that you wouldn't stake your life on a mere possibility either."

"I think that goes without saying, Mr. Delaney."

"Would you stake Mr. Brewton's life on a mere possibility?"

"Objection, your Honor," Rowland exclaimed, rising to his feet.

"I withdraw the question," Clay said. "Thank you, Dr. Willett. You've been most instructive. I have nothing further."

As Dr. Willett walked slowly toward the refuge offered by the courtroom door, Judge Armbrister recessed for the day to attend a judicial conference.

"Court will resume at nine-thirty tomorrow morning," the bailiff announced.

CHAPTER 15

▼

Clay stayed on in the courtroom long after Harco was led away, long after the courtroom had cleared of players and spectators. Solomon had something else to do, and Callie had to catch up with Mattie. Clay sat alone at his table, desperately trying not to unravel. More than anything else, he needed the soothing touch of time, that great healer. The events surrounding the brutal revelations of Harco happened so quickly, giving him no opportunity to deal with the enormity of his discovery. At a time when he'd been emotionally floored, he was required to be physically on his feet in a courtroom.

Clay knew he'd come close to breaking down. He'd tried to steel his mind for the beating he knew he'd take while reading a secret account of Chelsea's pain and agony to the unsuspecting Willett. It didn't work. It seemed his mind had a heart of its own.

He also had come as close as he ever would to trying Harco Brewton for the murder of his daughter. It was an odd sensation, secretly trying the very heart of his case against Harco within the body of someone else's case against him. But doing it was vitally necessary to the trial at hand. And, surprisingly, it served as a catharsis for Clay. Without really understanding why, he felt some sense of release. The pressure within him had vented slightly. Maybe it was the opportunity of standing in the room where justice could be found and being allowed to ask openly about motivations behind a crime he couldn't understand. Maybe it was the confirmation, if to no one but himself, and Chelsea if she was watching, of the nature of the beast that had ravaged their lives. Maybe it was simply dealing with the stark reality of truth. Whatever it was, it had a calming effect on Clay.

He felt bad about what he had to do to Dr. Willett, but it was right, and necessary. Seldom did one hit the bull's-eye of one target while aiming at a completely different one. An apology would be inappropriate, but an explanation would be in order someday. He had no idea if that day would ever come. If it didn't, neither Dr. Willett nor anyone else would ever know how right Willett really was in being wrong.

When he finally stirred and looked around, shadows were lengthening across the room. It was time to go.

Clay took a long time getting home. A stop by the office to read selected mail and give a few directions slowed him considerably. It also put him in the death throes of rush hour in Atlanta, an unusual event for him. He normally avoided it altogether. Working late enabled him to miss it. It was considered a perk of working for a large law firm.

On entering his kitchen, he saw the message button of his answering machine flickering. It was Callie. Mattie wasn't there when she got home. He called. As they talked, Fraidy appeared and sidled up against his leg.

"Hold on," he said, "I'll bet she's here. Isn't she, Fraidy?"

Laying the phone down, he looked through the great room and spied Mattie seated on the deck.

"She is," Clay said.

"I'll come get her," Callie replied.

Clay hung up and headed for the deck with Fraidy in trail. The sliding door was open. Mattie's back was to him. Her arms were folded across her chest. He called her name. No answer. Again. Still no answer. As he approached, he could hear her singing softly to herself as she rocked back and forth. Clay was right next to her, calling her name. No response.

Stepping in front of her, he noticed a far away look in her eyes. Then he saw a thin trickle of blood running down each forearm and dripping slowly off her elbows into her lap, where it saturated her white shorts.

"Mattie," he cried. "What is it? What—what's happened to you?"

Mattie stirred and seemed to return to reality. "Oh, hi, Mr. Delaney," she said, as if nothing was wrong. "I found my friend."

Clay gingerly pulled her arms from across her chest, and carefully removed from her tight grasp the silver framed photograph of Chelsea. Its broken glass had sliced into Mattie's fingertips as she clutched it to her breast.

"That's my little red-haired friend, Mr. Delaney. I didn't know where she went after Harco was so mean to her. I've been looking all over for her. Do you know her, Mr. Delaney?" Mattie said.

Her innocence broke his heart. One more time—and just when he thought he was over the worst of it.

"Yes. I did once, Mattie," Clay struggled to say. "But that was a long time ago. "Did you know her, too?"

"She was my friend."

Clay pulled a handkerchief from his pocket, ripped it in two, and tightly wrapped each of Mattie's hands to stop the bleeding. He then took her into a bathroom and began to clean and dress her cuts.

By that time, Callie had arrived and took over the bandaging. Clay explained that Mattie had cut her hands on the glass, then excused himself to get on the phone to his former mother-in-law.

"Gran," he said, "this is Clay. Just fine, how're you doing? Listen, the little neighbor girl who disappeared with Chelsea, did they ever find her? They didn't? What was her name? Matilda. Did she have a nickname? Mattie? Oh, no reason, just curious. Look, I'll try to explain later. Got to go now. Love you too. Bye."

Clay returned to the bathroom. "She was there," he said to Callie.

"What?"

"When Chelsea was killed, Mattie was a witness. Harco took two little girls that day. He killed one and must've kept the other one to torture. Mattie was the one he kept."

"Clay, I'm so sorry. But what are we going to do with her?"

"Keep her safe. That's all we can do for now. She's the only link between Harco and Chelsea. No wonder he's been hiding her from everybody, especially Rowland. Maybe she'd better stay here. Why don't the two of you move over here until this is all over? After that, we can decide how to get her safely back to her family."

"All right. I'll go get our things."

Later that evening, when Mattie was settled for the night, Callie and Clay stood shoulder to shoulder at the deck rail, looking up at the stars.

"When she was born," he said, "it was as if a delicate little star had fallen to earth and landed on my doorstep. And when I lost her, I tried to convince myself that she'd simply returned to her rightful place in the heavens. I know that sounds hokey, but it surely makes the night sky more beautiful to me, thinking that she's twinkling away up there somewhere."

"It's not hokey. It's a lovely thought. And what if some little child makes a wish on her?" Callie said, kissing him on the cheek.

He smiled. "I'd like that."

When the trial resumed, there seemed to be an undercurrent of excitement running through the courtroom. Members of the press had stationed themselves on the courthouse steps, trying to intercept any of the participants. Clay avoided them by coming in the back door. A few reporters had been hanging around from the first day, but now their number had doubled, and they'd become more aggressive. Harco Brewton's notoriety had edged up a notch. But more than that, the word was out that Celeste Lindsey was next up.

She was lithe, tanned, and her short blonde hair had bleached even more so by the sun. The predominantly female jury would react more to her motherhood than to her looks, Clay thought. But that was okay. That's the way it should be.

Rowland was at his very best, plucking every heartstring with a piteous touch. Celeste Lindsey had lost her only child. She'd scrubbed her, groomed her, put her in a frilly sundress and sent her bouncing off to middle school. She came back in a black body bag.

When it was Clay's turn, he handled her as gently as he could.

"Ms. Lindsey," he said, "we all sympathize with your loss."

"How could you, unless you've lost a child of your own?" she said stiffly.

"Yes ma'am," Clay said politely, stifling his desire to scream out that he had. "Maybe some of these ladies and gentlemen have. Let's not brush them aside so easily."

"I'm sorry, Mr. Delaney. You're right. Thank you for your concern."

"We can't return Carrie to you. God knows we all would if we could. But we can explore with you who may've been responsible for your loss. Would you allow us to do that?"

Clay's statements to Celeste Lindsey weren't proper examination, but they were so reasonable and sensitive Clay knew he'd get away with it because Rowland would be afraid to object.

"Yes," she said.

Clay walked over to where Harco was seated and placed his hand on Harco's shoulder. "Ms. Lindsey, do you believe that Harco Brewton killed your daughter?"

An uneasy hush settled over the courtroom.

"Yes!"

Rowland smiled and shook his head from side to side.

"Should this jury find him guilty and sentence him to death, based on what you know?"

"I don't know what you mean, Mr. Delaney."

"Let me put it this way," Clay said as he left Harco and walked over close to the jury rail. "Tell this jury what you personally know about Mr. Brewton."

Celeste hesitated for a moment. "I don't have any personal knowledge about him."

"Tell the jury where all your information about him came from."

"It came from Mr. Rowland." She nodded toward Rowland with her head.

"Did Mr. Rowland ever tell you that he had any personal knowledge about Mr. Brewton?"

"No. He never did."

"Where did Mr. Rowland's knowledge come from?"

"Several witnesses."

"Did Mr. Rowland tell you before you testified today that all those witnesses have already told what they know to this jury?"

"Yes. He said that."

"Have you ever talked to any of those witnesses?"

"No, I haven't."

"Do you know what they told this jury?"

"No. I do not."

"Under those circumstances, would you agree that this jury has a better idea of what all the facts are than you do?"

"You could say that, yes."

Clay moved away from the jury and approached the witness stand. He stood looking up a Celeste until their eyes met. His voice was calm and deliberate. "Do you believe that I killed your daughter, Ms. Lindsey?"

She recoiled and seemed to catch her breath. "No, I don't." A puzzled look came over her, and she kept her eyes on Clay's face.

"If Mr. Rowland told you I did, would you believe it?"

She thought for a moment before she answered. "It would all depend on the facts."

"But you don't know what facts have been given to this jury, do you?"

"No, I don't."

Clay turned and walked toward his table, asking his next question as he moved away from her. "Do you want the person who killed your daughter brought to justice?"

"Of course," she said quickly.

He turned back to face her. "Even if it was me?"

"Even you."

"Are you willing to allow the ones who have all the facts to make that determination?"

"I guess I'm going to have to."

"And that's the right thing to do, isn't it?"

"Yes, it is."

"Thank you. Now, Ms. Lindsey, since Carrie went into the eighth grade, hadn't you noticed some definite changes about her?"

"Well, she was growing up and becoming a young lady, if that's what you mean."

"Yes ma'am. But hadn't her taste in clothes changed?"

"Some, yes."

"Hadn't she started looking at fashion magazines and selecting both outer and inner wear based on what was considered chic?"

"To some degree."

"And you helped her?"

"Yes."

"What about makeup? Where did her knowledge of makeup come from?"

"Well, I treated her to a make over at the mall once, and then we bought some basic things, and we would work on it at home."

"Along with her change in taste in clothes and her new interest in makeup, didn't she also simultaneously develop an interest in boys?"

"What are you getting at, Mr. Delaney?"

"An accurate picture of your daughter, Ms. Lindsey. Would you help me?"

"If you are implying—"

"I'm implying nothing. I simply want you to describe to this jury the young lady you sent off to school on the morning of April third. Will you do that?"

"Yes sir."

Clay's voice suddenly became soft and gentle. He wanted to avoid the tone of an accusation. "Had she become interested in boys, Ms. Lindsey?"

"Yes, she had," Celeste Lindsey said reluctantly.

"As a matter-of-fact, her after-school behavior had changed significantly, had it not?"

"Somewhat."

"She wanted to spend more and more of her time with them, didn't she?"

Celeste looked away. "Yes."

"To the exclusion of her girlfriends?"

"To some degree."

"Did you know she was hanging out at the Zip 'N Mart?"

Rowland rose to his feet to object, but Celeste waved him off. "Yes. I was having a difficult time dealing with that. It was too soon. I tried to stop it."

"She should've still been playing with dolls, shouldn't she?"

"Yes."

"Ms. Lindsey, did you throw Carrie's rag-doll away?"

"No, Mr. Delaney. I couldn't have done that."

"Did she?"

"I don't know."

"Could she have?"

Celeste looked down at her hands folded in her lap and replied softly, "It's
possible."

"Thank you, Ms. Lindsey. I have no more questions."

The State's case against Harco Brewton ended shortly after Ms. Lindsey's testimony. It survived a perfunctory motion for acquittal, and Clay was on.

Clay had only two witnesses: Betty Sturgis, the manager of Harco's rooming
house in Montgomery, and Dr. Aubrey Brice, a meteorological consultant to the
National Oceanic and Atmospheric Administration's Climatalogical Research
Center in Asheville, North Carolina. Ms. Sturgis was home, mother, and apple
pie. Dr. Brice was Santa Claus in a rumpled, light-blue seersucker suit. Both witnesses took Rowland by surprise and set him back on his heels.

Ms. Sturgis told the jury that Harco had lived in her rooming house in Montgomery from January until he failed to show up again after the third week in
April. She presumed that he'd abandoned his room. She didn't know he'd been
arrested.

Rowland couldn't shake her. She knew nothing about a room in Atlanta. As
she put it, "He was in Montgomery all the time, why would he want to pay for a
room over here?"

One of Rowland's assistants left the courtroom after Ms. Sturgis testified, and
Clay assumed he was on his way to make contact with Ms. Gladdie. So be it.

Dr. Brice testified that a study of all available weather data, including radar
and satellite photos, showed no rainfall whatsoever in Georgia from the middle of
March until the middle of May. Except for central and south Florida, the only
rainfall in the southeastern states during that period resulted from some heavy
thunderstorms that developed along the Gulf Coast, and moved northward
through Alabama and on into Tennessee on April third. Heavy rain was reported

in Montgomery in the morning hours of April third, and Dr. Brice showed a twelve hour segment of radar photos compressed into a five minute video, depicting the build-up and passage of those thunderstorms, with emphasis on the time they passed over Montgomery. None of them touched the state of Georgia.

Rowland tried unsuccessfully to exclude Dr. Brice's testimony on relevance grounds, but Clay argued that Rowland himself had injected the issue of Harco's disputed presence in Montgomery on April third into the case. The evidence was relevant to that issue when viewed in connection with the wet doll found in the rusted-out floorboard of Harco's car. Armbrister allowed it.

On cross-examination, Rowland tried to discredit Dr. Brice, but couldn't. Clay had asked him to come to court and report rainfall in the Southeast during the months in question, without telling him what it was to be used for or whom Clay represented. Clay had figured that Brice's lack of knowledge of the facts of the case, or who might benefit from his testimony, would make Dr. Brice more believable. It would prevent Rowland from claiming he was biased and simply trying to assist the one who'd engaged him. Clay avoided going into Brice's ignorance of the nature of the case during his direct examination. He surmised that Rowland would get around to it soon enough.

"In how many criminal trials have you testified for the defense, Dr. Brice?" Rowland said.

"I've never testified in a criminal trial," he said and smiled. "Hope I never have to."

Rowland scratched his head. "You hope you never have to? What do think you're doing now?"

A puzzled look came over Brice's face. "I don't understand. Is this a criminal trial?"

Rowland took several steps toward the witness box, and stopped with his hands on his hips. He looked directly at Brice. "Are you trying to tell this jury that you don't know that you're testifying for the defendant in a murder case?" Rowland looked toward the jury and rolled his eyes.

Brice sat upright and gasped, "My Lord, I had no idea." He looked quickly at Clay. "Mr. Delaney, is that so?"

A faint smile crossed Clay's face as he nodded at Brice.

Brice looked back at Rowland with wide eyes, his mouth slightly open. "Mr. Delaney just asked me to come in here and tell the jury what the weather was like in this part of the country several months ago. He never told me why he wanted it or who he represented. I had no idea this was a murder trial."

As Rowland returned to his table after being hammered by Dr. Brice's innocent competence, Solomon chuckled and said to him as he took his seat, "You know, I learn something new everyday. Don't you?"

"Oh, shut up," Rowland said.

Clay knew that Rowland was disappointed to hear him announce that he rested his case. He knew Rowland thought there was a good chance Harco would take the stand to claim his innocence, and try to establish his alibi. Rowland had tried to tempt him to put Harco up when he called Harco's buddy, Marcus Bowman, to testify about the failed alibi attempt. But, Clay wasn't biting.

Clay presumed that Rowland had prepared well for Harco, and was itching to unload on him. But, he wasn't going to let it happen. Rowland was going to have to come up with something else. Clay wasn't surprised when Rowland asked for and got a short recess, then announced to Armbrister that he had something in rebuttal. Rowland advised the court that he wanted to present evidence to rebut Delaney's attempt to infer that Harco was in Montgomery on April third. Armbrister allowed it over Clay's objection.

Clay expected Gladdie to appear in court. Instead it was Detective Figuroa. Figuroa identified a Zip 'N Mart sales receipt he found in the back of Harco's car, dated April third at time thirteen-thirty, which Figuroa explained was one thirty in the afternoon. A murmur ran through the room, and several reporters exited the rear door.

On cross, Clay got Figuroa to admit that at one-thirty in the afternoon on April third, Carrie Lindsey was still in class. But as Figuroa pointed out, while it didn't show that the purchase was made when Harco was in the store with Carrie, it did show that Harco was in the Atlanta area that afternoon and not in Montgomery, as it had been insinuated.

Clay halfheartedly returned the receipt to Rowland as he made his way back to the defense table. The receipt didn't make it to Rowland's hand and fell to the floor. Having been blistered by Solomon time and time again, Rowland retaliated with his own smart comment, "Don't be a litterbug, Mr. Delaney."

The remark hit Clay right between the eyes. Yes. Oh, yes. "Don't be a litterbug, Daddy," rang in his ears. The bag. The paper bag he never removed from the back of his car. The one with the empty diet drink can and cracker wrappers in it. There should also be a receipt in there too from a Zip 'N Mart in Montgomery.

He could turn this around. All he needed was some time. Clay sent Solomon out with instructions to retrieve a brown paper bag and its contents from the back of his car, and then go make a purchase, any purchase, at a Zip 'N Mart, any Zip 'N Mart. He had to beg Armbrister for an early lunch recess, but he got it. That was all the time he needed.

Clay compared the receipt Figuroa had identified on the witness stand with the one Solomon had retrieved from the bag in Clay's car. Except for the date and time of day, they were exactly the same. The receipt for Solomon's recently purchased cigar was slightly different. It had some numbers on it that weren't on the other two. He needed Jeff Pilcher.

Clay made a call to Zip 'N Mart's corporate office under the pretense of being Jeff Pilcher's college roommate in town for the day, and wanting to take him to lunch. He learned that Jeff was already at lunch with his father at the Phoenix Club, one of the city's most exclusive downtown clubs. Only one thing to do— go get him.

Clay wasn't a member, but in exactly thirty-two minutes he'd gone from the courthouse to the club, walked uninvited and unannounced into the main dining room, escorted Jeff Pilcher away from a Caesar salad and a stunned father, and was back in the courtroom letting him view and explain the three receipts before anyone returned.

Jeff said he would testify, but Delaney owed him lunch, and he had to call his father.

When the jury was back in the box, Clay called Jeff to the witness stand. After he was sworn and had stated his name, Clay handed him the receipt that Solomon had just obtained, and asked Jeff if he would look at it and tell the jury what it showed.

Jeff looked at it and turned to the jury. "Someone made a tobacco purchase at eleven fifty-eight this morning at the Zip 'N Mart just down the block on Pryor Street."

Rowland rose to his feet, a slight smile on his face. "I'm not sure that I really want to object, your Honor, but I would like for Mr. Delaney to share with the jury what special expertise his witness has that allows him to interpret Zip 'N Mart receipts, other than being able to read, of course."

"I'm sorry," Clay said with a wink to Solomon, "I totally overlooked that. Mr. Pilcher, would you please tell the jury what you do for a living."

"My father and my brother and I own the Zip 'N Mart Corporation."

Rowland sat down without a word.

While Rowland was still reeling, Clay handed Jeff the receipt Figuroa had identified, and asked him to do the same with it.

Jeff looked at it, then stated, "Someone made a candy and soft drink purchase at one-thirty in the afternoon on April third of this year at our store in Montgomery, Alabama."

A roar went up in the courtroom, and Armbrister began to bang for order. Rowland sat there as if he hadn't heard, then turned and whispered to his assistant.

That was all Clay had for Jeff Pilcher, and he walked over and sat down. "Lane Morgan was right," he said to Solomon. "Rowland's 'need to' was greater than his 'want to,' and he exposed his belly when he threw that receipt in. He never checked it out."

Rowland struggled to examine Jeff about where the Montgomery store was located, and when the company left Georgia, and why no one knew about it, "Except Mr. Delaney, of course." In trying his best to recover from the blow, he got Jeff to admit that, if one broke the speed limit, one could drive from the Montgomery store to the one near the Lindsey's neighborhood in approximately two hours, depending on the traffic. That was the best he could do, so he quit.

With that, the evidence at the trial of Harco Brewton concluded. All that remained were the closing arguments of counsel and after that, the court's instructions to the jury on the law they should apply.

What had always been the most exciting part of any trial, Clay now viewed with considerable dread. Summation, final argument, closing, call it what you will, he'd still have to stand in front of this jury and dedicate himself completely to the only person in the world he'd ever despised.

He knew from his considerable experience that unless one had actually been the trial lawyer on the spot, one still wouldn't know how he felt when he faced the jury for the last time. For those few moments in time, though outwardly relaxed, every fiber, every muscle and sinew were stretched taut. Every ounce of remaining energy was poised and focused. His entire being was devoted to one thing and one thing alone: winning.

When Clay finished a trial, regardless of the result, he was drained and empty. His concentration had been so intense, and he'd sacrificed so much of himself for his client, that very little remained. The biggest chunk was lost when he finally stood before the jury, revisited the evidence with them, and attempted to persuade them of the logic and rightness of his client's cause.

Dedicated advocacy took its toll, and Clay well knew it. He'd paid the price before. No matter what the outcome, when he walked out of a trial for the last time, he left pieces of himself lying on the courtroom floor. Pieces he'd never have again. He knew he had only so many left, and he hated to give one up for a son of a bitch like Harco.

When he was assigned Harco Brewton's case, he knew it would be difficult. But he had no idea at the time how difficult it was going to turn out to be. He didn't realize that when he stood before a jury and pretended to care for his client, he'd actually hate his guts. When he was fighting to save his life, he'd want to take it himself.

"Mr. Delaney," Judge Armbrister said, interrupting his thoughts, "do you wish to make a closing argument?"

Clay wanted so badly to shout, "No! Haven't I gone far enough? What more do you want out of me? When is enough, enough? Uncle, goddam it! I give up!" Instead, he quietly said, "Yes, your Honor," and walked over and faced the jury.

"When Carrie Lindsey bounced off to school Friday morning, April third," he began quietly, "she left the protection of a loving home and caring parents. As she walked innocently home that afternoon with a friend, she unknowingly was walking in death's shadow.

"In many ways she was walking much faster than her friend, for a new interest and a time honored and respected curiosity of the young beckoned to Carrie. In pursuing that interest and in satisfying that inescapable curiosity, she innocently left a place of safety with someone who enthralled her, someone she didn't fear, someone who was part of the in-crowd to which she'd begun to aspire.

"Carrie Lindsey was a beautiful woman-child, any young man's prize, immediately recognizable as desirable, as well as extremely impressionable and naive. When the 'let me show you where it's at and what it's all about' boiled down to the sordid truth, Carrie was all alone and helpless. Something instilled in her by her parents told her to say 'no' and resist, but the person she undeservedly admired wouldn't be denied, not by a child, not by a mere middle-schooler. In order to have what he wanted, he was forced to take it. In doing so, he had to resort to his overpowering strength, and Carrie Lindsey, who beat him hands-down in morality, was no match physically."

Clay heard a muted sob behind him, and saw a woman juror shift her gaze from him to the audience. He glanced toward the audience and saw Celeste Lindsey with her head bowed, being comforted by her husband. Clay turned and faced in their direction.

"If through their grief, her parents can find a moment to be proud, they'll find it in the knowledge that she died living up to their expectations."

Celeste began to sob uncontrollably. Several jurors brushed their cheeks and dabbed their eyes. Clay felt a knot rise in his throat, and knew that if he spoke now, he, too, would be choked by tears. He waited quietly for Celeste to vent her grief, and to get a grip on his own emotions. He wanted to take her in his arms and tell her that he understood, that he lived with her pain every minute of every day. When he felt that all was back under control, he faced the jury once more.

"We would all do Carrie Lindsey an unforgivable disservice if we didn't give as much of ourselves vindicating her, as she did protecting the values her parents entrusted to her.

"It would be morally wrong and a gross distortion of the ends of justice to jump to the easiest conclusion, or simply to look for the easiest way to satisfy our own need to fix blame for her death.

"While placing the blame on the wrong person would be a great injustice of its own, leaving Carrie Lindsey in her grave without vindication would be worse. Her body is certainly beyond our repair, but maybe her soul would rest in peace if she knew we cared enough about her sacrifice to bring her violator to justice— not just for vengeance, that belongs to our maker, but to give some measure of meaning to her death and to make the walk home from school safer. It seems we owe that not only to Carrie, but to our own children as well."

Several jurors nodded slightly. Clay was finely tuned to them, and knew he was on the right track. He moved closer to his counsel table and to Harco, then turned back toward the jury.

"How do we find the truth, you ask? I can't in good conscience represent that I have the answer to that question, but I do have some suggestions. Why don't we start by considering the plight of Harco Brewton, and how he came to be here.

"He stops in front of the Lindsey residence on Wednesday, April first, after Carrie Lindsey has already gone to school, and immediately becomes a suspect to a crime that was still two days and over three miles away. Little did he know that by merely stopping there, he'd set in motion a chain of circumstances that would eventually thrust him into this courtroom, fighting for his life.

"Like the rest of us, he no doubt had heard at an early age that 'one man's trash is another man's treasure.' I doubt that anyone ever told him that one man's trash could be another man's death warrant. He's since learned that from Mr. Rowland."

As Clay began reciting the evidence in his unique way, he moved about in front of the jury, but not so as to distract them—only to maintain their attention.

"Little did he know when he stopped at the nearest convenience store that same afternoon to buy some candy before returning to his room in Montgomery, Alabama, that someone who saw him there for the first and only time would give in to the insistent urging of the police and claim that he was really there two days later.

"Little did he know that anyone would claim, much less believe, that a homely, rotten-toothed, thirty-five-year-old man would attract a beautiful young lady to the point that she'd be seen allowing him to buy candy for her in front of all the high school boys she was attracted to and wanted to impress, when no girl in the world at this stage of her life would even want to be accompanied by her own father under these circumstances.

"Little did he know, while he was driving around Montgomery in the rain with a discarded doll on the floor of his car and stopping to buy more candy at the only Zip 'N Mart outside the state of Georgia, that someone would claim that he was lurking around Zip 'N Marts in Atlanta, waiting to take Carrie Lindsey's life and a doll she'd long since abandoned.

"Little did he know that all the humiliation and pain of his childhood would be revisited in great detail before you by a career criminal placed in his cell for that purpose, and then fed to the distinguished head of the Psychology Department of our state's largest university, to be interpreted for you in a desperate attempt to link him somehow to this terrible tragedy."

Clay paused, then marched directly up to Harco, where he extended an arm in his direction, the palm of his hand pointing up. What followed—though true—came from Clay's mind, not from his heart.

"Take a good look at the person you have been asked to judge, ladies and gentlemen: Harco Brewton, a pathetic creature, ugly, trashy, unloved and, at this point in his life, probably unlovable. You've heard the expression, 'he was something only a mother could love.' Sadly, Harco Brewton doesn't even fit that description. If he did, Dr. Willett wouldn't have had anything to say to you, but Mr. Rowland would've come up with some other theory.

"Take a good look—you must. You're now sitting in judgment of him. And even though his life is in your hands, the only fact proven beyond a reasonable doubt is that he buys candy at convenience stores. The only opinion given to you is that he's capable of killing. Because that capability is unfortunately so universally true in our society, our government takes candy bars out of the hands of our high school boys and replaces them with rifles.

"I trust that when you pass judgment on Harco Brewton, you won't judge him for what he is or for what he's capable of doing, but only for what he's done."

Clay realized all too well the irony of his statement. He knew what Harco had done, and he'd already passed judgment upon him for it—judgment that must remain forever silent and unexecuted. He looked at Solomon, whose eyes encouraged him to persevere.

"My other suggestion to you for finding the truth is to listen to Carrie Lindsey. She's been speaking to us. We just haven't been listening. Her message is one of quiet eloquence. What she's been saying is, 'After you've looked at Mr. Brewton, look at me. The person who killed me didn't hate me. He desired me. He didn't beat me, torture me or mutilate me. He didn't punish me or try to get even with me. He was selfish, not vicious. He didn't listen to me and wouldn't stop. That's when he hurt me. When he saw what he'd done, it was too late and he was afraid. He tried to put my clothes back in place to hide what really happened, but he didn't know what he was doing. Some of them are on inside out. He was trying not to humiliate me in death.'"

Clay handed all the photos back to the jury. "I don't want to humiliate her either, but this is the only way she can reach out to us. Take a good look. What you see is not the work of the kind of animal Dr. Willett described to you. Even he finally admitted that. It's the work of a high school kid gone too far.

"By your verdict, tell Mr. Rowland to go back to the Zip 'N Mart parking lot and find him. Find him before he does it to some other child. Harco Brewton is not guilty."

CHAPTER 16

▼

Because it was so late after the lawyers finished their final arguments and the judge had given his instructions to the jury, they retired for the evening.

When Herb Solomon returned to his office to drop off his briefcase, he knew something was wrong when he walked through the main door. Enveloped suddenly in silence as he entered, he felt as if a dozen pair of eyes were burning holes in his suit coat as he moved across the room. Gone was the normal office chatter. Gone was the sound of hundreds of keys tapping out the law and the myriad reasons why motions or bail should be granted. The lonely telephone that normally went unanswered still rang incessantly. But with all the background noise now muted, its harsh call grated on both ears and nerves.

He saw Billy Rutledge and Juanita Crowley standing beside his office door. Brushing past them, Solomon said quietly, "Come in here and shut the door." When the three were all inside, Solomon turned to them and turned his palms upwards.

Billy hung his head and didn't speak. Juanita cleared her throat and said, "One of Billy's moles told him that the Commission Chairman's been privately interviewing lawyers with criminal defense experience."

"So?" Solomon replied. "Even though I'd like to interview them myself, we can always use good help around here."

Juanita cleared her throat once more. "They were interviewing for your job. Word is that one of them was selected and has accepted. He's replacing you, Herb. I'm so sorry."

Solomon pursed his lips, thought for a moment, then laughed. "Hell, thirty years in one job can get to be a bad habit. A changing of the guard may be just what the doctor ordered to get you lazy bastards off your asses. Look at you. None of you has hit a lick since I came through that door. Now get out of here and find me some goddamn justice."

As his young charges left, Solomon sat alone for a while. He knew who was behind it and why. He knew that if he had to do it all over again, he'd still be in Armbrister's face. He also knew that when the next day rolled around, he was still going to be sitting right beside Clay Delaney.

Court resumed on time the next morning, and all that was left was the wait.

Clay never handled that well—to him it was the worst part. At that point there was nothing more he could do. Everything was out of his control. He didn't need to be in control, but he didn't like it when he had none whatsoever. This was one of those times. He'd read a part of the paper he normally ignored. Walked down to the water fountain to drink when he wasn't thirsty. Sipped old coffee from a go-cup, then went to the bathroom.

He normally avoided his clients during this part. All they wanted to do was a postmortem. That wasn't productive. A million "why didn't yous" and "what ifs" would be thrown out, and while he certainly had the time to respond, he had neither the energy nor the desire to do so. They were nervous inquiries at best, and might not even be relevant when the result was finally sounded.

But this was a first for Clay. He was protected from his own client's insistent curiosity. His client was behind bars. Maybe there was some merit in that kind of work. At least he could wait nervously without interruption.

Waiting for the verdict was a special phenomenon to be endured alone. So much hung in the balance for everyone, and no amount of talk would change a thing. At that point, he was just along for the ride. It reminded Clay of being launched from the deck of an aircraft carrier, rolling to the end of the deck, either flying or splashing into the water.

Try as he might to repress it, never far from the surface of his mind was the lingering question, Should I have done anything differently? The answer was always the same: It's still too early to tell. That's why he was waiting in the first place.

As the hours wore on, the ticking of the old courtroom clock seemed to get louder and louder. The truth of the matter was the nearly empty room got quieter and quieter. A few people came and went, but Rowland, Solomon, Clay and Callie were constants.

Good old Callie, he thought, sticking it out to the bitter end. Without her he wouldn't have had a theory at all. He knew that her contribution to this case could ultimately prove to be the difference. Without it, Harco Brewton was dead. With it, at least he had an even chance. It was that chance they were all waiting for. It was good that she was there.

The banging open of the door that led to the judge's chambers brought them all to life.

"They have a verdict," the bailiff announced through the open door. "The judge is in a meeting, and we'll hold them till he's back. In the meantime, we'll send for the defendant." He was then gone as quickly as he had appeared in the doorway.

Apparently, the word about a verdict spread quickly, for as they waited for Armbrister to return, the courtroom began to fill again, first with courthouse personnel and interested onlookers, then with the press. It wasn't long before the hallway outside was plugged with light and camera-carrying crewman, jockeying for position.

If Clay thought the wait for the verdict seemed long, the time between the bailiff's announcement and the judge's arrival was an eternity. Clay's only solace was that Harco had to sit it out too.

"All rise," the bailiff finally drawled, as Judge Armbrister burst through his door and took the bench.

"Be seated," he said to the standing audience. "Bring the jury in."

As the jury filed solemnly into the box, Clay searched their faces for a clue. Many times a jury wouldn't look at a party they'd just ruled against. They were too self-conscious and couldn't bring themselves to do it. But no clue. Nothing.

"Ladies and gentlemen, have you reached a verdict?" Armbrister inquired.

"We have, your Honor," the woman juror in the first-row seat nearest the witness stand replied.

"In the matter of the State of Georgia versus Harco Brewton, how do you find on the charge of rape with bodily harm?"

"Not guilty."

"And on the charge of murder in the first degree?"

"Not guilty."

Clay Delaney didn't hear the roar that erupted in the courtroom. He didn't see reporters race for the door. He didn't blink at the incessant flash of strobe lights in his face. He stood, transfixed and numb, realizing what he had done. Reporters and well-wishers crowded around him, patting him, trying to shake his hand, posing questions that were neither wanted nor heard.

Amid all the crush, Clay turned to Solomon and said, as the tears started down his face, "I hope Chelsea will understand."

Solomon placed his hands on Clay's shoulders. "She will. It was right what you did, Clay. You know it was. God himself will tip his hat to you someday."

Several astute reporters had singled out Harco and moved in to isolate him from Clay and Solomon. They peppered him with questions. Harco reveled in all the attention, keenly aware that his words were in demand, and made the most of it.

Harco's voice suddenly rose over the din. "Where's my lawyer? Where is he? Where's the best damn lawyer in the State of Georgia? Where is he? Let's give that boy a cigar."

Harco came pushing through the crowd until he was at Clay's back. Grabbing Clay by his left arm, Harco swung him around, shouting, "Here's my main man."

If he'd seen it, Harco would've been witness to the world's fastest right cross. But he didn't. Nor did he hear or feel the savage thunk of knuckles to jaw. Only those standing closest to Clay saw him coil and strike. Everyone else heard a sound not at home in a courtroom, and saw Harco crumple at Clay's feet like a pile of dirty laundry. They saw his eyes glaze over and a trickle of crimson form at one corner of his mouth.

Rowland's view was blocked by Solomon. "What happened?" he asked.

"Oh, not much," Solomon replied. "Some Irishman just knocked Harco Brewton on his ass. And I'll bet you dollars to doughnuts some crazy Italian's going to kick him in the ribs before he can get up."

Rowland moved out from behind Solomon just in time to see his prediction come true. As a dazed and bleeding Harco tried to rise to his feet, Clay's right foot fired out and lifted Harco's body almost completely off the floor.

By now, Armbrister was banging away at the bench, and several deputies rushed over to stop Clay. It took more deputies to hold Clay back than it did to haul Harco's limp body out into the hallway out of Clay's sight.

"What's the meaning of this, Mr. Delaney?" Armbrister demanded, his voice rising almost to a squeal.

Clay didn't answer, but kept glaring at the door Harco had disappeared through.

"I'm talking to you, counselor!"

Still physically restrained, Clay turned his head toward the judge. He never said a word. He just glared at him.

"I'm holding you in contempt, Mr. Delaney," Armbrister announced. "And, Mr. Rowland, I also want charges brought against him for assault and battery. I'll sign the papers myself. I saw everything. Bailiff, escort these officers and Mr. Delaney to the court's holding cell for transfer to the county jail. Do you have anything to say for yourself, Mr. Delaney?"

"He's now represented by counsel," Solomon interjected. "All communications should be through me. And since you're now merely a witness, there's nothing either of us would like to discuss with you."

Armbrister whirled around abruptly and left the bench without another word.

"I'm sorry, Clay," Rowland said, as he directed one of the deputies to place handcuffs on Clay. "I truly am. Not so tight damn it," he said to the officer placing on the cuffs.

As Clay was led out into the hall, several reporters clustered around. One of them stuck a microphone in Clay's face and asked, "What was that all about, Mr. Delaney?"

Clay didn't answer. Several more questions were fired at him, but he remained silent. Then during a break in the questioning, a quiet but very deliberate female voice intervened. "Was he really guilty, Mr. Delaney? Would you tell me that?"

A hush fell over the crowd in the hall. Clay turned and saw her, alone against the wall. "No, Ms. Lindsey," he said, looking her square in the eyes. "He wasn't. God as my witness, he wasn't."

"I believe you," Celeste Lindsey said, then turned and walked sadly away.

When she was gone, a burly, black deputy holding Clay said, "Then why'd you coldcock the sucker?"

"It was personal, Mr. Justice," Clay replied, reading the deputy's name tag. "Very personal."

The knot of deputies escorting Clay passed quickly through the crowd and moved down the hall toward an elevator reserved for courthouse personnel. En route they passed a bench where an EMT crew was working over a still dazed and bewildered Harco Brewton.

A look of animal fear raced across Harco's face and hid behind his eyes as Clay approached. Then he noticed the handcuffs. "Well, well, well. If this don't beat all. You boys bring me in here in cuffs and take my lawyer out in 'em. It just goes to show you. Crime don't pay. Does it, Mr. Delaney! You crazy bastard!" Harco screamed. "What did I ever do to you?"

"You back off now and get out of my prisoner's face," deputy Justice said.

But, Harco persisted and followed them down the hall, still shouting, "You boys treat him as well as y'all treated me. I wouldn't want no discrimination or nothing."

As the group passed around a corner in the hall and stopped in front of the service elevator, Harco could still be heard cursing and calling out after them. "I sure hope your lawyer's as good as mine was, Delaney. You're going to need the best, you son of a bitch."

"Excuse me," the deputy said, and disappeared back around the corner. Just as the elevator bell rang its arrival, another loud flesh-on-flesh splat resounded up the now empty hallway, and the deputy reappeared, rubbing his knuckles.

"What was that for?" Clay asked.

"It was personal, Mr. Delaney. Very personal."

Armbrister saw to it that Clay remained overnight in the holding cell, claiming that it was for the contempt of court committed in his presence. The next morning, he instructed Rowland to release Clay and advise him that Harco hadn't pressed charges, and that he wouldn't either, unless he heard of a repeat occurrence.

Rowland appeared personally to set Clay free, apologized for having to be a part of his incarceration, then asked, "Just why did you hit him, Clay?"

"That's a confidential matter between my client and me, Jason. Please just leave it at that."

"Okay. Anything you say," Rowland replied, extending his hand. "Friends?"

"Friends," Clay said, and they shook hands warmly.

"Listen," Rowland continued, "thanks for the lesson in lawyering in there. I'm open to any suggestions you might have on the Lindsey killing. I owe them that."

"You might start by looking for the un-rusted white car little Julie Felton talked about. I'll bet you'll find some high-school kid driving one. But we'll talk later. Right now I need to go home and wash this jail stink off me and burn these clothes."

They both laughed.

When Clay arrived home, Callie was alone at the kitchen table in his terry-cloth robe. She rushed to him, enveloping him, beard stubble, slept-in clothing, jail smell and all.

"Where's Mattie?" he asked after a moment.

"Gone."

Clay pulled away from her, his eyes widening. "Gone? Where to?"

"I don't know. Herb and I went to the jail to post your bail, but they never brought you over. When I got home late last night, she wasn't here. All her things in the guest room had been cleaned out."

"Damn," Clay muttered, as he went into the great room. "Anything else missing?"

"If it is, it's nothing obvious to me."

Clay looked around a bit, then stopped facing the sofa end table. "The picture. She took Chelsea's picture. I put it right back where it belonged after cleaning the blood off of it the other night. It's gone."

"You don't suppose Harco found her and took her, do you?"

"I don't know, but why else would she leave? She seemed so happy here."

"We've got to get her back, Clay. She's not safe with him."

"I know. Let me freshen up and I'll think of something. There are a few things Mr. Brewton and I have to settle as well."

He showered and changed clothes, waited for the rush hour to end, then headed for town and Eleventh Street. If Harco and Mattie were together, that was the place to start looking.

Callie was a little disconcerted by Clay's comment about having to settle with Harco. Deep in her heart she had always feared what Clay might do to him, but until the previous day she had no reason to expect he would actually harm him. She'd seen the whole episode in the courtroom and knew it was prompted by Harco's arrogance. Now Harco had disappeared with Mattie, and she knew Clay wasn't simply going to let him walk away.

Clay had told Callie where he hid his gun, just in case she and Mattie needed it when he wasn't there. Overwhelmed by curiosity, she moved into his dressing room and felt among his socks. A lump rose in her throat when she realized it was gone.

The street in front of number 801 was crowded with cars, and Clay had to park up the block and walk back. The wide porch of the old rooming house was empty, so he simply walked in and made his way back to the kitchen. Expecting to find Gladdie there tending the coffee pot, he was surprised to see a much younger black woman occupying her chair. She appeared to be on watch, just as Miss Gladdie always seemed to be.

"Hi. Is Miss Gladdie around?"

The woman stared at him, then answered cautiously, "You trying to get her to come to court?"

"No. I need to ask her something. Is somebody trying to get her to court?"

"The police was here the other day. They was in an awful rush to get her to come to court."

"She in trouble? Maybe I can help."

"No. She ain't in no trouble. They say they wanted her as a witness for some trial that was going on."

"Well, I think the trial they were talking about is over now. Do you know where she is?"

"Yeah. She's up in Chicago, visiting her sister. Been there all week. Sorta like a free vacation."

"Free vacation? How's that?"

"Last week, some guy come by here and told her she done won a free airline ticket to any place in the United States, but she had to go this week. So off she went. She be back tomorrow."

"Did you see this guy?"

"Sure did."

"Was he short, chubby, and chewing on a cigar butt?"

"Sure was."

"Herb." Clay shook his head. "Maybe you can help me, then," he said, turning back to her.

Clay described Harco and Mattie to the young woman, and she said he'd come by himself the previous day and asked if his room was still his. He said he needed it only for one night, and then he'd move out for good. She said she never saw a young girl with him, but she thought she heard someone crying in the room last night. She thought she saw him leave the house that morning and assumed he'd moved out, because he had a duffel bag with him.

With her permission, Clay went back to Harco's room, listened very carefully, then knocked several times with no answer. Satisfied that no one was there, the young woman agreed to unlock the door.

Fearing the worst, he braced himself for what he might find. With heart pounding, he took a deep breath and quickly pushed the door open. The room was empty. Clay sighed and relaxed. A pall of fresh cigarette smoke hung over the room. The bedclothes were on the floor and a full ashtray sat on the end table. Candy wrappers cluttered the floor. The closet door was slightly ajar, and he walked over to look inside. As he pulled the door open, a broom leaning against the inside of the door crashed to the floor, and something akin to an electric shock coursed through his body because of the scare. Otherwise, the little cubicle was vacant.

None of Harco's or Mattie's personal belongings remained, and Clay began to look around for some indication of where they might've gone. Finding nothing, he sat down in the worn-out armchair by the window. Just like the first time, he heard the crunch of paper under the seat cushion. The porn magazine was still there. The police had never found it. No big deal. The one they found in his car was worse.

Clay rose, pulled the magazine out, and flipped through its pages. His heart froze. It had been completed. Where before only the faces of the models had been blacked out, now every breast was crisscrossed with slash-marks, and every vagina had been obliterated with a sharp instrument. Clay shuddered at the fury evident in the destruction of mere pictures of the women. Harco must have done that last night.

"You have a phone?" he asked the young woman.

"There's a pay phone out in the hall," she said. "But don't you write on the wall. That Harco man, he wrote on the wall last night. Gladdie gonna kill me."

"Show me where."

The young woman took Clay to the wall-mounted pay phone and showed him a ballpoint pen scribble off to one side. It was a phone number. Clay popped in a quarter and dialed it. Eight rings later he hung up. This was his only clue. If he couldn't get an answer, maybe he could get an address. But he needed it now. There was only one person who could get it that quickly: Rowland. Rowland would have to trust him. He couldn't answer any questions; at least, not yet.

Clay got Rowland's secretary and convinced her that despite what she said, he knew Rowland was there. He was returning Rowland's call, he'd said. That always worked. He got through. Rowland reluctantly agreed and in a few minutes was calling Clay back with the address: Cartouche's Tattoo Parlor on Peachtree Street in midtown.

Clay sped to the address and pulled up in front. It was closed. He couldn't believe the sign stating the hours of operation. "Eight p.m. to midnight."

He pounded on the door. Finally, a muffled, gruff voice could be heard in the back of the store. Clay kept pounding until someone appeared at the door. He flashed his wallet. "Please!" he said quickly. "Open up!"

The husky, shirtless proprietor grumbled something unintelligible and no doubt profane, and opened the door. He was a full head taller than Clay's six feet, and was obviously an admirer of his own art. Clay looked squarely into a tattooed four-masted schooner with chest hair growing out of it, and, incongruously, "sweet" and "sour" imprinted over alternate nipples.

"What do you want at this damn hour?"

"I got your address from the District Attorney of Fulton County."

That seemed to set the man back a notch or two, and his tone softened considerably. "Yeah? What can I do for you?"

"I'm trying to trace a man and a young girl, and the last information we had on them has led us here."

Clay then went on to describe Harco and Mattie.

"Yeah. They were in here late last night. Cocky little son of a bitch, he was. Had me tattoo a woman's name on his arm right in front of his wife. Said it wasn't her name, neither. And if that wasn't enough, he had me add it to a list of other women's names he already had on his arm."

"What was the name?"

"Let's see," the man said, as he rummaged through the clutter on an old roll-top desk. "I always try to keep a record of what I do, in case somebody comes back later and claims I made a mistake. Or, if they get an infected tattoo, say out in Long Beach, and try to claim I did it."

The delay was interminable for Clay.

"Helen," the man said.

"Oh God," Clay exclaimed as he whirled and moved for the door, where he stopped suddenly. "Call Jason Rowland, the District Attorney of Fulton County. Tell him to meet Mr. Delaney in Helen, Georgia. It's urgent."

"Listen, Mr. Whoever You Are. I don't play telephone tag with no cops."

Before the man could blink, the business end of Clay's nine-millimeter was in the rigging of his four-masted schooner, halfway between "sweet" and "sour."

"You call Mr. Rowland and tell him there's going to be a killing in Helen, or, so help me God, there's going to be one on Peachtree Street when I return. Now do it!"

"Yes sir."

Clay dashed for his car and careened away from the curb. He headed north through the city until he could access the interstate, then continued north toward the little faux alpine village of Helen. Under normal conditions, the drive to Helen was about an hour and a half. He had to reduce that. He needed to speed, but he couldn't be stopped.

Consequently, Clay was flying north on Georgia Highway 400, but his heart pounded every time he topped a hill or rounded a curve. Houses, overpasses, fields and farms passed by in a blur, caused as much by the speed of his mind as the speed of his car. His mind had already raced ahead to Helen.

Where would they be? Certainly not among the quaint Bavarian shops and eateries there, or among the tourists who thronged the sidewalks at that time of year. Where? Harco needed to be alone. He'd already planned everything. He always did. But where?

Helen was nestled in the mountains of North Georgia. It was surrounded by millions of acres of forest. Some private, and some belonging to the National Forestry Service. There were millions of places there to do his dirty work, secure and unseen. Mattie could scream and never be heard. She'd die helpless and alone, just like her little friend.

But Clay realized that if Harco was going to be true to his pattern, he wouldn't be too far away. Whatever place he chose, it had to be in Helen. And it had to be private. That would narrow the search considerably.

Clay was careful not to speed as he passed around the old square in Cleveland, Georgia. A local patrol car normally sat close by, waiting for just such an event as that.

When he finally passed through the outskirts of the small town, he could see Yonah Mountain's sheer rock face rising in the distance. Six miles to Helen.

After releasing Clay from Armbrister's holding cell, Rowland attended a sentencing hearing before another judge, then returned to his office. That was the first time in more than a week he'd been able to sit at his desk and read his mail. As he sifted the good from the junk, he happened on a several-day-old fax from the Highland County, Ohio, Sheriff to the Sheriff of Fulton County, a copy of which had been routed to him by the local sheriff. The simple sheriff to sheriff message read: "Do you know why Attorney Clay Delaney of your city would suddenly become interested in the attached autopsy report of his daughter, murdered in this county six years ago? Please reply."

Rowland rose from his chair and yelled at his secretary as he moved to put on his coat, "I'm on my way out, Shirley, have them bring my car to the front of the building. Now!"

He stuffed the fax in his coat pocket and headed for the elevator. He didn't know what was going on, but he was beginning to get goose bumps at the possibilities that were racing through his head. He was going to have to confront Delaney with it, face to face.

As he pulled abruptly into Clay's driveway, he almost hit Callie head-on as she was leaving. Their cars stopped bumper to bumper, and Rowland got out.

"Is he still here?" Rowland asked.

"No."

"You know where he is?"

Callie didn't answer.

"Do you know anything about this?" Rowland demanded, showing her the fax.

"I can't talk about that," Callie replied.

The radio in Rowland's car crackled out, and he turned away to answer it. He returned rapidly to Callie's car and said, "I've just received a message that there's going to be a killing in Helen and Delaney's somehow involved. Tell me what's going on!"

"I can't tell you anything, but you've got to get to him. Did you say Helen?"

"Yes."

"Oh my God! Mattie!"

"If he's thinking about killing Harco Brewton, you know I can't let him do that."

"There's more to it than that. You've got to find him."

"Okay, I'm out of here," Rowland said, moving back to his car.

"Not without me." Callie abandoned her car in the driveway and climbed in with Rowland.

"Suit yourself," he said, "but put on that safety belt."

As Rowland's car squealed northward toward Helen, he kept thinking about how he and Delaney had been locked in mortal combat for so long over the life of Harco Brewton, and now they may have traded places.

Clay's car crawled slowly over the narrow two lane bridge that spanned the Chattahoochee River in downtown Helen. "River" was really a misnomer at that point. No more than two feet at its deepest, it was more a clear mountain stream. These were really the headwaters, and it didn't become a full-fledged river until many miles to the south.

The traffic through the center of town was backed up. It normally was during the good weather months. Clay knew better than to blow his horn. If the people in front of him were tourists, they'd slow down. If they were "good old boys," they'd stop and get out. God knew what else they'd do.

Clay didn't really expect to see Harco and Mattie walking the streets. But he had to pass through town once or twice to look around and figure out what to do. He knew his best bet would be somewhere around the edges of this small town.

Helen was so contained, he decided to abandon his car and select a logical route to walk. Finding a convenient place, he pulled over and soon found himself close to the river, walking south along the bank, away from town.

He passed trout fishermen mixed with families tubing in the frigid water. As he followed the river downstream, the people thinned out and soon were no longer in sight. He noticed isolated chalets set back in the woods along the river. Most of them were rental cabins, where seclusion was the main selling point. That would be perfect for Harco: peace and quiet, all cash, and no I.D. required.

When the trail along the river's edge ended, Clay plunged into the cold water, shoes and all. One hundred yards downstream he saw enough of a trail emerging to climb back up the gently sloping bank. As he paused to pour water out of his shoes, the slamming of a screen door caught his attention. When his shoes were back on, he moved away from the river a few yards, toward the sound. Then he stopped.

A small mountain cabin sat in a clearing, framed by hardwoods. Parked beside it was the Pascagoula Special: a beat-up, white, four-door sedan, with rusted top and trunk.

Clay reached into his coat pocket, pulled out his pistol, slammed the receiver back, and listened as a shell slid smoothly into the chamber. That was the last thing he heard before a stout hickory stick crashed down on his head from behind.

Rowland's car sped northward, the blue light on the dash flashing hypnotically. Even when Callie closed her eyes, she could still see a strobe of varying colors pulsing against her eyelids.

In response to a radio call Rowland made, they were joined along the way by a state trooper. He positioned his patrol car in front of Rowland, and the two vehicles moved quietly through the traffic like a well rehearsed dance team.

The additional blue light was making Callie's head swim, so she kept her eyes tightly closed and simply dealt with the lights' aftereffect.

She and Rowland had spoken very little along the way. Only when they came into the outskirts of Helen did Rowland question her. But Callie knew nothing of either Harco's or Clay's whereabouts.

They decided that the quickest way to find them was to locate their cars. Callie described Clay's car to Rowland, and he described Harco's to her.

When Clay stirred back to consciousness, he was still lying on the ground near the edge of the water. Propped up against the trunk of a nearby tree was the motionless body of a young girl, eyes closed, her faced covered in mud. Glass shards littered her lap, and Chelsea's tattered photograph was clutched in her hand. Mattie.

When he sat up, he heard behind him the unmistakable click of the hammer on his pistol cock back. "You come up here to get me, Mister Delaney?" he heard

Harco Brewton say. "I wondered what you whupped up on me for back at the courthouse. But Mattie there, she done told me all about her little friend and how she found her picture and all at your house. Guess we sorta met before. Sure is a small world, ain't it?"

Clay didn't answer. He was trying to let the cobwebs clear. He needed it, but it was also a way of stalling for time. He rubbed the back of his head, and his fingers felt wet and sticky. He saw a dark stain on the ground where he'd been lying. When he looked at his hand, he saw blood from the back of his head.

"Ain't you in a talking mood?" Harco said, still behind him. "Now, Mattie was in a talking mood. All she could talk about was how nice you all were to her, and how you were going to protect her."

Clay could hear Harco's footsteps moving around him from his right. He continued to stare at the ground until Harco's feet came into view in front of him. Then he looked up. Harco pointed the automatic directly at him while holding an open folding-knife loosely in his other hand.

"You know what else she was talking about? She was talking about her little friend, who must've been your little girl, and how mean I was to her. Do you think I was mean to her, Mister Delaney? I couldn't have been too mean. Why this very knife was so sharp, she didn't even cry when I cut off her tit."

A primordial cry, buried for years, broke free and erupted out of Clay's mouth. He was catapulted to his feet by hatred and held up by some animal instinct to reach the throat of his enemy and kill with teeth and claws. But a nine-millimeter steel-jacketed slug took him down. He rose again in an instant, determined to survive long enough to reach his antagonist's belly. But, another bullet was stronger than the remnants of any prehistoric instinct, and Clay went down again.

The first hit was in the right shoulder, and it disabled his arm. The second was in the left lung, and breathing brought little air and intense pain. All he wanted was one more time on his feet. He was no match for the pistol, he knew that. He'd wait and see if God would give him one more chance at Harco.

He felt Harco's foot smash into his ribs. The blow rolled him over on his side.

Harco reached down and pulled Clay into a sitting position. "I don't like to kill a body when they're laying down. So just sit up so you can see the next one coming, 'cause it's going to make a nice blue hole right between those two blue eyes."

Harco grabbed Clay by the hair, pulled his head back, and placed the smoking muzzle of the cocked pistol on his forehead. The two men were now looking at each other, face to face, no more than eighteen inches apart. The only thing Clay had left was a mouth full of spit, and he put it squarely between Harco's eyes.

A strange expression suddenly came over Harco's face. He turned Clay's hair loose and stood up. The hand with the pistol went to his side, and he turned and took two steps toward the river. As he did, Clay saw something that seemed to be pinned to his back. It was the picture of a smiling little Chelsea, held in place by a long sliver of glass, deeply embedded in Harco's back. Harco collapsed and fell face-first into the Chattahoochee River. His body floated slowly away in a swirl of red-stained water.

It was then that Clay saw Mattie, her hands bloodied from wielding the broken glass from Chelsea's picture frame, standing where Harco had been.

"My little friend told me to do it, Mr. Delaney. Was it okay?" Mattie asked.

"You and your friend did the right thing, Mattie," Clay said. He smiled and passed out.

CHAPTER 17

▼

Callie kept a constant vigil until Clay had recovered from surgery and was awake in his room. After that, it was a full week before he was able to have visitors. Then, the first one through the door was a very talkative Rowland.

"We got the whole story from Mattie. We've contacted her parents, and they've come to get her. She's going to require a lot of help getting over this, but knowing her friend's dad has given her a head start. The information we got from Cartouche has closed a lot of unsolved murders in Ohio."

"Cartouche?"

"Yeah. The big tattoo guy. That list of names, or places, on Harco's arm. Cartouche had written them all down when he did the last one."

"Why'd you need Cartouche?"

"To tell you the truth, Delaney, we haven't found Harco's body yet. It's moving slowly this way, but we'll get it. You know you're the talk of Atlanta, don't you? You've got everyone shaking their heads. None of us knows how you did what you did. Once we got Mattie's story, the press got the word, and it's all over the state. I've put some of our deputies out in the hall to keep them out of here. Hope you don't mind."

"Certainly not."

"On the Lindsey case, I took your advice, and we set up surveillance at the Zip 'N Mart parking lot. We brought in three different teens who cruised through in white autos. Two were clean, but we found some fiber evidence on Carrie's clothes that matched the third one's car. When we confronted him with it, he tried to hassle us, saying we couldn't touch him because his uncle was a judge."

"A judge?"

"Yeah. Seems our boy's mother is Jack Armbrister's sister. The grand jury is hearing evidence against the judge this afternoon on an obstruction charge. He's going down, Clay. He thought he had you set up from the beginning. He had no idea who he was up against."

"I'll have to introduce him to Callie someday."

"That's it for now. I'll be talking to you later." He smiled. "By the way, my mother sends her regards."

When Clay was ready to leave the hospital, Solomon volunteered to drive him and Callie home, and he appeared at the hospital in a Fulton County van used by his office. Instead of heading straight for Clay's house, Solomon headed downtown. Clay didn't notice this immediately, because he was so interested in hearing Solomon talk about his new job.

"The productivity study the County Commission did on the Public Defender's office consistently showed the highest number of cases handled by the smallest number of lawyers in the entire state," Solomon explained. "Marshall Bishop was so impressed he prevailed upon the Governor to appoint a task force to revamp indigent programs throughout the state, and he recommended that I head it up. I start next week—at twice the salary and with weekends off, I might add."

Clay expressed his pleasure at Solomon's promotion, but also asked why they were headed into the city. Solomon sheepishly said that he had to complete some business at the courthouse before they went home, but that it would only take a minute.

As they neared the courthouse, Clay could hear the noise of a crowd chanting something. When they turned the corner, he could see the courthouse steps were full of people.

"Who are all those people, Herb?" Clay asked.

"The kids from my office, and it looks like everyone else from the courthouse has joined them."

"What do they want?"

"You."

It was then he realized what they were saying: "Delaney. Delaney. Delaney."

Clay smiled self-consciously and waved as Solomon drove the van slowly by the crowd.

"It was their idea, Clay. It was the only way they could say thank you for giving them the lesson of a lifetime."

Clay couldn't speak, but he knew Solomon understood. He always did.

With Mattie gone, there was no reason for Callie to stay at Clay's, so she returned home, but checked on him from time to time. In a few weeks, Clay felt strong enough to start exercising his right arm. He figured that the most enjoyable way to do it was to use his kayak. He could paddle as slowly or as rapidly as he wanted, and once again enjoy his love for the river.

Late one evening as he moved downstream from his home, soaking up the ever-changing colors of the setting sun, the soft melody that had tantalized and enchanted him before began to drift over the river. It was the closest he'd ever been to the music, and he decided to find out where it was coming from.

As he moved farther downstream, the sound of the piano melody grew louder. It was beautiful. He stopped paddling and floated closer to it.

When he realized that he'd discovered the source, he beached his little boat on the bank in front of a small cottage. He walked toward the little house, hoping not to frighten anyone, but he was irresistibly drawn there, nevertheless. As he neared, he could barely see the pianist through the large bay window. It was a woman.

She didn't know that it was her music that had set Clay free from the memories of his past, that her music had totally changed his future, and given him the assurance that love was out there for everyone. Like the music, one just had to go out and find it, and bring it back.

He thought of Callie. He wanted to share it with her. He'd felt that way for some time now, but she was never around when the music was. He wondered what she would think of his sneaking around someone's yard at dusk simply to hear them play the piano.

Clay was brought suddenly back to reality when the music abruptly stopped and he heard, "Clay? Is that you?"

"Callie?"

"What are you doing sneaking around my yard? Are you listening to me play?"

Clay's eyes widened as Callie stepped out into the grass. "I didn't know you lived here. I didn't know you played the piano."

"There are a lot of things about me you don't know."

"Is there some way I can change that?"

"How much time do you have?" she replied.

"I've got a whole lifetime. How about you?"

"That sounds an awful lot like a proposal, Clay Delaney."

"It is," he replied with a grin. "Say, what are you doing?"

"I'm unbuttoning your shirt, dummy. Now hold still. Can't you see I'm busy?"

In Hillsboro, Ohio, Mattie's parents sat on their front porch in the gathering darkness and smiled as they listened to their long lost little girl recite a favorite evening rhyme.

"Star light, star bright, first star I see tonight. I wish I may. I wish I might. I wish my wish comes true tonight. Good night, Chelsea," she whispered.

978-0-595-37371-
0-595-37371-2

Printed in the United Kingdom
by Lightning Source UK Ltd.
112690UKS00001B/97